The Blasphemy Box

By

Mandy Behbehani

Breedon Avenue Books
Copyright © 2013 Mandy Behbehani
All rights reserved.

The Blasphemy Box
ISBN: 0-6157-3683-1
ISBN-13: 9780615736839

Why is divorce so expensive?

Because it's worth it.

—PlentyofFish.com

Chapter 1

DAY 1 OF SEPARATION

Marriage is the chief cause of divorce.
—Groucho Marx

You know that nightmare you've always had?

The one where you wake up one day to find yourself fat, frumpy, fifty, and alone?

I'm living it.

It's barely nine on a frigid January morning. The three children have gone off to school, and I'm in the kitchen in my pajamas on my laptop working on my novel when Steven comes lumbering through, toward the front door of our Victorian house in San Francisco, dragging two of my large Louis Vuitton suitcases.

It's been only a week since he said he was leaving. Not even a week. Six days. We'd only just celebrated the kids' birthdays. After twenty years of marriage, I just didn't believe it. I thought maybe he had a cold and was feeling out of sorts. Sure, we'd been bickering a lot lately, mostly about how he was working until all hours of the night with no convincing explanation. And about how he was sick and tired of seeing my nose in a book and that I should take it out and pay more attention to him. And about why he hadn't touched me for several months. And about that wooden box with a slot on the top, which suddenly appeared on the kitchen table to remind me not to curse. Steven called it the Blasphemy Box, and I was to insert a quarter into it every time I swore. (I'm from England where cursing is the second language.)

He told me he was leaving while we were perusing the baking aisle at Whole Foods. It was the first time he had been grocery shopping with me in a long time. All I could see through my tears was a row of boxes of "No Pudge Fat-Free Fudge Brownie Mix." I kept asking him if he was joking. He said it was no joke. I blinked the tears away and tried to maintain my British cool—public grief is just not done in England after all, where I come from. I babbled about needing bitter cocoa powder, mascarpone, and ladyfingers for tiramisu. I asked him if he wanted something other than tiramisu. But he just stood silently next to me, not looking at me, far away, already gone.

Had I seen this coming? No! (Well, not exactly.) I thought we were just used to each other, just comfortable with each other, the spark gone, the flame tamed, but still together as one. I guess not. We didn't talk about it again in that intervening week. I couldn't. It's called denial. I thought if I didn't talk about it, it wouldn't be real. It wouldn't happen. But it has. It is. Happening. Now.

As he lumbers toward our front door, I look up. "So, that's it. You're really leaving."

"Maddy, don't start…We've been through this. It's over. "

No matter how many times he says it, I still can't believe it.

"Because of some bimbo half your age?"

"And half your size."

Ouch.

"Her name is Gabriela, Madeleine."

Gabriela. I want to skin her and wear her like last year's Dior.

"Yeah, right," I say, furious, then numb as I get up, pull my stomach in and try to stand straight. I am trying to hold back my tears. I really am. I dig my finger into my thigh, hoping the pain will distract me from the other pain and humiliation. Of course it doesn't. I just feel the cellulite growing there like kudzu.

"You're pathetic." Steven glances at my laptop. "Still scribbling away, are we?" he says, as he turns to me one last time. "Still dreaming of that brilliant literary career?"

"It's my novel. What if I am?"

"Now you're truly pathetic. Why do you always answer a question with a question?"

"Why not?"

Steven sighs heavily, shakes his head, and walks toward the door. He reappears immediately. "Don't give the kids too many bagels."

"But they love bagels."

"So do you, and look what happened."

How had I ever loved this man? Had it been his gorgeous, sun-swept face? The promise of a new life in the New World? Was it his kinder, gentler self, the one at the beginning? The one who saw flower-child, creative me as a risk, yet took it anyway? I may have lost my much-vaunted looks, but he's no Brad Pitt anymore either, I catch myself thinking. Lines crisscross his face, and a soft paunch protrudes from his waistline, punctuating his once-svelte form.

"How the fuck can you just leave like this?"

He reaches into his pocket, pulls out a quarter, and tosses it to me. I let it plummet to the floor. "Twenty-five cents in the Blasphemy Box. Gabriela doesn't curse."

"Screw your effing box!" I cry, taking it off the counter and dumping it in the trash. "And screw Gabriela! Oh, sorry," I say, "you already do."

Steven walks down the steps toward his Lexus, opens the trunk, and tosses the suitcases inside.

I follow him to the front door.

"Steven, how can you leave your children?"

He closes the trunk and opens the car door.

"I'm not leaving the children. I'm leaving you."

I just stand there. It's really happening. He's gone.

I slam the door and head for the fridge. The magnet Steven put on the door months ago, reading, "By the Time I'm Thin, Fat Will Be In," mocks me. I rip it off the door and throw it in the trash. Inside, the last piece of a princess cake from Amanda's birthday looks as lonely as I feel. It beckons me insistently. I know I will feel better after I eat it.

I don't.

I sink onto the floor, knees to nose, feeling very sorry for myself. I'm crying and have to keep swallowing to clear my ears. The house is quiet, which makes my sobs sound even louder.

I think I hear the door open, and I look up, thinking it might be Steven. But the doorway is empty, and I'm still alone. I wander into the bedroom, barely noticing the spectacular Bay views, and get into the bed, pulling a pillow toward me. My head throbs, and I doze on and off for some time, trying to turn off my brain, hoping to escape my situation and what it means.

It doesn't work.

I can't help thinking of the night I first met Steven. My best friend Suzy and I were both still unmarried at twenty-nine, and it was at a party in Chelsea hosted by a strange woman who said she had dyed her hair purple, because she had exhausted every other option. Suzy was in the corner, snogging with some lusty German guy called Hans. Or was it some lusty French guy called Florent? Anyway, I was in a tight little ruched floral Ungaro. Very chic for the time. Steven, who was surrounded by women, was a money manager from San Francisco in London on business. After several glasses of Pimm's, I eased my way through the gaggle and started to flirt shamelessly.

"And where have they been keeping *you*?" I said.

He smiled. "What do you do?" he asked, polite but interested.

"Anything that feels good." I couldn't believe my brazenness, even then.

His eyes locked with mine, intrigued. "Well..." he said, "That's very un-English."

I smiled and said, "You'd be surprised."

"Well, I like surprises."

At that moment, "Brown Sugar" by the Stones came on, and I pulled him into the flat's living room to dance. He demurred, but I would not let go of him. With much looking around and a red face, he started dancing, if you can call it that. No wonder he said he didn't want to. It was like watching Pee Wee Herman do the Macarena. At the end of the dance, he threw off his jacket and got a Pimm's for himself and one for me, and then he pulled me out back into the dance area for a slow dance to "Whiter Shade of Pale."

"You know," he whispered in my ear, "I'm only here for a few days."

"No time to waste then."

He burst out laughing and without any prompting from me, pulled me closer to him. The rest, as they say, is history.

We were so good for so long. When had it changed? He was always a bit of prig, but we worked well together. I loosened him up. Made him laugh. At least until recently. He got so critical, so stingy. Never wanted to do anything alone with me. I tried. I truly did. I guess it wasn't enough. Miss Young, Perky, and Willing won out. I guess you never really know a man until he leaves you.

I pick up a book. A chapter or two of Henry James always makes me feel better. Not today, however. I get up, shower, put on jeans and a white sweater, and make my way to the kitchen. Passing by the gold-leaf hall mirror, I glimpse my reflection. My face is plump. I've got dark circles around my eyes, frown lines, and a growing wattle under my chin. Gray is pushing through my dark hair at the roots. My skin is pasty and dry. Who is this woman I see? Not the pretty, fashion-conscious, well-groomed person I always took pride in being. The past week has been hell, and it shows.

I swallow two Advil with some water and curl up on the couch, my head buried in my chest. I must have sat like this for hours because suddenly, I hear the scampering of feet in the foyer. The kids are home.

"Mom!" Amanda bursts through the kitchen door yelling. "Dad bought me an iPhone!"

"Did he? When? How? Did he just drop you off?"

"Yes, he picked us up from school," Amanda says. "Look, look, here it is! And I got the hot pink cover! The boys got iPods!"

And with that, my baby girl, fourteen years old, flings her hot pink velour Juicy Couture backpack onto the kitchen counter, sending a half full coffee mug onto the floor. My beloved Amanda has always been like this. She is so gifted—plays piano like a dream and can ably wield a tennis racket—but she always leaves havoc in her wake. Privately, I call her my weapon of mass destruction.

"Amanda," I call after her.

"What?" She's halfway up the stairs to her room.

"Come back here and clean up this mess you made."

"I'm busy, Mom. I have to get Adele on my new phone."

At that moment, my adorable, button-nosed, ten-year-old twins Charlie and Colin drop their backpacks on the floor and plop themselves down at the kitchen counter. All three kids go to a French Catholic school where they are meant to be learning French, but so far the boys seem only to have learned the word, "bon."

"Hey Mom, can we have some milk and Oreos?"

I tiptoe around the shards of porcelain on the floor to get to the fridge. Then I tiptoe around them again on the way to the pantry to get the cookies.

"So how was school today?" I ask them.

"Bon," they say in unison.

"Anything happen?"

Without looking up from their iPods, they both say, "Nothing."

Whoever said children should be seen and not heard doesn't know what they're talking about. That's a mother's job.

I look over to the boys again. Until now, skinflint Steven has balked at giving the kids the rather expensive iPods and iPhones. Now, I suppose, he's trying to assuage his guilt at leaving by getting them the electronics of the day.

I hear Amanda chattering excitedly in her room and walk to the bottom of the stairs.

"Amanda," I call up to her, "you really need to come down here and clean up this mess."

Before I know it, she's barreling down the stairs, clutching her iPhone. I follow her into the kitchen, where she actually picks up the pieces of my mug and deposits them in the trash. I hand her some paper towels to clean up the spill.

"Thank you," I say, planting a kiss on her forehead. "Now, how did your day go? The boys won't give me any details."

"Well," she says, "Madame Berry's beehive collapsed during French lit, and Miss Read was crying in the bathroom. Someone said it was because Mr. Trent dumped her."

"Well, if Madame Berry will insist on wearing a hairstyle from the sixties, que fait-elle attendre?"

The boys' heads snap up, and Amanda stares at me as if I've said something rude.

"Mom, please." And she runs off to her room.

"What did I do?"

Colin giggles and heads off after his sister.

I shake my head and start to gather up the plates and the tumblers ringed with milk-sodden cookie crumbles and put them in the dishwasher. I need to start working on dinner, I think. Steven always likes to eat early. He might like duck à l'orange tonight, with fingerling potatoes and creamed spinach…

But then, I remember he won't be here for dinner. Ever.

At that moment, Charlie looks up at me and says, "When will Daddy be home? I need help with my stupid math homework."

But I turn toward the sink. "Oh, he'll be late…"

Before I am forced to make up some kind of story, Amanda bursts into the kitchen again with her new iPhone.

"Mommy, I can't get this damn thing to text my photo."

"Don't swear."

"But can you help me?"

"Sweetie, you know Mummy's not really good with this kind of stuff. Maybe you could ask…"

And then I realize the person she could ask is no longer here to ask anything of.

"OK, I guess I can wait until Dad gets home," she says.

All I can do is nod.

"I can't believe you can't help me with this." Amanda is whining now. "Didn't you have technology when you were at school?"

"Technology?" I say. "At school, we had detention."

Chapter 2

There is love of course. And then there's life, its enemy.
—Jean Anouilh

"Hello?"

"Did he come back?"

"Suzy! Every time I've thought to call you, something happens. After school today, the boys barricaded themselves in their room and put up a sign reading, 'No Moms Aloud.' No, it's been two days, and His Majesty hasn't come back. What am I going to do?"

As I said, Suzy is my best friend. We are fellow Brits who grew up and went to school and university together in London. She and Rex, her husband, have been in Los Angeles for two years. She's a research scientist at UCLA, and when they moved to the States, it was the first time we'd lived on the same continent in two decades. Only Suzy knows so far. I have been too embarrassed to tell anyone else.

"Maddy, you'll be fine," she says, somewhat unconvincingly. "Steven has always been so full of himself. If he can't appreciate what he has, screw him and the horse he rode in on."

She pauses then, and says, "I didn't want to ask you before, but where did he meet this gold-digging you know what?"

"At work. She was his personal assistant. With the emphasis on *personal.*"

"How mundane. But Steven was never the creative type."

I want to laugh, but it hurts too much.

"What am I going to do? It's all so overwhelming."

"Did you write it all down in your journal? Everything he said?"

"Yes."

"Good. It will help if things progress further."

I pause, not wanting to even think about the D word.

"Well, at least you've got your writing to keep you sane."

"You mean my novel?"

"And your articles."

"I can't focus on them with all this going on."

"Why not start a blog for now? It will you keep going. Give you an outlet."

"A blog? Who would want to read about my problems?"

"Every woman who got dumped by her cheating husband, that's who. It'll help you process. People will post comments, which might be helpful as well."

"It *would* keep me busy...."

"Who knows where it might lead," Suzy says. "You could build a following."

"Where would I begin?"

"Start with the break up. You don't need to mention names or anything. Just write about the emotion of it all."

"It's too personal, and anyway, I can't think about all that right now," I say, suddenly feeling exhausted. "To me, the whole Internet thing is just one gigantic Saks Fifth Avenue that I've missed a good sale on. Besides, I don't know how to set one up."

"That's why you have me," Suzy says. "I will set it up for you."

Suzy's always been savvier about the technology than me. "Sounds lovely, dearie," I say, the idea not thrilling me one whit.

"So, how are you doing? Really?" Suzy asks.

"Awful."

"I know, but you do realize that Steven's leaving could be the happiest day of your life."

"God, I fucking hope not," I said. (Twenty-five cents.)

"With him gone, you can be you again."

"What are you talking about?"

"You know what I'm talking about."

"No, I don't," I say. But of course I do.

"A few of us couldn't really understand why you married him in the first place. You're so full of vim and vigor, and he's so restrained and controlling. You'll be free of all his whining and criticism."

"I know," I say sheepishly. "But we really loved each other. And I still love him. With me he was different. He wasn't always such a priss. He was a bit uptight and straitlaced, I grant you, but he said that was why he loved me. Because I wasn't. And now..."

"He got his midlife-crisis bimbo to loosen him up. It's sooo clichéd."

"Clichéd or not, it still happening, and I'm a wreck over it. All I wanted was to make him happy and share our lives together."

"Well, now you can want something else. Besides, he's gay anyway. That girl is just a beard."

Laughter catches in my throat.

"No, he's not."

"Of course he is. Look at his relationship with his mother. Positively incestuous. And wearing all that Tom Ford. *So* obvious."

"Oh, Suzy," I say, a bit indignantly, "just because your hubby just left you for another guy doesn't mean Steven is gay, you know."

"Well!" Suzy says, huffily. "It's something to consider."

We are silent for a moment, and I can feel Suzy's anguish.

"I don't know what to say about Rex. Did you suspect anything at all?" I ask her.

"Once or twice over the years something kind of pricked at me, but not really."

Suzy is still recovering from a horrible shock. Not long after she and Rex arrived in Los Angeles, he left her. She said that one day he took a ride over to West Hollywood and just never came back.

There's a silence. "How's the research going?"

"Fine," Suzy says. "There's so much more money for everything here than in London. Although I do get sick of the scientist's life, sometimes. You know you've been in the lab too long when you wonder what absolute alcohol tastes like with grapefruit juice."

I laugh out loud. And then I feel sad again. "I miss him," I say. Tears threaten to come again. "I miss being a family."

"Of course you do," Suzy says. "I know exactly how you feel."

"I try to remember all I do have, try to embrace the being-grateful concept people always blather on about. But it's hard to do."

"Listen, darling girl," Suzy says. "You just have to try to accept that you will be a different kind of family from now on. I know how hard and awful and bruising all this is, but you have three lovely kids, and you need to think of them. Go online and read a few blogs. Call me when you're ready to plan yours. It'll be fun."

"I still don't know what's wrong with just writing entries in my journal."

"Nothing, but a blog is a way to get you out into the world. Share experiences with other women."

"Why do I want to share my situation with women in my position? Why would I want to hear more stories like mine?"

"It's all in how you view things, Maddy girl. Trust me. It helps to know you're not alone."

I say good-bye and return to the chaos that reigns in the house until the kids are settled in for the night. I kiss their sweet faces and tell Colin to turn his iPod off. He grudgingly complies.

I return to the kitchen to file the dinner plates in the dishwasher and wipe the counters down when the phone rings again.

"Hi, Maddy. It's Cameron."

Cameron is one of the mothers from the neighborhood. Her daughter goes to school with Amanda, and she's the former wife of one of Steven's college mates. I like her a lot, and she seems to like me. We've become quite close, in fact. Like some of the other mothers I know, she's younger than me—forty-five—but we get along quite well. She's the one who favors black eyeliner and leather pants and makes care packages for her airplane seatmates of ear plugs, candy, and a meditation.

"How are things?"

I'm going to have to tell her at some point anyway, I think, so it might as well be now.

"Well, Steven has moved out. Seems he has a girlfriend."

"He does?" Cameron is spluttering with shock. "I know you said things weren't perfect between you but I didn't think it had reached this point. How are you coping?"

"It's all just been a bit wretched. I don't know whether I'm coming or going."

"I know, I know," she says. "I'm coming to take you out to dinner and a stiff drink."

"Oh sweetie, that's very nice of you," I say. "But I have the kids."

"Well, shall I come over, then? We can chat, and I'll cheer you up."

"I really appreciate it, but I just feel so ragged, so beat, right now. Not very good company. "

I just want to be quiet. I don't want conversation. I can't deal with commiseration.

"Fine," Cameron says. "I'll check in tomorrow. Love."

"Love," I say.

I head for the shower. Under the water I scrub myself vigorously, hoping to wash away my problems with Cetaphil and pumice stone. All I get is red. When I fall into bed, it feels as big and empty as Neiman's on New Year's Eve.

Chapter 3

All marriages are happy. It's the living together afterward that causes all the trouble.
—Raymond Hull

"Darling."

"Hello, Mother." I just got the kids off to school, and I'm already exhausted. The last thing I need is a call from my mother.

Mother and Father moved from London to the States several years ago so my father could take a job teaching classics at the University of California-Berkeley.

"Darling, how are you?"

Being English, Mother calls everybody darling, from the butcher at Andronico's in his blood-stained apron pointing out the marbling on a nice piece of beef, to her best friend's husband, Jim Gordon, who, she likes to insist, always tries to flirt with her.

I take another sip of coffee. Steady, girl.

"Mother, he left."

"Who left, darling?"

"Steven. You know, my husband."

"Where's he gone, darling? I didn't know he had a trip planned."

"He has not gone on a trip, Mother. He has left me."

"Really? Goodness gracious. What happened? What did you do?"

"What did I do? I did nothing. He's the one at fault."

"Really?" Mother says. "Well, come over for dinner tonight with the kids, why don't you? We can chat."

When we arrive at my parents' 1913 house on Grizzly Peak, the highest point along the ridgeline of the Berkeley Hills, it's getting dark.

In front of us we can see the Bay and the lights of the Golden Gate Bridge and San Francisco blinking and glittering. Father opens the door.

"Grandpa!" the kids yell and barge right past him into the house.

He shakes his head. "Your mother is in the kitchen," he says, rolling his eyes. We both know about Mother's dearth of cooking skills. He follows the kids into the living room, and I make for the kitchen.

I find Mother chopping cucumber with surgical precision. *Aida* is on the radio. She's in a stylish Tiffany blue sweater and pants, elegant as ever.

"Oh darling," she says as I join her. "There you are. Where are the kids?"

"They're in the living room, fighting over the TV remote. I'm surprised you can't hear them."

"Oh, this opera drowns out everything," Mother says happily.

"What can I do to help?"

"Perhaps you can make the salad? I have radicchio and endive in the fridge, and the strawberries and kiwis are over there."

I make no comment on the idea of putting kiwi and radicchio in a salad that children will eat. Instead I wash all four and start chopping alongside Mother.

"So tell me," she says, now seasoning a chicken breast for herself and steak for everyone else with what looks like half the container of garlic powder.

I tell her.

"Well," she says, "I wouldn't upset yourself too much about it." She has never been what you would call a doting mother.

"Is that it? I'm telling you my husband of twenty years has left me for some tramp, and that's all you can say?"

"Well, what else is there to say, darling?" She lights a cigarette and puffs away on it. "I mean, maybe it's for the best."

"For whom, Mother? You were the one who urged me to marry him. You kept carrying on about old maids and gout and crochet and how you had already been humiliated enough by having to tell everyone your daughter worked for the gutter press and that you couldn't bear the further humiliation of having a daughter who worked for the gutter press *and* might never get married."

"But darling, of course we encouraged you to get married." Mother's tone is indignant. "You were in love, and he was handsome and well off and so nice and sensible. And he was American. You know how an American husband is the holy grail for all English girls. Besides, you *wanted* to get married. All your friends were married, and there you were, still single, and all tied up with your wretched writing career all day. Time was marching on, darling. How could we have stopped you?"

"Very easily," I say. "You were never one to withhold your opinions. You could have warned me."

"Warned you of what, darling? He was the son of someone your father knew and liked. We loved him. We still do. And he held your attention, which God knows it's not easy to do. You know how you are. You've never been easy to reach. I mean I tried, believe me. But often you're not, well, not quite there. Don't you remember Madame Laurent, your French teacher? If she told me once, she told me a hundred times: '*Madeleine? Ouf! Elle est dans la lune. C'est tout. Elle est simplement dans la lune.*"

"Yes, yes, Mother. That's only the trillionth time you've told me that. Thanks for the sympathy." I pour myself a glass of Pellegrino and stare out at the view of the San Francisco Bay.

"Now, now, Madeleine," Mother says. "Don't get upset. I am your mother, after all. And as such I've always tried to guide you. Anyway, after dinner you have to help me choose something to wear to the Lintons' on Friday night. You have such a good eye for what looks best on me. Although I must say, you have let yourself go in that area. Maybe that's…" Her voice trails off, and her tone is no longer insouciant.

"I'm going to go check on the kids," I say.

I find them settled on the couch, watching *American Idol*.

"Madeleine, how are you?" my father says, rising from the couch, the *New York Times* in his hand, his reading glasses perched on his nose. His khakis are wrinkled, and he's beginning to get a hint of the paunch he swore would never appear, but he's still handsome in that college-professor, pipes-and-cardigans way.

"Well, compared to Syria, I'm fine. It's been difficult."

"Yes, your mother told me."

Father shifts uncomfortably. "Don't worry now, old girl," he says. "It'll all be OK." And he sits back down on the couch and opens his newspaper again. He has been married to Mother for fifty-one years, so I don't expect him to relate or understand.

"Dinner is ready," Mother trills from the dining room.

Dinner—overdone salad and underdone steak—is a hectic affair with Mother asking the kids questions nonstop and the kids answering her questions nonstop.

"How is your piano playing going, Amanda? You are so talented, isn't she, Gerald?" she adds, looking indulgently at Father.

"Great," Amanda says. "I've been invited to play in another recital soon."

"Now that's nice, dear. I wish your mother would have learned to play. It's good for a young girl to know an instrument."

I don't bother to comment.

"What are you boys up to?"

"Dad gave us iPods."

"Eye pads? Is something wrong with your eyes?"

The kids shriek with laughter. "They're called *i*Pods, Granny," Colin says. "They're for listening to music."

Mother winks at the boys. "Well, I hope you like them."

"A *lot*," Charlie says.

"Is Amanda going to be in the Christmas play at school this year? She's the greatest actress since Meryl Streep," Mother then says.

"Yes, she is, isn't she?" I say, rubbing Amanda's arm.

I help Mother clear the dishes and settle the boys in front of the TV. Amanda sits in the corner, chomping down on cookies and tapping on her iPhone. I hear her saying, "This thing is amazing."

"Yes, but can it scrub a toilet?"

Amanda salutes heaven with her eyes and turns her back to me. Mother beckons me to follow her upstairs.

"I just wanted to show you this, darling. Do you like it?" she asks, pulling out of her bedroom closet a yellow floral dress that looks like a carpet at a Marriott hotel. "I got it at Loehmann's. Such a bargain. The Queen wears a lot of yellow, you know."

I demur.

Mother points to her bed. "Come sit down here, darling. We can have a nice chat."

I don't feel like a nice chat.

"So, darling, I was thinking," Mother says, smoothing down her pants as she sits down and crosses her ankles daintily together. "Why don't you ring Steven up and meet him somewhere for a chat?" (Mother loves chats.) "Maybe he can give you an idea of the problem."

"I already know what the problem is," I say. "She's twenty five and a size two."

Mother mutters something I don't hear.

"What?" I say.

"Oh nothing, darling. I'm just thinking that this is all just a fling, you know. Nothing serious. Men and their midlife problem. Once he's had his…well, you know what I mean. He'll come to his senses. They all do."

"I'm not sure he will."

"Well, darling, you just have to make him. I mean, you have to."

I say nothing. A wave of pain is washing over me.

Mother takes my hand. "Now listen, Madeleine. You need to get together with your husband and work things out. You need to ask him what he wants and then provide it. You have to wake up and get in the game."

"Get in the game? What have I been doing these past twenty years if not playing the game? He's not easy to be married to, you know."

Mother looks surprised. "Really? He's always been pleasant when we've seen him. Look, darling, at a certain age, men see they're getting old, and they get a bit frisky. Your job is to make sure that doesn't happen and that if they get frisky, it's with you."

"Steven used to get frisky with me. Well, up until recently, he did."

"Hmm," Mother says, unconvinced. "Well darling, you know you really could pay more attention to your appearance. After the children…" And her voice trails off.

"What do you mean, Mother?" I ask, knowing exactly what she means. "I might have put on a few pounds, but he always liked my full figure."

"Now, Madeleine. You're being deliberately obtuse. You know there are areas in which you can improve. I've always stayed slim and trim, haven't I?" I feel bile rising in my throat.

"I know, Mother. I am aware of that. It's just not that easy to shed the pounds right now."

"I know, darling, but everyone diets. Why can't you? I can't eat what I want."

"Oh, Mother, you've been on a diet for forty years."

"Exactly, darling. That's my whole point. Do you think your father would still be wearing out the carpets in this house if I had gained fifty pounds and not made him feel like the king of the castle?"

"Oh I don't know, Mother," I snap. "I guess I'm not the perfect wife like you."

"Darling, please don't be cross with me. I don't mean to upset you, but it's my job to advise you, isn't it? For instance, you need a haircut. Do you know that?"

"Of course I know that."

"And your house, well, it's a bit of a mess. When I was there the other day, I could see dust on the tables. Whatever happened to your housekeeper? Didn't she use to come three times a week?"

"I'm not sure how much money I'm going to be getting from Steven, and for now, she's only going to be coming once a month. How many cleaning ladies do you know who accept credit cards?"

"Well, you just have to *make* Steven send enough money, darling."

I just nod. Mother has no idea how stingy Steven can often be. At least with me. I bought most of my own clothes with the money I earned when I was at the *San Francisco Chronicle*. I always said he has deep pockets and short arms. "It's time for us to get going."

"Oh darling," Mother says. "So soon?"

"It's a school night. The kids need to get to bed."

"Well, if you say so, darling. Just think about what I've said. And please continue to take the children to church. Father Ralph will be so unhappy if you don't."

I take a deep breath and walk to the living room, where Colin is asleep on Father's lap and Charlie and Amanda are bickering over who dresses more bizarrely—Lady Gaga or Nicki Minaj. I gently smooth down Colin's blond cowlick and pick him up in my arms. "Let's go, you two," I whisper.

As we drive off, I see Mother standing rather forlornly by the front door, waving the royal wave.

I see the kids to bed. When I get into my own bed, I run, as I have been doing a lot of lately, revenge scenarios through my head. A letter to the principal of Steven's company, telling him all about his so-called family man. Seven machetes to the exterior and two gallons of Kelly Moore Very Cherry paint to the interior of his Lexus.

Chapter 4

The secret of a happy marriage remains a secret.
—Henny Youngman

The kids have just left for school, and I'm cleaning up bagel crumbs from the kitchen table.

The phone rings. "Hello?"

"Hello, Madeleine."

Steven is at his most serious and sober-voiced. It is the first time we have spoken since he left, and I feel my stomach clenching. There have been e-mails back and forth about money. About how he isn't sending enough. And about who should have the children when. For now, Steven gets them most weekends. But this is our first conversation.

"The kids' principal requests we go see her next Wednesday at five."

Why isn't he saying I love you, I made a mistake, I am a miserable wretch not fit to lick your boots (or rather your blue suede Cole Haans)?

"Why wouldn't the school call me directly?" I say instead.

"I told them not to bother you because of your fragile state."

Rage sears me. "Fragile state? How dare you say that about me to the principal?!"

"I didn't mean to upset you. I was just trying to—"

"Oh fuck off." (Twenty-five cents.)

Stevens sighs heavily. "Look, none of this will help, you know. And keeping the kids from me won't either."

"I'm not keeping the kids from you," I spit back at him. "You can see them anytime you want but not for overnight, not when Lolita's there."

Steven sighs heavily again. "I just—"

I hang up.

The prospect of meeting with the kids' principal, Anna Langley, is not one I relish. She reminds of Mrs. McNeagle, the prissy headmistress at the school I went to in London—hair scraped back so tightly her pink scalp shows and ice in her eyes. Miss Langley always makes me feel "unsuitable." Like Steven deserves a wife who sports a laser-cut navy tweed Chanel suit with a miniskirt and tulle lining, not loose-cut jeans and T-shirts. She makes it obvious that I don't fit the bill of the glamorous wife and looks at me with such puzzlement and disapproval I almost beg her to send me to detention. The meetings always go on for so long it feels like *Seven Years in Tibet* without the popcorn. Miss Langley—emphasis on the *Miss*—is always criticizing. I'm sure this one will be torture.

I turn on the television, and what are they showing? *Heartburn.* Just what I need. I flip channels. Talk shows about divorce. Infomercials about new fantastic weight-loss programs. It's all so abysmal, I turn it off.

I take my laptop into the library, a paneled affair that is my favorite room in the house. It's small, tucked away near the bedrooms. It originally was the house's attic, but I prevailed on Steven to convert it into a library and writing room for me. He hemmed and hawed about it a bit, calling my writing a "hobby, and not a very remunerative one at that." Finally, however, he was made to understand that if I had a library, he would not be, as he put it, "falling over at every turn," on my admittedly large collection of books.

The Bay is gray and choppy as I sit down to finish an article on great stores and boutiques in San Francisco only locals know about, a rather time-consuming, overly detailed exercise that included visiting more than fifteen stores and scribbling down descriptions of their innovative inventory, trying to run down their owners, and a lot of feeble conversation about how the latest look is the bell-shaped skirt in a color designers call burnt sienna and I call brown.

I have kept my hand in journalism since quitting the *Chronicle* just before Amanda was born by freelancing here and there. Even though I am less than excited about the content of my current project and the writing is going slowly, I comfort myself with the thought that I am trying (successfully so far) to resist the rum raisin ice cream I know is residing in my freezer.

The phone rings. It's Suzy.

"How are you?"

"Just going along, I guess."

"What are you doing?"

"I'm finishing an article, and then I will start writing in my journal, all the while trying not to succumb to my ice-cream craving."

"Good for you, but we need to start that blog we talked about."

Sigh. "I can only manage one new thing in my life at a time right now. Why don't we change the subject?"

"OK, what to?"

"Steven called to tell me we have to go see the principal at the kids' school."

"What for?"

"God knows. Probably some silly bit of nonsense. The worst of it was that it was he who called me to tell me about the meeting, not the principal."

"Why?"

"He told her it was better if he did it because of what he called 'my fragile state.'"

"Sanctimonious arsehole," Suzy says.

Exactly.

"So what's going on with you?" I ask.

"Rex the Ex is coming over Friday night with his new love—whom I am calling Boy Joy—for dinner. Am I nuts?"

"No comment."

"Of course I am. But we have two children together, and no one wins if we're enemies. Judge Judy says you have to love your children more than you hate each other."

"Judge Judy? I didn't know you watched her. I kind of like her straight-talking ways. I loved it when she told one plaintiff not to pee on her leg and tell her it's raining. And then she said to one woman, 'You spent seventy-two dollars to have your hair done? You wasted your money.'"

Suzy and I shriek with laughter.

"As to building bridges, I'm just not ready for that yet."

"Fine," Suzy says. "But just read some blogs, and let's get to it. You'll love it."

I type "divorce blogs" into Google. A long list appears before me, and I move from one to another. Most are dreadful. One woman suggests that if you are unhappy in your marriage, you should go on a "divorce diet." Meaning get off your marriage diet. Meaning get a divorce. Very insightful.

I move to a website dealing only with divorce where there is a thread related to dumped wives writing to the "Other Woman."

One such wife writes, "Dear OW: U think u should ask urself a few questons? One would be do you wanna be with someone who don't even suportt his own kids? He might be mad with me right now, but, honeybun, han't u heard? Men always come home. And where does that leave u? Have ur fun while it lasts. And if he don't come back I will be here with bills to pay and a juge and lawer to tell him to support his three butiful kids. And then *u'll* be suportting him. And, by the way, everything's in my name."

Lovely.

Do I really want to join the ranks of these disgruntled women? You bet I do. But at least I'll do it with style and correct grammar.

Chapter 5

After all my erstwhile dear, my no longer cherished;
Need we say it was not love, just because it perished?
—Edna St. Vincent Millay

THE BLASPHEMY BOX

This is my first blog entry. My BFF says I have to call it a post. So this is my first post. BFF set up the blog for me. She says it will help me process the breakup of my marriage. This and a lot of ice cream and shopping, I think.

First, something about the title. Months before he left, His Majesty (HM) thought he'd teach me a lesson about good language. So he put a small wooden box on the kitchen table into which I have to drop a quarter every time I curse. He dubbed it the Blasphemy Box. It's a symbol of everything that was wrong in the marriage, so it seemed like a fitting title for my blog.

Anyway, I'm fifty. I'm a journalist and worked at the San Francisco Chronicle *until fourteen years ago when I quit to start a family. My husband has left me after twenty years of marriage and three children, and I feel so adrift, so alone, so goddamn bewildered. (Oops! Twenty-five cents). I'm as sad as a snowdrop in summer.*

To add insult to injury, I also have to live with the fact that he has a twenty-five-year-old girlfriend (Girl Bambi), who my kids now see on a regular basis.

Sometimes, at the grocery store or while making the kids dinner, a huge surge of panic overtakes me, and I have trouble breathing. I'm terrified for my future, my old age, the kids with their own families, me alone. For twenty years I was part of a "we." Now it's "I" and "he."

I feel so pathetic. Alone with my laptop refreshing my e-mail every two seconds and watching that K9 Advantix commercial we both loved— the one with the singing yellow Lab puppy who writes home from camp thanking his parents for sending him flea and tick control. I stare at the phone, trying to think of any reason at all that I can call him. I've got to control the urge. We were so great together for so long. At least I thought so. And now…It's as if twenty years have been eviscerated from my life, and I'm walking around without my internal organs.

BFF says over 55 percent of American marriages end in divorce and that I shouldn't feel such a failure. She cites the London lawyer who sells divorce gift vouchers as Christmas presents—that it's almost fashionable.

She'll say anything to make me feel better. That's what BFFs do.

Anyway, perhaps one of the most frightening things, at least for me, is the thought of seeing my ex for the first time since our breakup. I know I should make sure to brush my hair and keep it cool and civil. But the thought of it makes my heart race and my mouth as dry as Palm Springs.

Help!

It's Monday morning and a blustery one out on the Bay. I get the kids ready for school. In addition to the usual "Mom, where's my backpack? Mom, where's my lunch box? Mom, where's my jacket?," it's also now "Mom, where's my iPhone? Mom, where's my iPod? Mom, where's my laptop?"

"As I've told you kids before," I say. "All those items are where *you* left them."

Once I see them into the carpool car, I walk back to the kitchen and look at the digital scale with ill-concealed hostility. Dear Steven bought it for me a couple of years ago, hoping, I imagine, that it might prompt me to once again become the size four he married. I had hoped that just by looking at it every day, I would once again become the size four he married.

I get onto the scale and step back quickly. I'm Ten-Ton Tessie. I can't bring myself to speak out loud how much I weigh. Maybe I can. A hundred and sixty pounds—at least forty over optimum. Surely this can't be right, I tell myself. There must be something wrong with the scale. Sure, I've put on bit around the middle, and my hips have suffered from the aftereffects of childbirth, but 160 pounds is just not possible.

Shaking my head in disbelief, I take a cinnamon bun from the fridge, heat it up, and scarf it down. There, that'll show the scale something. I shower, get dressed, and get into the car. I need to go to the pharmacy to find eye drops for one of the boys. When I get there, I wander the aisles looking at the signs. There's an aisle for oral care, feminine care, skin care, and every other care in the world it seems. Except husband care, of course. I would love to see what might be in *that* aisle.

My route takes me past some scales. For a lark I decide to try one. Maybe it will give me my correct weight. At least I'll get an accurate reading. A hundred and sixty-two pounds! I pick up the drops and make for the cashier, where I pull my coat tightly around me so the perky clerk won't notice my expanded middle.

Does anyone remember me when I was thin and young and pretty? I don't.

࿐

This afternoon is the meeting with the school principal. Yesterday I got my hair tinted and highlighted and raided my closet for a slimming outfit, a black sheath dress with white stitching. I apply some makeup, hoping that it will make me feel better, which it does, and thinner, which it doesn't. I fling down the mascara, make my way to the garage, climb into the car, and turn the key in the ignition. I see my hands are shaking, and I feel nauseous. With the exception of brief glimpses as he picked up and dropped off the kids, this will be the first time I have seen Steven in the month since he left.

When I arrive, he is almost at Miss Langley's door. My nerves feel like harp strings ready to snap. He turns around and sees me, a half smile on his face. I want to say, listen, let's forget all this nonsense. Come home. But he doesn't wait for me to say anything; he just graciously holds the door for me.

I can already hear Miss Langley start up her customary sickeningly ingratiating greeting and inviting us to sit down. Steven pulls out one of the two chairs in front of her impressive, ornately carved mahogany desk and gestures to me to sit down on one of them. Putting on a show for Miss Langley, I see. I haven't received this kind of courtly solicitude since Clinton was first president. Steven then sits in the second chair and focuses his attention on the headmistress.

She begins with her usual condescending tone, describing the twins as more unruly than usual in class and Amanda as not paying as much attention to her studies as to boys. (I could have told her that.) She reminds us again that at last year's school social, Amanda danced too closely to Nicholas, forcing her to separate them with a ruler and the admonition: "Save room for Jesus." It's a Catholic school, after all, and she's a nun in everything except the habit.

"She was getting As and Bs, and now she's getting Cs and Ds." Miss Langley is droning on. "Amanda has always been a good student, if a bit headstrong. Have there been any changes at home that might account for her behavior?" she says, her beady eyes boring into me.

I look at Steven, who does not look back. He doesn't like public conversations about private matters, and instead of answering, he is tapping the floor with the loafers I bought him last Christmas, something he does when he's annoyed.

There's silence. I keep waiting for Steven to say something, but he doesn't. So I say, "Well, we are separated. For now."

Steven looks away.

"I see," Miss Langley says, her eyebrows raised. She doesn't approve of separations, obviously. But then, neither do I.

"Well, have you thought of any kind of counseling?" she says. "It's not good for young children to be in limbo."

Steven finally speaks. "We know what is best for our children, and we thank you for alerting us to this situation. We will certainly address these issues."

Miss Langley seems about to discuss the matter further, but Steven is up and out of his chair. "Thank you, Miss Langley," he says.

Even after this brush-off, the principal seems inclined to keep talking, but all I can think of is that Steven is leaving. I thank Miss Langley and we leave, retracing our steps down the hallway plastered with paintings of bleeding martyrs and along the breezeway toward the parking lot.

"Her attitude is a bit inappropriate for what I'm paying for that school," Steven says. "Treating us as if we were insubordinate children."

"She's always been like that," I say. I am silent then, hoping he will say something else, continue the conversation.

We are in the parking lot now, and finally I say, "Hang on a sec, would you? I was hoping we could talk a little. You know. About us. About our situation. I'd like to discuss what the problem is, see what we can to do, well, to fix it."

"I have to go back to work."

"But can't we, I mean…we really need to talk."

"Madeleine," he says, looking around to see if anyone can hear us, "there's nothing to talk about. This is where our children go to school. Please don't make a scene."

He inserts the key into the door of his car as I step backward, feeling foolish. I'm an embarrassment to him, someone to be shushed and hushed, like when Charlie was four and asked the nun on a bus in London if he could see her knickers. I feel like Queen Elizabeth doing a lap dance.

"Look," I say. "I understand about the affair. I get it. Twenty years of marriage and all that. But we can work through this. It doesn't need to mean the end of us."

"Madeleine," Steven says with a sigh. "This won't help. It's over between us, and it doesn't matter why."

"It doesn't matter why?" I repeat. I am numb with shock. Who *is* this man? I just want to feel normal again.

"How could you do this?" My voice is a whisper, raspy with tears. "What happened? We were OK, weren't we?"

He turns on the ignition. "No, we weren't and aren't, and I have to go now."

He rolls up the window, and as he drives away, I've never felt lonelier in my life.

When I get home, I call Cameron, who has been married and divorced three times, and blubber on the phone to her for a while. She says all the right things and tells me I'm a wonderful, beautiful person. I feel so much better.

Not too much later, the kids arrive.

"How did the meeting with Miss Langley go?" Amanda says tentatively. There's a wary look in her eyes.

"She says you need to concentrate more on your studies, and Daddy and I agree."

"Am I grounded?"

"No, of course not," I say.

She looks at me unwaveringly, then. "Are you OK, Mom? You look like you've been crying."

I want to tell her I could cry and cry, like a seabird in the wind. But I say only, "Oh, I've been chopping onions, that's all."

Amanda is unconvinced but says nothing further.

At 2 a.m., she crawls into bed with me.

"Daddy's not coming back, is he?" she says.

"I don't know," I say. "I don't think so."

I stroke her long, dark hair and kiss her on the temple. How did she ever get so big? Soon I can hear the rhythmic sound of her breathing. She's asleep.

Chapter 6

If love is the answer, could you please rephrase the question?
—*Lily Tomlin*

THE BLASPHEMY BOX

When you are newly separated or divorced, there's nothing more glaringly obvious than Valentine's Day to remind you just what a loser in love you really are. This year, V-Day snuck up on me in the sneakiest, smarmiest fashion and here it is, all sweet and syrupy, yet at my house, there's nary a red rose or a box of See's Candies Nuts and Chews in sight. The Sinatra channel keeps playing "Isn't it Romantic?," cable TV keeps replaying The Way We Were, *and I'm feeling like Santa in June. For the first time in a number of years, I have no plans for tonight. What about you all, out there?*

It's Valentine's Day, and all I want to do is bury myself in the sheets with my old friends Häagen and Dazs. Or throw myself off the Golden Gate Bridge. If I do the former, however, I won't be able to eat again in this century, and if I do the latter, my children will be motherless, and I'll never again get a Valentine card from Charlie reading, "Mom, you are my Valentine because you give me food and water."

Though it may surprise you to hear this, Steven could, at one time, have been accused of being something of a romantic. He more usually than not surprised me with a lovely dinner at a lovely restaurant for Valentine's Day and brought me sprays of dense red roses and chocolates. We always had a babysitter for the evening, and after dinner we would meet friends for a nightcap. It was all very enjoyable, and even if, lately, we were not in the bloom of young love, we both still managed to enjoy the evening as if we were. Now, it's the day for lovers, and Steven is not here offering flowers and candy. No one else is here, either. And there's the rub.

I give myself a good talking to, recalling all the things Suzy has been telling me to do lately. Like think of what I have, not what I don't have. As Suzy says, happiness is not having everything you want, but being able to be happy with what you have. But when I was with Steven, I was happy, mostly. At least I had a built-in partner with whom to share the holidays. Particularly this holiday. I was half of a couple. Now I'm just one of one. I know intellectually that I should create new rituals for myself around Valentine's Day—around every holiday, in fact. But the notion brings on such a depression I want to stick pins into a Steven look-a-like voodoo doll and destroy every single goddamn (twenty-five cents) wedding photo in my albums.

I sit staring out at the Bay. And then I decide that instead of moping around all day while the kids are at school, I will give myself flowers and candy, and while I'm at it, I'll get my hair done, too. I'll put it all on the credit card and hope the charges go through.

I call the salon, and they can get me in at eleven.

I shower and dress and make my way downtown, but when I get there, the traffic signals aren't working, and it's more frustrating than usual to get into the public garage. After parking, I saunter down Geary and see all the stores have Valentine's Day themes: sexy red lingerie in one window, tight little crimson tube dresses in another—dresses that would just about fit around a normal woman's arm.

I fight back feelings of sadness as I head to the salon. I'm looking forward to having my hair done. But when I get there, the windows are dark. A small sign hangs on the door: NO POWER UNTIL THIS AFTERNOON. SEE YOU THEN.

I decide to go get something to eat, but none of the cafés have electricity, either, of course. No reason to kick around for three hours, so I get back into my car, pay three dollars for ten minutes of parking, and drive home.

Once there, I pick up the phone to call Cameron to see if she wants to go to dinner. But then I remember she has a hot date, and even if she didn't, Gracie, my babysitter, has a hot date, and I wouldn't be able to go anyway. Everyone has a hot date, it seems, except me.

Breaking my promise to myself not to mope, I mope. I make tea, then throw it out untasted. I turn on the television and flip through every channel on the guide from Cloo and Nicktoons to DIY, where the host is instructing the viewing audience on the ten best fire pit designs and how you can do one backsplash in seven different ways. Fascinating.

I get up, I sit down. I try to work on my novel, but the cursor just blinks mockingly at me. I just can't believe I am now facing years of Valentine's Days flying solo. Not to mention all those Katherine Heigl movies I'll be watching in the fetal position.

I go into my bedroom and throw myself on my bed. As soon as I do this, I sit up again and stare grouchily out at the roiling gray waters of the Bay. I just don't know what to do. I just don't know what to *do*.

I lie back down again and close my eyes, praying to whoever is out there to have mercy on me. I hear the mailman drive up and walk out to the mailbox.

I wave at him.

"Happy Valentine's Day!" he says cheerily.

I grimace and wander back into the house. Rifling through the letters, I see what looks like a greeting card of some sort. Maybe I have a secret admirer who knows that after twenty years I am single and available. One can hope, can't one? I open the envelope and pull out a card with a red velvet heart on the front. I open it and see Suzy's familiar handwriting. "Dear Maddy: as someone once said, the heart is the only broken instrument that works."

I am so cheered and so guilty I didn't send her one too, I get on the phone to the florist we've always used and order roses.

"Can they be there today?"

"It's cutting it a bit fine, but we'll call down to our LA shop and do our best," the owner tells me. "It might be much later."

I go into the kitchen and start preparing dinner. At least, I think, I have my children on Valentine's Day. At that exact moment, the carpool arrives. The kids alight, take our stairs two at a time, and land in a heap on my living room carpet. Colin is clutching a bunch of red roses in his hand, squashed into a pressed state perfect for the pages of a book.

"Happy Valentine's Day, Mom," he says, my darling, angel, child. At that moment I realize I am not alone, after all. I have these precious lovelies.

I kiss him on the top of his head, ruffle his hair, and say, "Thank you, to all of you. You've made my day."

Amanda is watching me carefully. "We figured you might be a little sad today, Mom," she says.

I blink back my tears. "Not at all," I say. "How could I be sad when I have you three?" And I pull all of them to me for a group hug. Amanda twists away as quickly as she can, but the twins stay so close I can smell them.

"I made you a card," Charlie says, rifling through his backpack, from which he draws out a fraying linen card with a huge red heart drawn on the cover. Inside, he has written, "To the best Mom in the world."

This time I cannot blink back my tears. I hug the boys again, but not Amanda. She's too old to be hugged, it seems. "Thank you very much again. OK," I say, "wash your hands for dinner."

"What are we having?" Amanda asks.

"I was going to make grilled salmon with roast potatoes and spinach."

"Really, Mom?" Amanda's tone is wheedling.

"What's wrong with salmon?" I say.

"Mom, it's Valentine's Day. Can't we go out? Everyone goes out."

"But sweetie, Valentine's Day is for well…you know…romantic partners. It's a day to celebrate romance."

"Well," Amanda says. "Madame Berry said today that it's a day for love and that there can be all kinds of love between all kinds of people."

I am about to debate the question but stop myself. Madame Berry, despite her towering beehive, is right.

"I don't know where we could get in at this late date," I say. I can just see us ending up at the Burger King just off the freeway next to some soused old woman stinking of smoke and urine chowing down on a Double Whopper with no teeth. "And it is a school night, you know."

"Oh Mom, we can be back early," Amanda says. "It doesn't have to be anywhere fancy. Let's just go for pizza."

The Blasphemy Box

"Pizza!" The twins start screaming and jumping up and down. "Let's go for pizza!"

"OK, fine," I say. "Upstairs right now to take showers and put on some warm clothes."

The kids run upstairs like a herd of elephants, and I follow them. What, I wonder, does one wear to go out for a platonic Valentine's Day dinner? I don't know. I've never done it. I shower, pull out a sweater and tailored pants from my closet, and brush my hair until it shines. Frankly, I'm dreading this dinner. I just know that everyone's going to be in couples, and there I'm going to be, big loser herself, forced to eat pizza on Valentine's Day with my kids.

When we get to the restaurant on Lombard Street, it's jammed and the wait is an hour. The boys' faces drop, and Amanda just stands there, disconsolate. She has never taken disappointment well. I guess she's a spoiled brat.

"Well, I guess we need to find somewhere else," I say. "Let's see now. What's near here that has pizza?"

The kids don't know, and neither do I. I go back to the restaurant and ask the hostess if she can enlighten me.

"On Chestnut there's this brand-new place where they have all these exotic kinds of pizzas," she says. "Maybe because they're new, they won't be totally slammed?"

"Good idea," I say. "Thanks."

I motion the kids to follow me, and we walk down Steiner to Chestnut. Within minutes of arriving at the new place, we are given a large, comfortable red leather booth, and soon we're poring over the menu composed of the strangest pizzas known to man.

"I want the bacon cheeseburger pizza," announces Colin. (See what I mean about strange pizzas?)

"I want the nacho pizza," Charlie says.

This can't be healthy.

Amanda fixes her eyes on me. "Don't worry, Mom, it's just this once. The twins won't die from one fatty pizza."

I smile. "You're right. And what will you have?"

"Pesto pepperoni," she says.

"Great idea. We can share."

- 37 -

The boys turn on their iPods, and I turn to my daughter—my suddenly so-grown-up daughter—who seems to be able to read my facial expressions in a way that is unsettling.

"So, did a boy give you a Valentine's card today?" I ask her.

Her face creases into a moue. "Mom. You can't ask me stuff like that."

"Why ever not?"

"I'm not a kid anymore. My private life is my private life."

Hmm. I didn't know she had a private life.

"I didn't know you had a private life."

"Well, I might not, but if I do, I'm not going to tell *you* about it."

"OK," I say, wrapping my arm around her and laying my head on her shoulder. "It would just be nice to know who he is."

"You should be more worried about yourself, Mom," Amanda says. Her eyes are this aqua kind of color that's quite mesmerizing.

"What do you mean?"

"I mean about the situation with you and Dad."

"Ah, here are our pizzas," I say, sending a prayer of infinite gratitude up to the heavens.

We eat happily, the twins bickering as usual, this time over how many pieces of each other's pizza the other's going to get. Amanda and I eat our pizza while she regales me with tales of Madame Berry, who, she says, gets very involved in the French literature she is teaching Amanda's class, forever siding with the unfaithful protagonist.

"Like who?"

"Like Emma Bovary," Amanda says.

Hmm. Not exactly what I sent Amanda to this school for. To learn that it's OK to commit adultery. Especially now.

"Well, what do you think about that?"

"About being unfaithful?"

"Yes."

Amanda's eyes bore into me as if they can see into the utmost reaches of my soul. "I would say it isn't a good idea," she says.

I hug her then and tell the boys to stop arguing over the last piece of pizza.

So that was my Valentine's Day. I wonder what everyone else did.

Chapter 7

Never rely on the glory of the morning, nor the smiles of your mother-in-law.
—*Japanese Proverb*

THE BLASPHEMY BOX

One of the most awkward and uncomfortable things about getting a divorce is being forced to continue dealing with your former in-laws. (Especially if you don't have the warmest of relationships with them.) How do you manage their stern disapproval, as if you're the one who ran off and shagged someone new? That look of undisguised hostility that says, "I knew it wouldn't last. Thank God he finally came to his senses"?

In a divorce, you worry that your in-laws will take their child's side (they will) and that your kids might suffer because of it (they might). And then you worry that if your in-laws do indeed still want to be in your kids' lives (which you want), it means they still have to be in yours, too (which you don't). You can divorce your husband, but not his parents.

I knew mother-in-law and I would never be chums. When I found out she had "accidentally" thrown out my engagement ring (which I had taken off to wash the dishes, and which I discovered later in the trash rolled up in a paper towel), I should have known she was Satan incarnate. Same goes for her Christmas gift to me one year: a membership to Weight Watchers.

It's a wind-whipped morning, and Steven's mother, Anita is at the door. With hair hard as cement and perfectly frosted, wearing a crisp Chanel jacket and tailored pants, and smelling of the thousand-dollar La Mer face cream she's always prattling about, she barges in.

"Madeleine," she says in her gravelly smoker's voice.

"Good morning, Anita."

"Are the boys ready?"

"Almost." She drums her knuckles on the demilune table just inside our front door.

"I want to arrive at the Disney museum early, so we can get to the Cliff House before it gets too busy. I want a table over the water and plenty of those popovers. The children love them almost as much as I do."

"I'm sure you'll get there in plenty of time."

Anita coughs and then checks her makeup in the hallway mirror.

"Would you like some coffee?" I say.

"Don't touch the stuff," she says abruptly. "Bad for the complexion."

"You drank coffee when we were all in Rome," I say.

"Well, that's Italy. Italian coffee. That's different."

I look at her, waiting for her to mention the Big D.

She coughs again. "Do the kids need anything?"

"Yes, their father."

Anita sighs. "Now, Madeleine," she says, "people divorce all the time. You're not the first woman whose husband has left her. I'm sure he had a good reason for doing so."

"Yes, Anita, I am sure he did. Her name is Gabriela, and she's twenty-five years old, and the kids say it's serious."

Anita takes a step back and actually pales. It's perfect. Steven hasn't yet told her how far things have gone with Girl Bambi. She is so taken aback she can't speak for a while, which if you know Anita, is completely out of character. I can practically feel her shock and anger vibrating in waves toward me.

"Is this your idea of a sick joke?" she says, sniffing as if she had just passed a sewer. Just when she thought she was rid of one daughter-in-law, another one seems to be rearing her head.

But there is no time to answer. Two voices cry "Nana!" and two children hurl themselves down the stairs en masse and fling themselves at Anita, whose stone face softens into genuine affection.

"And how are we all today?" she cries. "Amanda not coming?"

"Not today," I say. "I think she has plans with her friends."

"Well," Anita says, trying not to show it matters. "Ready for the Disneyland model and popovers and ice cream?"

The boys scream in delight, kiss me on the cheek, and are gone in a flurry of parkas and electronica. I look out of the window and watch my babies climbing into the car. In the past, Steven would have been here watching with me, smiling indulgently at the kids' excitement.

At least I don't have to worry about keeping the relationship going with Steven's father. He was a money man, just like his son, but he died when he was only fifty-one in a car accident on the way to Stinson Beach. I never met him, but I get the impression from people who did that he was just like Steven—a bit aloof and rather prissy. Much like his wife. And much like all their relations. At least all the relations I've met. If I had my druthers, I'd wad the entire Nelson clan into a tight little spitball and shoot it down the San Francisco hills into the Bay.

I wouldn't suffer one whit from not having Anita in my life. But as Judge Judy says, children are entitled to the widest circle of love and attention, and I cannot deprive mine of their grandmother.

Everyone tells you that marriage is just an unending series of compromises. But what it really is is just an unending series of sacrifices. And who wants to make sacrifices unendingly? No one, that's who. Who wants to sacrifice the peace and enjoyment of every holiday so that dear mother-in-law can sweep in and play Lady Bountiful to everyone except you? Oh, she's willing to help the kids wreak havoc in the kitchen making Creamy Dreamy Peanut Butter cookies, but never around when said kitchen needs cleaning up by the exhausted mother of said kids. I didn't want to sacrifice my career to have kids, but I had to. When I suggested we get a full-time nanny, mother-in-law said we don't need that, we have you.

I make myself walk into the library, determined to use the time to work on my unfinished novel, knowing that it might be difficult with the specter of Anita still dancing in front of me. I sign on to my blog only to find my first comments from readers. Yippee! Can't believe it!

Wow. Your MIL sounds exactly like mine. She never made a secret of the fact that any other woman in the world would have made a better daughter-in-law than me. Five years after we got married, she arrived on Christmas Day with a box. I thought, great, finally she's willing to

play nice. Intrigued, I opened the box and inside found hair dye. She apparently didn't like my hair color.
Posted by SereneCoreen

My mother-in-law is the bane of my life. I got her a really pretty Swarovski crystal bracelet one time, and when she didn't thank me, I asked her if she liked it, and she said, 'Yes, I've put it with all the other costume jewelry I never wear.'"
Posted by Givemeagun

I reply:
On the subject of jewelry, my MIL has some really nice pieces. Once, when my daughter was admiring them, she said to her grandmother, "I love these, Nana, how lucky Mom will be to inherit them."

My MIL was apoplectic. "Your Mom?" she cried. "Oh, no, dear, these will come to you...not to..."

My mother-in-law is just some perma-tanned, shriveled-up old string of spaghetti who lives in Palm Desert and still insists on wearing sleeveless dresses at 78. She's always saying how fat and pale I and my children are and how I should give us less food and more sun.
Posted by HatemyMIL

I reply:
Can my MIL come live with your MIL in Palm Desert? Maybe they can desiccate together?

In response to your Valentine's blog: wanna know what I did the first Valentine's Day after my divorce? The same as I did when I was married. Nothing.
Posted by is-happy

My husband waited until Valentine's Day to tell me he wanted a divorce. It was our fourteenth anniversary.
Posted by tigress1

Chapter 8

Ask yourself whether you are happy, and you cease to be so.
—*John Stuart Mill*

THE BLASPHEMY BOX

BFF suggests I go for therapy.

"What on?" I ask her. "Buttons? Therapists don't take credit cards, you know."

And then I remind her of our school friend Angela, who was seeing a shrink after her divorce and quit after a couple of sessions, saying why should she go to a head doctor when she could stay home and talk to the ceiling for free.

I mean, really, how can it help you solve your problems to sit on a scratchy, polyester tweed, fifties sofa in some stranger's office telling him your troubles, while he says, "Really? And how did that make you feel?"

Then she says I could always join a support group for women whose husbands have left them. She says getting mental-emotional services is just as important as getting legal services and nowhere near as expensive. Widows are showered with compassionate phone calls and chicken casseroles. What have I gotten? A lot of "What did you do?" and silence. A dumped wife is a source of embarrassment to the people she knows. BFF says joining a group will help me to not fall prey to depression.

At least it's free.

My first session was yesterday. There are six of us, from all kinds of backgrounds and socio-economic groups, but all of us are fifty or over. You have to be fifty. Frankly, this is not the scenario I envisioned when I thought of turning fifty: sitting in some drafty Victorian flat over a store that sells Guatemalan textiles with babies crying outside and women crying inside.

I found the group through a friend of a friend, and we are meant to meet twice a week. I drive around and around for ten miles looking for parking. What a surprise. No parking in San Francisco. As the headline for one of my early articles for the *Chronicle* said, "A Night at the Opera, but Where Do we Park?"

Each new member has to introduce herself and tell her tale of woe. I hate that. Just hate it. That's why when I went to my reading group for the first time, I stood up and said, "I'm Maddy, and I've always wanted to be a plant morphologist in Australia." Nobody laughed. Hmm.

Anyway, I hate the whole lame introduction game. Do these women really have to know my *real* name and everything about my sad situation?

Unfortunately, yes. It's mandatory. Like AA, where you have to admit you have a problem.

"My name is Maddy, and my husband, er..." is how I begin. I just can't bring myself to say the words.

"Your husband dumped you," says the group leader, Rachel, who sports five nose rings, puce nail polish and Goth makeup, and sells Manic Panic hair color and pasties at a store for working drag queens on Haight Street.

"For a younger woman," says a gorgeous petite brunette who looks about forty-five and is wearing enough ice to reverse the greenhouse effect. I can see her sizing me up as the candidate most unlikely to be wearing the latest fire-engine red Donna Karan cut-away jacket and Yves Saint Laurent poppy-print wedges. I'm not wearing either. She is.

"Yes," I say.

They wait for more, but I just can't bring myself to say more at that minute, so they start updating the group on how they're getting along in the wake of the breakups of their marriages.

Their stories are as sad or sadder than mine and mostly familiar, although today, when Angie handed out copies of a letter she had written to her husband asking him why he wanted to "sepperate," how she had had a "gut ranching feeling" that he was "cheetin" on her and "lie-ing" to her, I nearly asked her if it was because she can't spell.

But most stories are what you would imagine. Sally's husband (an electrician who took the plug off the television every morning before he left for work) had an affair with her best friend. (Horrid.) Lillian's husband had an affair with her daughter. (Even more horrid.) Rachel's husband with her mother. (Unimaginable.) I guess it means that it's sex that is the cause of all the trouble. But Steven and I never had that problem. Not until recently, anyway.

Why is it I never hear about women being unfaithful? Rarely, that is. We know they are—we know they just have to be—but in my admittedly limited circle of experience and friends, I know of no marriage that broke up because the woman was having an affair. Maybe it's just that women can hide it better or that men are clueless. Maybe it's true what they say: "Infidelity in a woman is a masculine trait."

The gorgeous brunette, whose name is Myla, lifts her hand. In a breathy, Jackie Kennedy voice she says, "I have something to share."

We fall respectfully silent and train our eyes on her. "My husband has been unfaithful to me," she announces.

Of course he has, I think. Why would she be here otherwise?

"*And*," she says, "I have incontrovertible proof."

Well done using the big word, I want to say. And great plastic surgery. No original parts. And then I tell myself to cut the bitchiness.

"What is it?" I ask.

"Well," she says, leaning toward me, "Two weeks ago, on a Saturday, I had a nine-thirty appointment with my trainer, and when I got back to the house around eleven, the housekeeper told me a man had been calling every fifteen minutes asking for me and refusing to leave his name or number."

Rachel looks at her askance at the word "housekeeper," but continues to listen carefully with the rest of us.

"Anyway, I thought nothing of it. I went to answer my e-mails and then the phone rings. I answer it, and a guy asks for me. When I say who I am, he says my name is Robert James, you don't know me, but my wife, Linda, is having an affair with your husband."

She pauses then. I know exactly how she must have felt.

"Anyway," Myla continues. "I tell the guy not to be silly and ask him who he is and why is he calling, telling me these awful things, and it's harassment, and I'll call the police, and so on. And he says if you don't believe me, ask him where his car keys are when he gets home."

The group is agog now. This is some story.

Myla continues in her breathy whisper, so low that we all have to lean forward to catch what she's saying.

"I make him tell me what he means by that, and he does. He says he followed his wife that morning and saw her getting into a car with a man downtown and then driving to the Ritz-Carlton. When the man— my husband, Justin, apparently—and the man's wife, Linda, pulled into the courtyard, Justin got out, presumably to check them in while Linda stayed in the car. Then this Robert guy got out of his car, ran to Justin's car, grabbed the keys, and drove off."

We are all listening intently. Myla's eyes are wet, and I want to wrap her in my arms and cry along with her.

"What happened next?" says Rachel, who's intrigued by the story in spite of the anti-proletarian lifestyle it evokes.

"When Justin came home, I confronted him," Myla says. She's really crying now. Sally's mouth is open. "We had the mother of all fights, and I ran out of the house."

We wait for more, but Myla's coughing and sniffling too much. I leap up and hand a wad of tissues to her.

Gulping, she says, "Thanks. I'll get him, I'll fucking get him." (See, I'm not the only one who curses.) "He'll see," she keeps saying, "he'll fucking see. Nineteen years we've been married. I'll ruin him. I'll take all his money and the children, and he'll only be able to see them on Father's Day, and then he'll go bald and get fat and his dick will flop around like a wet seal, and we'll see who wants him then."

And I thought I hated my husband. That's nothing to how Myla feels. I believe she will make this breakup as public and as difficult as she can, and you know what? Good for her. We sit in silence for a while and I notice I am crying. Why do people make the people they love and who love them so unhappy?

When I get home around five, everything is whirring around in my brain. I feel exhausted, and I'm grateful the kids are having dinner with

Steven. I pour a glass of Pellegrino and sit on the couch facing the Bay, which is gray and choppy.

I didn't suspect a thing. That's worrying. They say a wife knows instantly—or not at all—so I guess I must be in the latter category.

I should have known and/or suspected. Shouldn't I? I mean, Mother would say I should have. Knowing or suspecting are on the top of Mother's list of the skills every good wife should have.

Perhaps I should have become suspicious when he left home smelling of Dial and returned smelling of Irish Spring. Or when a survey arrived in the mail from the Ritz-Carlton in San Francisco about his latest stay there, a hotel he and I have never even been to together. (Why didn't he choose the Ritz down the coast a bit in Half Moon Bay, where we *have* been together? After all, they say if you're unfaithful in another city, it doesn't count.)

But I didn't. I was driving the kids from ballet to karate to piano to soccer to basketball to swimming. I was making breakfasts and dinners. I was arranging playdates and putting on parties and going to parties. I was making sure the drinks cupboard was full of just the right tequila (Partida) and single malt (Glenfiddich). I was making vol-au-vents for Steven's boss and his beady-eyed wife. I was planning vacations and supervising the housekeeper and helping with homework and making gourmet dinners for Steven once the kids were in bed. We didn't have a lot of sex or together time, but I didn't worry too much about that. We had been married a long time, and you lose track of romance in the distractions of everyday life, don't you? I didn't have time to suspect. I didn't have a clue I should suspect.

I'm dozing on the couch when the kids come in. They know better than to disturb me, but I hear them anyway. I don't let on, and they go to bed. An hour later, I make my way to the bedroom and collapse.

When I wake up this morning, my dumped-wife situation surges into my brain with alarming alacrity. I get out of bed out of sorts. I yell at the kids to get ready for school and trudge down into the kitchen to make breakfast. Thank God the school provides lunch. The boys come down, and I fix their white button-down oxfords. Amanda is dawdling, but finally joins us. She's not eating.

"Amanda, eat your cereal, we'll be late."

"I'm not hungry."

"We go through this every day. Why do I even bother?"

She looks at me then with those clear aqua eyes of hers, that level, steady, disapproving gaze adolescents give their parents. "You know, Mom," she says, "just because you're upset with Dad doesn't mean you can take it out on me."

I open my mouth to say I am more than *upset* with Dad, that Dad is a faithless, ungrateful pig. But I quickly close said mouth again. "You're right," I say. "I'm sorry. Let's go."

We pile into the van—it's my carpool day—and zoom up and down the streets of Pacific Heights and Presidio Heights, studded with gorgeous multimillion-dollar Victorians, half-timbered Tudors, and Mediterranean-style homes.

We pick up Nicholas, the boy who Amanda likes, then go over to Washington Street for the twins' friend, Milo, who informed me last week that the duodenum is located in the southern part of Delaware. (He's also the one who told me that the opposite of complimentary is rudimentary.) The boys immediately pull out their video games and start playing. Then it's over to the house of Amanda's best friend, Sabrina, who is wearing earphones and dancing down the marble steps.

"Good morning, Sabrina," I say.

She takes her earphones off, smiles at me distractedly, puts them back on, and gets into the van. I recognize the strains of Justin Bieber.

After dropping off all the kids, I drive to the drycleaners. The owner, Han, smiles widely at me. "Mrs. Nelson," she says. "So lovely to see you."

"You, too, Han," I say. "I have a sweater and a shirt here, I think. I'm not sure what else."

"Let me check for you," Han says, peering into her computer. "Yes, that's right." She presses the button to the revolving rack, and it grinds into action. Soon, she is handing me my items.

"Thanks, Han," I say.

She shifts uncomfortably. "Some other lady comes now to pick up Mr. Nelson's shirts. Is that OK?"

My stomach jumps and I feel sick, but I just smile and say, "Yes, of course."

Back in the car, I breathe deeply and ignore the urge to cry. Then I drive to Safeway for milk and other basics. Steven is keeping a tighter-than-tight rein on the budget, and so my normal forays to Whole Foods are pretty much over. By the refrigerated section, I see Dana, the fiancée of Mark, one of Steven's close friends. She has the tall, lean body of a runner, and she's highlighted her dull brown hair so much she looks like a Marin County realtor. They returned from vacation three weeks ago. Steven and I have spent quite a lot of time with them, golfing and such, and though we have never been very close, she is someone I see regularly and talk to.

I smile and wave as I walk toward her. I'm sure she has seen me, but she turns away and pretends to be choosing from among the eight hundred and thirty-three organic yogurts in the case in front of her.

"Dana!" I cry. I'm at her side now.

"Oh, Maddy, hi," she says, her gaze still on a row of Cultural Revolution Vanilla Complete 5% yogurt. She reads the label first on the blackberry flavor and then on the peach.

"How are you?" I say. Why isn't she asking me how *I* am? I think. "How was your trip?"

"Oh, just fine," she says, running a finger along a line of yogurt cartons and finally turning to look at me. "Do you know anything about organic yogurts? Mark's on a kick for everything organic."

My husband has left me, and she's talking about yogurt?

"I'm afraid I don't," I say.

"Well," she says, popping three or four into her cart, "I just don't have any more time to spend on this."

I wait, willing her to show any sign of knowing about the divorce, of caring about it. Nothing.

I stroll along beside her to the produce section. "So you heard that Steven and I..."

"Yes," she says. "I've been meaning to call. We've been away."

Yeah, great, I think. I've been wandering around like a lost soul in Hades and she's been where? At the Mauna Kea, that's where. And meaning to call. And she's been back for three weeks, and I haven't seen or heard from her. I hold back tears. The last thing I want is for everyone to know I cried over the artichokes.

"Do you think it might be for the best?" Dana fixes me with a schoolmarm look.

"The best?" I say, a little too sharply. "The best for whom?"

"Oh, I don't know, but when a relationship has run its course…"

I want to say, just wait for *your* relationship to run its course, sister. But of course I don't.

"Are you coming to the committee meeting and lunch coming up for our charity?" I ask her.

"I don't know," Dana says. "I think we're away then." *They're* away then. She's firmly part of a "we." I'm not.

I signal my goodbye and move on. I can't talk to someone like this. I throw some broccoli, asparagus, and fingerling potatoes into my cart and go to the dairy case where I check the expiration dates on milk: whole for the kids, fat-free for me.

At the cashier, I empty my items onto the conveyor belt and cringe when Dana gets into line right behind me. I stand silently in front of her, biting my lip and feeling so alone. When the pink-haired, tattooed clerk has rung the total, I swipe my credit card.

"It didn't take, ma'am," the cashier says, looking at her screen. "Could you run it through again?"

I swipe the card again, and this time the clerk looks more closely at me. "It's saying it's at its limit."

Heat courses through my body, and I feel myself flushing. "Are you sure?" I say. "There must be some mistake."

Dana's interest has finally been engaged, and with raised eyebrows, she is peering over my shoulder watching this humiliating drama unfold. Steven didn't cancel my credit card, but he put a limit on it, and apparently I've reached it. In fact, I've reached my limit on a few things.

"Just take back the steak and salmon," I say. I can't look at Dana. I just can't.

This time, the credit card goes through. I toss my items into my own grocery bag and wave to Dana. "Lovely to see you," I say.

"And you," she says, unloading her cart.

Back in the car I am consumed with rage and embarrassment.

I get out my cell phone and text Steven.

"Increase the limit on the credit card immediately. Your children need to eat."

Chapter 9

A lawyer with his briefcase can steal more than a hundred men with guns.
—Mario Puzo

THE BLASPHEMY BOX

The divorce process is not pretty. Apparently, getting served with divorce papers from your rotten, stinking spouse is the first step. Tandy Michaels, one street over, had her eighteen-year-old son do it, which everyone thought was quite bad form. And Annie Craven, the Jessica Rabbit of our block, got herself a boyfriend soon after Todd left and had him serve Todd with divorce papers.

And you should hear all the stories about lawyers! They may be nice, they may be good, but to them you are only a source of income. Sally, someone in my divorce support group, said last week that her lawyer didn't inform her he would be charging her $50 for every five-minute phone call and for each e-mail. Another woman said her lawyer did an abysmal job on her case, got her screwed out of everything, never once sent her an itemized statement, and then, after refusing to take or return her calls, charged her for talking to his secretary. Talk about scary.

I keep expecting things will get back to normal any moment now, and I will start up my former life again. But it hasn't happened yet. At least I haven't been served with official papers. Hope springs eternal. That is, until the pizza man cometh.

When I come home from dropping the kids off at school and errands, some burly, acne-infested kid holding a large square pizza box that reads, "Best Pizza," approaches me as I get out of the car. Best Pizza is my favorite pizza joint.

"You Mrs. Nelson?" he says.

"Yes."

He hands me the pizza box, shoves a brown paper bag on top of it, says, "Consider yourself served," and runs back to his car and speeds off.

Served pizza in my driveway? What on earth could he mean?

I get to the kitchen and open the box. It's my favorite pizza of all time, the Combo—pepperoni, meatball, bacon, sautéed mushrooms, and black olives—the one Steven always said was too fattening and that I shouldn't eat. I close the box and open the bag, hoping for the dried spices in little plastic cups.

But what I see are documents. Divorce papers. Along with a note on impressive-looking legal letterhead telling me I am to go to a settlement meeting a few weeks hence. I burst into tears.

The house is so quiet that my footsteps echo loudly as I make my way into the kitchen. I throw the pizza in the trash, retrieve my groceries from the front door and put them in the refrigerator, take a "Skinny Cow Only 140 Calories" ice cream sandwich out of the freezer, and scarf it down standing up at the kitchen window. Then I go into the bedroom and sit down on my bed and look out at the Bay. My bed. Used to be our bed. Now it's only my bed.

Surprisingly, I fall asleep. When I wake up, it's nearly noon, and I make for the family room, where I happily collapse onto the couch and turn on the television. Though I would never admit this, I have been watching a lot of television lately, trying to fill this empty house with sound, noise, anything. The children will be coming home late today because of soccer and ballet.

I half watch a few minutes of vile but oddly addictive talk shows. Then I watch CNN for ten minutes, and then I flip back and forth between channels until I see a rerun of Dr. Phil is on. The mustachioed talk show host's always good for killing some time.

Dr. Phil says he helps people solve their problems for all the world to see. The English would never have a show like that. The English never talk about their problems. (Too many to talk about?)

The good doctor (who isn't even a doctor) does shows with themes like, "Are You Having an Affair With Your Friend's Mate?" Everyone cries and carries on, and it's like some huge, unbearable sob fest.

I punch the remote to turn off the television, and silence invades the house again. I try not to remember the pizza and the divorce papers and Steven's cruelty and the absolute inanity of life and how it can change in one act, one word, one day. I remember Suzy telling me I should find a divorce lawyer. And quick. She said she would have given me hers but that he just died.

I call my friend Annette at the *Chronicle.*

"Hi, it's Maddy. Are you on deadline?"

"No, I just turned my story in."

"How are things going over there? I'm hearing about more lay-offs."

"Things aren't great," Annette says. "But we're all trying to hang on. How are the kids? How's hubby?"

I swallow. "Well, that's why I'm calling. I need the name of a few good divorce lawyers."

"Ah," Annette says. "Going to be joining our ranks, are you? Best thing that ever fucking happened to me."

I laugh. Annette's the only person I know who swears more than me.

"What happened?" she says.

"A twenty-five-year-old whose face hasn't fallen below the Mason-Dixon line, is what."

"Oh boy. Same thing here. I'm so sorry, Maddy. I'll e-mail you the list I used. These are the absolute top lawyers in the city. I included them when I did that story on prenups last year."

"Will they go for the jugular? I have a feeling I'll need them to."

"All divorce lawyers go for the jugular, Maddy. They're out to make money off your misery."

"Bloody hell." (Twenty-five cents.) "I'm not cut out for this."

"Listen, Maddy," Annette says. "I know it's tough, but you'll get through it. It's about survival. And next time, don't get married. Get a pet. At least they're loyal."

I sit still for several minutes after I hang up. I still can't believe I have ended up here, fifty years old with three young children and a husband doing the horizontal hula with someone other than me. Now, there's the bitter pill of fighting for money. Not my strong suit. Never has been. It's all so…unpleasant. Once I sign with a lawyer, everything will essentially be over. I will have conceded to the divorce. I will have given up any hope for reconciliation.

I make myself a second cup of tea and have a donut to go with it. I steel myself as much as I can and pull up my e-mail, open the message from Annette, and scroll through the six names on the list. Then I lift the receiver. My finger shakes as I punch in the first number.

"Smythe and Greenfield." The woman's tone is polite but firm.

"I wondered if I might speak with Simeon Smythe."

"Mr. Smythe is in court. Can I take a message?"

"Well, I'm looking for a divorce attorney."

"I see. Could I ask you a few general questions? Mr. Smythe likes to have some information about potential clients before he consults with them."

"I'd prefer to speak with him directly."

"It is our policy."

"All right, then."

"Thank you. When did your husband file for divorce?"

"I was served the papers today."

"How long have you been married?"

"Twenty years."

"All those in California?"

"Yes."

"Is there a specific reason for the divorce?"

I pause. "I'm not sure what you are asking. It's all his idea."

"I see. So, it is not by mutual consent."

"Of course not."

"Is this your first divorce?"

"Yes."

"Are there substantial shared marital assets?"

"Yes."

"Any children?"

"Yes, a fourteen-year-old girl and twin ten-year-old boys."

"Thanks. That's all the information we need at present. Now if you can give me your full name, address, e-mail, and phone, I'll be sure Mr. Smythe contacts you."

"Thank you. My name is Madeleine Nelson, my address is…"

I hear the clicking of computer keys stop.

"Excuse me, but is your husband's name Steven?"

"Yes. How do you know that?"

"One moment please."

I hear classical music. Why does everyone assume that we like to listen to music while we are on hold? It is pleasant, though. But a few seconds later, it stops.

"I'm sorry, but Mr. Smythe will be unable to represent you. He has already talked to your husband."

My stomach clenches. "I'm sorry. I don't understand. Isn't your business to represent people getting divorced?"

"Yes, it is; however, our policy precludes Mr. Smythe from taking a client whose spouse has already consulted with him."

"Steven met with him already?"

"Several weeks ago. We keep records for this very reason. I'm sorry. It is a matter of professional ethics. Thank you for calling Smythe and Greenfield." I hear a dial tone.

I call the next firm on the list.

"Lawton, Lane, and Boucher."

"I wondered if I might talk to Karl Boucher."

"I'm afraid he's with a client. Can I take a message?"

"Yes, thank you. I'd like to speak with him about his representing me in my divorce."

"Your name?"

"Madeleine Nelson."

"One moment please."

This time, it's Frank Sinatra singing "All of Me." Somehow it's bizarrely fitting. After the first refrain, she comes back on.

"Mrs. Nelson, I'm afraid Mr. Boucher won't be able to meet with you. Your husband has already consulted with him, and it is our policy to…"

I cut her off. "Yes, I know. Professional ethics."

"Right. Thank you for calling. Have a nice day."

I slam down the phone.

Fuck her. (And fuck the twenty-five cents). It's just like Steven to cover all the bases. I'll bet he knew about this ethics thing and planned to prevent me from getting the best lawyers. Harvey Bilkman, his high-powered attorney friend with the trophy wife, probably put him up to it. They all belong to the Olympic Club. No point calling the other numbers.

Determined not to let Steven win, I resort to Google. Divorce Attorney San Francisco. Dozens come up. I choose the first one and dial.

"Jenson, Allen, and James."

"May I please speak to Mr. Jenson?"

"Your name?"

"Mrs. Madeleine Nelson."

"What is this in reference to?"

"I'm in need of a divorce attorney."

The female voice immediately becomes warm and kind. "I'm Paul Jenson's assistant. Unfortunately, Mr. Jenson is on medical leave at the moment."

"I see."

"But, if you like, I could refer you to Alec Brown in our offices. He's an excellent attorney and works with Paul on all of his cases."

"Thank you." At least he hasn't consulted with Steven.

"Fine, one moment please."

No music. What a relief.

"Alec Brown."

"Oh, good afternoon, I'm looking for a divorce lawyer."

A pause. "Well, that's good, because I am one."

Hmm. Not too friendly.

"I assume you've received divorce papers. Who is your husband's lawyer, Mrs. Nelson? It'll be on the papers. Do you have them handy?"

"Sure," I say, picking up the papers and scanning them quickly. "It appears to be John Harrison at Harrison & Harris."

"Fine. I know the firm. How long have you been married?"

"Twenty years."

"Children?"

"Yes, three."

I hear him taking down notes. Very professional.

"OK, I suggest that you come down to the office so we can go over how all this works. Would this afternoon be convenient, say around four?"

I really want to say no, forget the whole thing, and have a nice long soak in the tub, but I know that I can't.

"Yes, that would be fine."

"Thanks. Terry will give you directions. Please hold on."

I jump in and out of the shower and then run to my closet to choose something to wear. But what does one wear to meet the person who will sever you from your husband? My ex-friend Dana says something sexy; you might be meeting your next husband. That's how she met Steven's friend, Mark. I haven't heard anything from her since that incident in Safeway, I think to myself. Why not?

I know I should probably not wear jeans or sweats, but should I wear khakis and a shirt and jacket or a suit or a dress and matching jacket? Ultimately I decide on a black turtleneck and pants with a camel wool jacket.

The law firm is in a luxurious high-rise overlooking the Embarcadero and Bay. The elevator zooms up to the forty-fourth floor and deposits me in the lobby of a huge suite of offices, all plush with dark carpet and dark wood, very quiet and subdued. I feel like I am going to a funeral. Which, I guess, I am.

"Hi, I'm Maddy Nelson," I say to the receptionist. "I have an appointment with Alec Brown."

"Please have a seat."

I sit, tapping my foot and wishing there was something to read other than *California Lawyer.* Do attorneys really think their clients want to read about a surprising ruling in the Second Circuit that holds corporations cannot be held liable under international law violations of the Alien Tort Act?

After about twenty minutes, a rather dry-looking woman in a starched white blouse and black pencil skirt appears. "This way, please."

Alec's office has windows on three sides with sweeping views of the Bay over to Alcatraz and is lined with rows of law tomes and serious, high-minded literature.

"Hello, Mrs. Nelson. I'm Alec Brown." He stands and extends his hand. I take it. "Please sit down," he adds, indicating a chair across from his large teak desk.

A man about my age, he is extremely good looking. He has flecks of gray in his full head of dark hair and sports a white pocket square in his well-tailored sport jacket with the studied nonchalance of George Clooney.

"Now," he says, his hands clasped together, "why don't you tell me everything."

"Everything?" I say. I can feel the pulse in my neck hammering away.

"Shall we start with the reason for the divorce, Mrs. Nelson?"

"Ah, yes," I say. "Well, it turns out he has someone else. Someone half my age."

I wait for him to say there, there, now, now, and offer me tea, but he doesn't. He merely flicks some imaginary lint off his thousand-dollar pinstriped Zegna suit and starts to shuffle the papers on his desk in a fashion that even he won't know where they are when I'm gone.

Then he looks at me again. "I see. Go on."

I tell him as much as I can bear to. Just talking about all this is so painful and shocking.

He takes copious notes, and when I finish, he says, "And how, Mrs. Nelson, do you intend to pay?"

Gosh, I say to myself. I hadn't thought of that. Steven always handles all that payment stuff.

"I imagine my husband must pay you, because I have no money."

Alec grimaces.

"We can certainly ask the judge, Mrs. Nelson, to make your husband contribute, but if there is no such judgment made, you will be on the hook for all the fees. Furthermore, we also require a retainer."

No problem, I think to myself. I can manage a few thousand. "What is the amount?"

"The minimum retainer is fifteen thousand dollars."

No wonder he and his partners can afford these offices.

I nearly have an apoplexy right there on his expensive, blue silk Isfahan carpet. I don't have that kind of money. I don't have access to any of the accounts, and Steven is sending barely enough money for household expenses. Alec is looking at me.

I am flushed, panicked, trying to figure out what to do. And Alec is still looking at me.

"Would you excuse me for a moment?" I say.

"Of course."

I get up and walk to the bathroom. Once inside, I fan myself with my purse and try not to get more panicked. Then I have an idea. I get out my phone.

"Cameron?"

"Maddy, how are you?" Cameron's voice is deep and soothing.

"Well, I'm having a bit of a crisis. I'm at the lawyer's office, and I need to pay his retainer. It's fifteen thousand, and I don't have it."

"Whoa!" Cameron says. "It's up to fifteen thousand now, is it?"

"Yes," I say. "It's outrageous, but there it is. Could you...could you..."

"Of course."

"I'll pay it back."

"I know you will."

"When I get my settlement."

"Of course. Don't worry. Give the secretary my number, and she can call me to get the credit card number."

"Thanks so much, Cameron. I don't know what I would do without you."

"Listen, honey, I've been through three divorces; I know how it is."

I return to Alec's office and give Cameron's number to him.

He writes it down, presses a button on his phone, and in sails Miss Sensibly Dressed. She takes the piece of paper, exits, and five minutes later returns and nods at Alec. She also has me sign a fee agreement, which looks like it spells out the terms and conditions of Alec's employment and his hourly rate, which is so huge that my heart fairly punches up against my chest. I look up at Alec.

"Does this mean that you have agreed to represent me?"

"Yes."

I sign it and hand it back to Miss Sensible. She quietly leaves.

"Now, Mrs. Nelson—"

"Please call me Maddy."

Alec's head turns from his computer, where he is entering some of his notes.

"As I was saying, Mrs. Nelson, I will call you tomorrow so we can go over more details. Right now I have another client."

He gets up and motions me out. I walk toward the door, wondering why I didn't stay in law school and get an office like this.

Back home, I sign onto my blog. The comments on divorce lawyers stretch to three pages. Most of them are in the same vein.

I was married to a lawyer. We've been battling for a while. My bill: $50,000. His? Zero. He knows other lawyers, and they work for him for free: professional courtesy.
Posted by StarB

My lawyer neglected to file my pleadings on time, didn't tell me about court dates, made decisions with my ex's attorney without consulting me, and basically got me nothing in my divorce except credit-card debt and the hamster.
Posted by Mizz1234

Chapter 10

The first time someone shows you who they are, believe them.
—Maya Angelou

THE BLASPHEMY BOX

I've never liked competition. I hate Scrabble and lacrosse and soccer and pedro and all those other endeavors where you're pitted against someone else. I don't want to fight with others. It seems so impolite, somehow.

Divorce, I am unhappily finding, is very much like competitive sports. One wins and one loses, and you'd better not be the latter. Your mate takes everything he knows about you—all your weaknesses, foibles, eccentricities, and idiosyncrasies, all those things you keep buried inside—and uses them against you. It's blood sport of the worst kind.

But here's the worst thing: even if I win everything I am going to ask for in this divorce, when it's all over, what will I truly have gained? I might have a little more money, yes. But I will have fought so hard that the man I love, I mean loved, will be the man who hates me. And I him. In divorce, winning only leads to losing.

"Mrs. Nelson? Alec Brown."

It's two in the afternoon the next day, and something in my stomach jumps. I have a lawyer now and must expect these kinds of calls out of the blue.

"Hi, Alec."

"I have had a short conversation with your husband's lawyer, Mrs. Nelson," he says.

"Already?"

"Indeed."

I feel panic surging through me. "I just want you to know, before we go any further, that I cannot lose my kids."

"I think that's highly unlikely, since you are and have always been their primary caregiver. And, from what Mr. Harrison said, your husband is not asking for full custody."

Relief descends on me like a warm shower.

"What happens now?" I say.

"Well, we try to negotiate a settlement so as not to go trial, but first we have to file a response to the divorce petition and do discovery, so everyone knows the facts of the case."

"What facts are there to know?" I ask. "My husband dumped me for his chickadee. That's the only fact one needs to know here."

"Not exactly, Mrs. Nelson." I wish he would stop calling me Mrs. Nelson. "It's a little bit more complicated than that."

"What do you mean?"

"Your husband's lawyer says he has been unhappy for some time in this marriage and frustrated by what he feels is your less-than-healthy way of raising the kids."

"I don't have a clue what you're talking about."

"Well, your husband says the kids get too many carbohydrates, you know, bagels for instance."

Bagels. My husband's divorcing me because I give the kids bagels?

"And the house," Alec continues, "is often in disorder."

"Of course it's in disorder," I cry. "We have three children. He just goes to work and comes home. I do all the rest."

"Quite right," Alec says. "Your husband's attorney says your husband is not interested in an ugly divorce and that the two of you have just drifted apart and that you've just had too little time for him lately."

I try to control the anger shooting through my body. All I can do is laugh.

"I've been at his disposal for years. He's the one that's never around."

"Of course," Alec says.

"I gave up my career for him. I kept things running smoothly at home. I surrendered my youth and beauty to him, and now I can't get them back. What else does he want?"

"Exactly," Alec says.

"I did everything."

"Absolutely," Alec says. "And that is what we will prove."

I say nothing for a moment. I am just so hurt. How can the man I've lived with for twenty years be regaling a stranger about the problems in our marriage and blame me for them? It's insane.

"I need more money for me and the kids to live on," I say then. "My husband is paying the school and all the other regular expenses but is sending me only a thousand dollars a month for us to live on."

"I will file a request for an order of support for more than you are currently getting."

I am relieved. "Thank you. That would be great."

"Is there anything else?" he says.

"Well, school will soon be out, and I wanted to sign the kids up for camp like every summer, but I don't have the money. I don't know what I'm supposed to do about those kinds of costs."

"I'll talk to his lawyer and get back to you," Alec says. "Please try to have as little contact with your husband as possible. Although I hate to say this, in a divorce anything and everything is fair game. So the less interaction, the better. OK?"

No worries there. "Fine with me."

Having a lawyer to deal with the nasty, difficult stuff isn't such a bad idea after all.

On my blog later, someone has commented: *I have a jar on my kitchen counter that reads "Ex-Husband's Ashes."*
Posted by WishTheyWereReal

Chapter 11

We like to be deceived.
—Blaise Pascal

THE BLASPHEMY BOX

Now that I have a lawyer to deal with HM, I thought I should attack another area of my life that needs attention: my figure. It's true I've never been a great advocate of exercise. (The English don't exercise, really. Our idea of a workout is raising a glass to Manchester United.) My friends and I started a walking club when the kids were small, but that didn't last. I did yoga and Pilates (well, sort of) and even had a trainer come to the house three times a week for a while. But we mostly ate bear claws and watched exercise videos. HM did get me a membership at the fancy Bay Club but canceled it recently, saying that if it weren't for the fact that the television and the refrigerator are so far apart in our house, some of us wouldn't get any exercise at all.

I said, "And by some of us, you mean?" and he rolled his eyes and walked away.

Truth to tell, I have become a bit lazy. I truly understand the reasoning behind exercise. But middle-aged spread has a mind of its own, and only vast amounts of dedication can make an impact. Drastic times, however, call for drastic measures.

I decide to get going on an exercise program by going for a jog. I put on some black leggings I haven't worn since forever and am a bit shocked I can even get into them. Thank God for spandex. I pull on one of Steven's Giants T-shirts he left behind, which hides a multitude of sins, pull my hair back and slip into my sneakers. The weather has been nice, and there's a park on the hill opposite us. I think a short jog might even be fun.

Five minutes into it, I am already winded, huffing and puffing, and have to stop to catch my breath. These San Francisco hills are brutal. Runners as thin as incense sticks jog by, looking at me in sympathy. One of them stops and says, "You need to get into shape before you start running seriously, otherwise you can hurt your joints."

I summon up the iciest stare I can muster and say, "I am in shape; round's a shape, isn't it?"

I talk tough to myself and start running again. But everything hurts, and I can't breathe. My knees hurt, my back hurts, my ankles hurt, and even my fingers hurt. Now I remember why I never kept up with jogging. I manage to jog for five minutes more, then I collapse onto a bench with a view of San Francisco. The only reason to exercise is because you die healthier.

After I've recovered, I take myself over to my support group. Construction crews are hammering and pounding away on Rachel's street, and parking is even more difficult than usual, if you can imagine that. San Francisco has never met a construction project it didn't like, and most of them are useless, I have always thought. There has not been one day since I arrived here twenty years ago that I have gone anywhere at any time and there have not been brawny men in hard hats pummeling and pulverizing what seemed to be a perfectly good street.

Once inside Rachel's flat, I greet my cohorts in the world of dumped-wifedom and plop down on the eight-legged couch in Fanta orange velour that looks like a mutant caterpillar wearing an Early Walmart bathrobe.

Rachel says something, but no one can hear above the incessant drilling outside. She shrugs, and we all wait in silence, hoping the cacophony will stop. Myla, gorgeous in a snowy wool jacket with black leggings, begins.

"I really did it this time."

"What did you do?"

"Justin came over to get some of his things last night." Her smirk goes from her lips to her eyes. "He had left about twenty pairs of shoes behind."

"And?" Rachel says.

"He went straight into the master bedroom closet. I waited. Then he came down screaming, 'Where are all my left shoes?'"

It takes a moment, but then we all get it, and Rachel and Sally give Myla the thumbs-up.

"He loved those damn shoes," Myla said, laughing.

"What happened then?" I say.

"He said, 'You fucking bitch, those shoes belong to me.' And I said, 'Only half of them do. California's a community property state.'"

We all burst out laughing.

"Myla, I cannot believe you did that," I say. "It's brilliant."

"It certainly sent him the message not to fuck with me."

Rachel gives her another thumbs-up. "All's fair in love and divorce. Now, what's the latest with you, Maddy?"

I flush. I don't really like talking about myself. It's too personal. "Well, I decided I'd better lose some weight, so I went for my first jog in perhaps twenty years. Or ever, actually."

The other women smile.

"I call it the Tale of Two Nipples," I say. "Mine kept bobbing up and then flopping all the way down. I now understand the power of the sports bra."

Everyone laughs.

"Aging sucks," Angie says plaintively.

"Too right," Myla says.

"And they never prepare you for that," I chime in. "I mean, do they? They always say, don't drink, don't smoke, don't do drugs, don't have premarital sex, but nobody in the world ever tells you not to get old, now do they? They don't tell you you'll get the size of Texas, that your skin will dull, that you'll have blubber hanging from your upper arms like one of those fringed kitchen curtains from the sixties, and that when you walk, your thighs will rub together so fiercely you'll worry they'll set your tights on fire. They don't tell you you'll not recognize yourself in photos, that everything, even your attractiveness, is finite. Or that your husband will leave you and do his best to screw you in the divorce. And then that exact thing happens. And there you are. With nothing.

Alone. You've given him your youth and beauty, and at the very moment you need them again, they're gone."

The women nod their heads frantically in agreement.

"On a brighter note," Myla says with a mischievous grin. "Just think of all those shoes Justin lost."

The drilling starts up, and as a group, we get up and get the hell out of Dodge.

Chapter 12

The older we get the more we should accessorize. Or is that exercise?
—Birthday card

THE BLASPHEMY BOX

This exercise thing doesn't get any easier. It takes discipline to get on that torturous jogging path every day. Not my strong suit. I use every excuse in the book not to go. It's too cold. It's too hot. The plumber's coming. You name it. BFF says I should join a gym with classes. At least then, I'd be motivated once I get there. She says a lot of gyms have smoothie bars, too. Now, that's incentive. Oops. I'm supposed to be dieting, too.

His Majesty is sending so little money I can't join a proper gym. And I certainly don't want to ask any of the other mothers I know from school and the neighborhood for recommendations. I don't want any of them to know I am joining anything less than the fanciest place in town. If a health club doesn't have locker rooms with travertine floors and Calacatta marble counters, they simply don't want to know.

On reflection, I decide I should look for a place where none of these ladies would think of going. What happens in the gym, stays in the gym.

I go online and look up health clubs in the city. There are quite a few, and I start calling to find out initiation and membership rates. They are all so expensive. They're like day spas with exercise rooms. Then I hit on some place called All Day Fitness. It's cheap, twenty-five dollars a month, not too far, and has free parking for members.

I get in my car and drive down Bay toward the waterfront and go around in circles for ten minutes looking for the club's parking lot—a holy grail for San Franciscans—and just as I am beginning to give up and go home, someone pulls out of a metered spot. When I get to the health club, I find parking is on top of a grocery store, hence the free parking. I could have just parked there. I go through the glass doors, look around, and sniff. I look around and sniff some more. It doesn't reek of body odor or cleaning fluid.

So far, so good. There are even a couple of huge plasma televisions tuned to ESPN and the Food Network. Gee, I think, maybe dear old Rachael Ray will appear and teach me how to make *chicken francese with gremolata.*

I walk toward the front desk and stand there hesitantly. The young woman residing there has muscles so toned I could bounce a ball off them. I am not looking forward to having her look me over, clap her hand to her mouth, and say, "What took you so long?"

The woman raises her eyes from her computer and sees me standing there. "May I help you?"

"Er..."

"Do you want to sign up?" she says.

"I'd like to look around first, if I could."

"Of course. Let me get a trainer to give you a tour."

Before I can say I don't want a trainer, I just want to wander around, and then get out, she picks up the phone, mutters something, and in less than one minute, a hulking great man with the most gorgeous face and obsidian hair comes bearing down upon me. Poured into some tight little turquoise Lycra outfit that does nothing to hide his rather generous anatomical gifts, he looks twenty if he's a day. He extends his hand.

"Hi, I'm Duane," he says, flashing a smile wider than the Grand Canyon.

"Hi, I'm Maddy."

"OK, Maddy, come with me, and I'll show you around."

Duane begins chatting about abs and workout routines and where I've worked out before. I demur mostly and try to look interested.

We pass a large room with hardwood floors where a bunch of skinny women are leaping and squatting and lunging and dipping about in a way that looks painful. They're all in chic, color-coordinated outfits. The average age is about twenty-four.

"We have the best fitness classes here," Duane says. "This one is called BodyCombat. It's pretty advanced. We've classes for whatever level you like."

"How about first-timers?"

He smiled. "No problem. There's a few of them."

He then leads me into a cavernous room filled with an assortment of machines that look more like torture devices than exercise equipment. "We have a huge array of workout and weight machines," Duane says. And then he starts enumerating them: "Stairmasters, treadmills, recumbent bicycles, steppers, rowers, pec decs, lat pulls..."

I'm in a daze now as I watch some huge man lift what looks like a ton of metal over his head.

"Where's the juice bar?" I say.

"We don't have one. The women's locker room is to your right. Why don't you check it out?"

I stick my head in and then wander through a rather too utilitarian facility for my liking.

"Where are the towels?" I say when I walk back to Duane.

"You bring your own." Talk about barebones.

Soon we are back at the front desk.

"So, that's about it," he says, shaking my hand. "See you around."

"Thanks," I say and get ready for the pitch from Miss Muscles.

"Would you like to sign up?" she says.

"Do I have to?"

She smiles. "No, you don't have to. But you're here for a reason, right? Might as well get on with it."

What she says makes perfect sense. But I still hesitate.

"You get one free personal training session if you sign up."

"Well," I say finally. "Why not?"

"Here's the contract for you to sign, and Duane has a ten a.m. open tomorrow to get you started. Will that work for you?"

"Yes," I say and sign the paperwork.

I drive home with a renewed sense of purpose and decide I will fully commit to getting into shape. Once there, I rifle through my drawers in the bedroom to find my exercise gear, the stuff I used to wear at home when the trainer came or when taking the occasional class at The Bay Club. As I pull out and try on each top and each pair of shorts, I find something remarkably similar to what's called a muffin top spilling out over the waistline of my shorts, and a definite belly line visible under the tops. Won't do. Until I can fit into the gear I already have, I'll just go shopping for some more…well, more comfortable stuff.

I get back into the car and sail down to some chichi little store on Chestnut Street in the Marina that's known for trendy exercise and swim wear.

"I need some exercise clothes," I say to a bronzed young woman called Jody who has the body fat of a Sony Ericsson flip phone.

"We have Nike and Lululemon, plus a whole bunch of designer fashions," she says gaily. "Why don't you try on a few outfits, and I'll tell you what I think?"

I know Nike, of course, but I'm not familiar with Lululemon. Either way, I'm not looking forward to displaying the cellulite on my thighs, which, lately, seems to be advancing like the Red Army. I turn around to see if anyone else will be watching me model. Happily, the store is deserted except for Miss Tanned America and me.

I stand there looking at my toes. When I look up, Jody is nodding encouragingly toward the racks of clothing, and I slowly make my way there. I go through the options, searching for something that will cover me up but willing to settle for something that will just fit. But even the large sizes look too small. They must make exercise clothes much smaller than regular clothes.

I try some psychedelic Pucci-style halter bra so low-cut it gives new meaning to the words "belle poitrine" and shorts that only accentuate my slightly burgeoning middle. I refuse to let Jody see me in them. After a lot of "What about this?" and "Do you like that?" from Jody, she wrenches open the changing room curtain and thrusts a hanger at me. "How about this?" she says. "This is a three-hundred-and-sixty-degree shelf bra. Very sexy, don't you think?"

What the hell is a shelf bra, I think to myself. To her, I say, "Oh yeah, great," and throw the bra and hanger on the floor.

Then she wrenches back the curtain again and hands me an über-sexy plunging triangle bra in a color called sunburst. It has a metal ring in back connecting to the straps, and comes with matching shorts. "These are from Brazil!" she says.

Can't she see I'm not Gisele Bündchen?

Apparently not, because she's on a roll, chucking me bras and tanks and shorts and pants in RIO CORAL! IPANEMA PINK! SAMBA SUNSET!

"How do they look?" Jody says from behind the curtain.

Like I'm going to actually show her.

"Oh," I say, "they're just not me."

Why can't I wear plunging fuchsia Lycra bras and midriff-baring boy shorts like all those women doing aerobics around the corner?

"Do you have anything else, something more basic?" I say.

Jody sounds affronted. "We don't have too many *basics*," she responds. "If we did, we'd be Walmart."

"Right," I say, emerging from the fitting room. "I guess that's it then."

But Jody is dashing toward me.

"Here," she says, handing me a black tank top that covers and minimizes my stomach and some black capris. I try both on and even let her see me in them. Soon I'm handing over that please-don't-reach-the-limit credit card.

It's amazing how much thinner one looks in black.

It's the next morning, and I wake up thinking about exercising and feeling very pleased with myself for doing so. My black tank and capris are lying on the tufted armchair in my bedroom, the first things I see when I open my eyes. My appointment with Duane is at ten, so I leap out of bed and run to the kids' rooms to roust them out of bed. Then it's into the kitchen to make scrambled eggs and bagels. When my three lovelies arrive, there's the usual chorus of "I'm not hungry, Mom" from Amanda and "Mom, where's my shirt?" from the twins.

I just smile and kiss the tops of their heads, put the food in front of them, and smile some more. Somehow it works, because they eat, even Amanda, who says, "You know, Mom, Dad doesn't want us to have too many bagels."

"I know," I say. "And he's right."

Amanda's head snaps up from her plate.

"These are the ones left over from yesterday," I say. "After this, no more bagels. Dad's right, and from now on, the Nelson household is going to be a healthy one."

Amanda's staring at me in disbelief. "Whatever," she says.

Once the carpool mom of the day has whisked my offspring away, I eat some eggs and the remaining bagel and dress for the gym.

At 9:55, I'm parking in the lot, winding my way past shoppers with huge carts, and at 10 a.m. I am standing at the reception desk, waiting for Duane.

He appears within seconds, poured, this time, into some Lycra number in electric teal. I just don't know how he moves in this stuff, I truly don't.

I notice the floors are scratched and that it's awfully stuffy inside and a bit humid. I sniff for BO and get a faint whiff. Duane leads me to the cardio machines.

After surveying a row of machines, most of which carry a "Not Working" sign, he puts me on the treadmill, (which, after today, I will call the dreadmill) and turns it up to four miles an hour. After eight minutes, even though I'm huffing and puffing and gasping for water, he says, "This is really good for you," and transfers me to the stair master with what feels like the incline of Mount Kilimanjaro. Why should I climb stairs when there are escalators do it for me?

After I've scaled the Empire State Building, Duane smiles daz-zlingly at me, and I imagine he's going to take me to the café I saw next door for a latte, or maybe in his case, a glass of something green and disgusting-looking. Instead, he bundles me off to do weights.

In the free weights room, a group of large Asian men with shaved heads, tank tops, basketball shorts, and an unseemly number of dragon tattoos are clustered around the weights, guarding them as if they were gold ingots. Their attitude makes it clear no one had better get near them. There's that faint of whiff of BO again.

They watch me relentlessly as Duane instructs me. I can barely hear him, what with the Red Hot Chili Peppers blasting away on the sound system, making me more than uncomfortable. I do hear Duane say "biceps" and "delts," and then he sits me down at a machine to do something he calls "bicep extensions." This involves me lifting the handles of a bar up to my shoulders. It's really heavy, and after five repetitions, I'm ready to stop. But Duane is having none of it.

"Maddy," he says, one eye on the replay of a Giants game, "keep going. Great! How does it feel?"

"Like childbirth," I say.

Duane chuckles, and we move to another machine, where he says I will be doing triceps extensions. This is where I push the bar down from the top instead of up from the below. The sides of my upper arms hurt. Sweat is pouring down me, and I beg Duane to let me stop, but he keeps saying, "Ten more, nine, eight…"

At seven I give up.

"Maddy…" he says. His voice is cajoling.

"I'm not used to lifting anything heavier than an ice cream tub," I say. "Can I go home now?"

"No, you can't," Duane says, smiling.

"Is there someone I could pay to exercise for me?" I say. "I am a single mother of three, you know. I'm very busy."

Duane is no longer smiling. "You have to be serious about this," he says as if talking to a recalcitrant child.

He makes me do crunches, squats, abs, resistance bands; it just goes on and on. I sweat like a soldier in Iraq, but he never lets me rest for even one second of the fifty-minute session. Every time I say, "Gee, this is like that root canal I had last year," or "Gosh, that apple muffin at the café next door sure looked good when I walked past it forty frigging long, unbearable, torturous, painful minutes ago," he stays squarely on the motivational path.

"Awesome!" he cries. "You're doing great! You can do it!" And he keeps telling me to breathe. What does he think I'm doing? Taking air in through osmosis?

"Can I go home *now*?" I cry.

"No," he says. "We mustn't forget the legs."

I sigh to myself and get up. The Asian men are still staring at me.

"Now, why don't you sit down at the hip abductor machine, and we'll do some exercises to strengthen and sculpt your outer thigh muscles."

I've never really thought much about my outer thigh muscles to tell you the truth, or how to strengthen and sculpt them, but there it is. Anyway, Duane instructs me to put my legs inside the side pads, grab the side bars, and move my legs apart as far as possible.

"Are you serious?" I say.

"Deadly," he says.

I gird my thighs against the pads and open my legs wide. As I do so, I look up and see the Asian contingent staring straight at my crotch. I feel like poor Princess Diana when the owner of the health club where she worked out took illicit photos of her on the leg press and sold them to the tabloids. I jump out of the chair, leaving the metal machine parts to crash together.

"What's the matter?" Duane says.

I am embarrassed, so embarrassed. How can I say I'm not used to exercising in public like this? "Oh, I'm just a little tired," I say, unable to meet his eyes. "Could we continue this next time?"

He raises one eyebrow and decides not to take things any further. "Fine, let's make our next appointment. I have a really good special going on right now. Two sessions for fifty dollars."

I feel myself flushing. I don't want to make another appointment. I don't want to be here. Ever again. But I think, then, of my situation. I think of being fifty and being single and not being at my very best and having far less money than I'm used to. I sigh and say, "Fine."

"I'm off on the weekends, but I think we should train twice a week, and you should come in on your own an extra three days as well," Duane says.

"Really?" I say. "That much?"

He smiles. "That much."

"OK," I say. The price he quotes is not astronomical, and he's so good looking and pleasant, after all. We make a date for two days hence, and I start to hobble off. All of a sudden, Duane is back. "They have great spin classes here. You should try one."

"What the heck is a spin class?"

"Bicycling. On stationary bikes."

I haven't bicycled since Suzy and I stole Mrs. Runyon's prize plums from her front tree and got away on my tandem by the skin of our teeth.

"It would be a good idea to start that tomorrow, and I'll see you the day after that."

"Fine," I say. It's stationary bicycling, I think. How bad can it be?

Chapter 13

The only solid and lasting peace between a man and his wife is, doubtless, a separation.
—*Lord Chesterfield*

THE BLASPHEMY BOX

The bombs never stop landing in the divorce process. And even if you get them filtered through the sympathetic voice of your lawyer, they're bombs all the same, and they just keep on coming. Here I am, the injured party, and I'm on the receiving end of a litany of demands and complaints from His Majesty, who really shouldn't be making any of either, since he's the idiot who started this whole ballyhoo in the first place. And it's not only demands I am getting. It's information. Kick-in-the-stomach information. Information that just brings you to your knees.

I had forgotten my healthful eating kick and butter a bagel this morning for Amanda, which, with an arch to her brow, she refuses, saying, "I thought we were going to stop eating bagels like Dad said."

"Once the bagels run out, we'll start. Waste not, want not, after all."

"Whatever," she says, pushing the bagel aside.

I load the kids into the car and drive over to Presidio Heights to get three other kids so I can drop them off at school. When I get back, I start cleaning up the kitchen, and while I'm wiping down counters with 409, my lawyer Alec calls. He says that Steven wants particular items from the house.

"What do I do?"

"I'll just tell them that there will be a settlement as to property and to wait until then to take any items out of the house."

"What does the creep want, anyway?" I ask.

"Oh, the leather sectional, the TV."

"No way. I have three children who spend too much time on that sectional watching that TV, and that's how we like it."

"It's going to get uglier, Mrs. Nelson."

"What do you mean?"

"It appears he wants the house."

"Where the heck are the kids and I going to live, then?"

"Well, now, apparently, he wants the kids along with the house. He needs more space. His, er, girlfriend appears to be pregnant. She's two months gone and due after Christmas."

My stomach drops—fairly drops—out of my body. The oldest trick in the book, and Steven fell for it. I lurch away from the counter onto one of the kitchen stools. "She's *pregnant*?"

"I'm afraid so, Mrs. Nelson," Alec says, and then he's silent, thank God.

When I can actually form words again, I say, "Can he really get everything?"

"It's unlikely, but he's going to try."

"You tell that sorry excuse for a husband he's not getting any-thing." I am hyperventilating with rage. "He's not getting the house, the couch, or the television. And he sure as hell isn't getting the kids."

"I agree. We'll make him fight for everything. Is he still paying the monthly bills along with support?"

"Very little support."

"Well, I wouldn't surprise me if he cuts back a bit in response to our position."

"He can't. We're barely surviving as it is."

"I'll communicate that to him and let you know what he says."

"And while you're at it," I say, anger surging through me, "tell the bastard his bit of fluff is not allowed to be around my children. *And* he didn't send Amanda's soccer shoes back with her last time."

Wisely, Alec makes no comment. "Talk to you later," he says, and hangs up.

How could Steven be so cruel? He's treating me like the devil in a dress. I gave him the best years of my life. I'm angry and hurt and afraid, all at the same time. I feel so helpless.

൞഻

Despite my aching muscles, I go to the gym. Suzy says it's great for working out anger and aggression. If that's true, I'm going to need to stay there all day.

I arrive a little late for my session with Duane, and see he's not over there by the spin studio looking at himself in the mirror like he normally is. I search around for him, stopping to ask at the front desk. They tell me he's in the weight room, and when he sees me, he runs over.

"Maddy, there you are." He's in this blindingly shiny teal romper-style getup, and his biceps (see, I'm learning) are vibrating.

"You didn't answer your cell. I've had an emergency and can't train you today. But just go take the spin class. It's really fun and great exercise." And with that, he's gone.

I remain outside, waiting until he is out of sight to plan my escape, and just as I am beginning to wander nonchalantly off in the direction of the exit sign, a hand descends on my arm and wheels me round.

"Now you weren't thinking of not joining us, were you?" A pert little miss who looks a little like Betty Boop introduces herself as Chelsea, grabs my hand, and steers me into the spin studio.

I walk reluctantly behind her to find the place filled with an army of the carrot-stick Barbarellas I am already heartily sick of seeing.

The bikes are positioned very closely next to each other, in order to dissuade, I imagine, anyone larger than a size two from taking the class. All the bikes are taken save for one. In the front row.

"There's only one bike left," I say, with as much concern in my voice as I can muster. "I would just hate to deprive one of your regulars. Why don't I just go home and…"

"Come right back here," Chelsea says. "I told Duane I would look after you. Let's go."

I turn around. Everyone is looking at me, and I feel a flush take over my entire body. I clamber gingerly onto the bike and find a triangle seat the length and shape of a licorice stick—and myself flailing away, because my legs don't reach the pedals.

Chelsea sees me struggling and helps me adjust the seat level, then walks over to fiddle with the stereo and her headphones. Soon she has set the music loud enough to shatter glass and is back on her bike.

"OK, ladies, let's go!" she cries.

All the spinners start pumping furiously to the music. I watch everyone else and try to copy them. I am already sweating like the blazes, and my legs are on fire. Chelsea keeps yelling, "Smooth circles. Keep it going!"

Nothing's smooth about this ride. I am panting so much now I can barely breathe, and Chelsea's yelling, "Back straight! Abs in!"

"Don't you feel great?" she cries. Her legs are going so fast I expect her to take off flying through the air. I'd so much rather be sitting on the couch eating bonbons and watching reruns of *Columbo*.

"Heels down!" she cries. "Hover!"

All of a sudden, everyone has their butts off the seats and in the air, still cycling. I am only able to stand up for an instant and only for the second of relief I get for my butt. I'm feeling dangerously dizzy. Suddenly, I lose my balance and nearly fall off the bike. I am wracked with humiliation. Everyone is watching me. I have had enough. I have to get out of here. I try to get off the bike and stand up, but I can't. My legs give way beneath me, and I feel like I'm drowning in my own sweat. Chelsea's still screaming. "Heads up! Spine straight!"

Clutching at the bike, I stand up and hobble off the floor, ignoring Chelsea's cries to come back. I manage to haul myself onto a bench outside the spin room and seriously consider calling 911. But my cell phone's in the car. I sit there for ten minutes, mustering the courage to move. I wish I were at the airport and could call for a wheelchair.

When I get home, I'm walking like John Wayne. But I'm also three pounds lighter overall after a month of exercising. Maybe all this get-off-your-bum stuff really works, after all.

My face looks thinner. I even feel better once the pain subsides. When I manage to drag my sorry arse down to Safeway later, my favorite clerk, a nice young college boy with shaggy blonde hair, even comments. I never thought I'd live to see the day when attention from a store clerk would bring me joy. The boys haven't noticed, but Amanda has.

"You look good, Mom," she says. "Better than I ever remember."

That one comment makes it all worthwhile.

Later, I log on to my computer to check for new comments on my blog.

When my husband announced he was divorcing me and that I should move into the garage so he could move his girlfriend into our house, I was 183 pounds. And I'm only five foot three. I got mad, sure, but I also got in shape. It was torture, agony, but I lost sixty pounds, and the other day, I bumped into him at Safeway, and he didn't even recognize me.

Posted by JemmaL

Chapter 14

Celebrating Mother's Day without flowers and presents is like celebrating Christmas without Jesus.
—Molly Buffet

THE BLASPHEMY BOX

When your husband has left you and it's Mother's Day, there are all kinds of self-pity to wallow in. Like who the heck is going to supervise the kids' making of your breakfast in bed? To which you look forward to all year. Without your husband around, it's easy to wake up to incinerated toast and eggs on the wrong side of salmonella. And there's no one to carry that tray. One year, when HM ran out for lattes (it's hard to believe, I know, but once in a while he did do something for me), Colin took it upon himself to carry the tray to my bedroom, where he promptly dropped it and three pieces of French toast smothered in strawberries and yogurt and mascarpone all over our prized Persian carpet.

And then, of course, there's no spa day gift certificate or small tasteful piece of jewelry gently pushed across the table toward you. No husband around to make you feel it has been worth being a mother. (Your children never thank you, that's for sure.)

I read somewhere that ten million mothers currently awake to no husband/father in the house on Mother's Day, and let me tell you, it's not a great feeling.

However, if I'm looking for an upside, and believe me, I am, it's that I don't have to spend the day with dear old MIL. Yippee!

For the past few years, we have gone to the Palace Hotel for brunch on Mother's Day. Several other families we know from school and the neighborhood go, too, descending on the hotel's spectacular, glass-domed courtyard restaurant like an invading army and trying, I am certain, the patience of the wait staff.

It has always been fun, if slightly marred by the presence of my mother-in-law, Anita, who has always insisted on coming along, never tiring of reminding us that she, too, is a mother.

I always tried to sit as far from her as I could, but somehow, by some maleficent intervention, she would end up next to me or across from me, glaring at me if the children dropped their forks on the carpet or played too loudly with the other hooligans under the table. After a few years of this, I asked Steven if just he, I and the kids could go, that Mother's Day was meant to be my day, a day when my wishes should count. He would always say that Anita was on her own, a longtime widow who deserved our compassion, not our avoidance. And frankly, what could I say to that?

On this Mother's Day, however, I am not obliged to go to brunch with Anita, not forced to endure her frosty looks, her quiet disapproval, her unmitigated resolve to let me know who's the boss in my house. (I mean her, of course. Steven would do anything for that old cow.) As I'm reveling in this lovely thought, my bedroom door flies open, and two little tousled-hair boys in Harry Potter pajamas tumble in and jump on my bed.

"Happy Mother's Day, Mom!" they cry in unison.

I embrace them in a huge hug. "Happy Mother's Day to you!" I say.

They look a little confused, so I say, "You know what I mean. Where's your sister?"

"Downstairs," Colin says. "She's—"

"Shh," Charlie says, putting his finger to his lips. "It's a secret."

"It is? Oh my, how exciting."

They hand me their handmade cards, with blocky, uneven writing that falls down and almost off the card, and I squeeze them to me until they can barely breathe. "Thank you. I love them!"

Right then, Amanda appears in the doorway, carrying what looks like a plate and a cup on a large coffee-table book.

"Thanks, sweetie," I say. "But why didn't you use the tray?"

"I couldn't find it," she says, which means she couldn't be bothered to look for it. She gingerly sets the book down on my bedside table.

"Thank you so much," I say, surveying a previously—and still partly—frozen waffle with what looks like a pound of butter and some strawberries on top, along with a cup of something that looks like brackish water.

"Coffee and a waffle!" Amanda trills.

"Mmm," I say, reaching for the cup, "delicious. Can't wait to taste it. Now, why don't you three go have your showers, and we'll go off somewhere lovely."

"Where, Mom? Where?" Charlie is jumping up and down. "Brunch at the Palace?"

I cough. "Well, I thought this year we might go somewhere different. What do you think?" I can't sit in the Palace's Garden Court with all those other couples watching me, or worse still, come face to face with Steven and Girl Bambi and my soon-to-be ex-mother-in-law.

Charlie's face drops, and Colin looks at me questioningly. Amanda gives me a knowing smile.

"Like where, Mom?" Charlie says.

I desperately try to come up with somewhere the kids will like. For a minute I can't think of anything, so unused am I to making this particular decision on this particular day.

And then all of a sudden it comes to me. "How about that place in the Presidio?"

"What place?" Amanda says.

"It's this great old historic army barracks that's been converted to a retro kind of diner, and someone told me they have a great Mother's Day brunch. After, we can go down to Crissy Field and walk along the Bay over to the Golden Gate Bridge."

The boys watch Amanda's reaction. She looks intrigued. "Fine," she says, finally. "I was getting sick of the whole Garden Court thing and all the screaming kids there, anyway."

I smile. Then I take a sip of the coffee, which tastes like fermented bracken, or, at least, how I imagine fermented bracken would taste, and a bite of the waffle, which is still frozen with visible slivers of ice.

"This is yummy!" I say, smiling as widely as I can. "Now, off you go and get ready."

In record time we are all showered and dressed and getting into the car. We drive into the Presidio via the Lombard Gate, and soon we're parking and walking up to the restaurant, which sits amid a eucalyptus grove and has a large porch with red geraniums cascading from a row of planters. There is a short line, but we are soon seated on a very sunny deck and perusing the menu. I am worried about how much it will all cost, but I refuse to stint on Mother's Day. Steven can just pay it, one way or another.

I order a rum-soaked challah French toast with a side of eggs, while the kids have the brioche beignets. As we wait for our food, children and dogs play in the lush green grass around us. I glance around and see families everywhere, each one of them including a father, and a sharp pain shoots through me. I put on my sunglasses so the kids can't see my tears and chatter inanely about the restaurant and the food and Lord knows what else. Sadness settles on me like a fur cape, and soon I stop talking and just sit there. The kids do not seem to notice, thank God. The twins are their usual cheerful selves, and Amanda, as usual, doesn't say much. I realize how lucky I am to have them with me today.

Afterward, we stroll down to Crissy Field and walk along the shore. Dogs are splashing in the water, children are flying balloons, and the bridge sits suspended in front of us like some hanging Christmas ornament. The air is fresh and the scenery breathtaking.

As the boys run ahead, picking up and throwing sticks, Amanda stays close. I put my arm around her shoulder and lean my head toward her. For once she doesn't try to get away immediately.

"Are you really OK with not going to the Palace?" I ask. "Are you OK with Dad and I…well…Dad and I not being together? I read that children can get very angry and upset when their routines are interrupted."

Amanda smiles at me. "It's sweet of you to worry, Mom, but I'm fine, and I honestly haven't heard the twins talk much about it. They seem to be fine, too. And remember, this was Dad's decision, not yours, and all three of us know that."

I want to say, you bet it was that son of a bitch of your father's idea to break up this happy home. But I don't. I say, "Well, I don't want you to hate your dad because of this decision."

"You sure about that?" Amanda says.

I grin. "Well, maybe a little. Just kidding. He's your dad, and these things happen, and we all have to accept it and move on, right?" I can't believe how grown up I sound.

"Exactly," Amanda says. "Lots of kids I know have parents who are divorced, Mom. It's not that unusual. And as long as both of you are still in our lives, we can definitely deal with that."

Joy surges through me. Perhaps my children won't be damaged forever after all, I think.

When I get home, I go online to see if any readers have posted comments. I'm beginning to build up readers in a way I never thought possible.

This is exactly my experience! Brunch every Mother's Day with the only mother who ever counted for anything with hubby—his own. That first Mother's Day after he left—when I didn't have to grit my teeth all through brunch as the discussion centered, as per usual, on MIL and all her aches and pains and her disappointments (main one being me)— was such a gift I found myself thinking, gee, why didn't he leave sooner.

Posted by my salgal

Chapter 15

Divorce is the one human tragedy that reduces everything to cash.
—Rita Mae Brown

THE BLASPHEMY BOX

Why does everything in life have to be about money? School, college, dining out, skiing, ornithology? And relationships! I'm finding they're all about money. Are marriage and divorce always overshadowed by economics? Is that because they are about the beginning and ending of a business? I mean, that's really the sum of it, isn't it? The marriage contract is a business deal, right? So is the divorce decree. As my friend C says, marriage is about love, and divorce is about money.

I mean, here I am, in a most precarious financial position with no prenup, no money, a lawyer who needs paying, children who need raising (along with a new pair of sneakers every five minutes), and a soon-to-be- ex-husband who's dangling his pregnant nymphet on his knee and fighting me on support. It's enough to sour you on relationships forever.

"You husband is pleading poverty," Alec informs me not too long after the bombshell call. "He's saying he doesn't have a lot of money and can't pay the upkeep of the house, the private school, child support, and alimony. And the new baby, of course."

I laugh. "Steven is all about money. He's been hoarding it away for years in all sorts of funds and accounts. It's all a big lie."

"That may be, but that's his position going into the settlement talks. It's going to come down to how much you will want to compromise in the end."

"Compromise?! He's the one who walked out."

"True, but he's the one with the money. And if he can convince the judge he doesn't have much...well..."

"What should I do?"

I still just can't believe how Steven and I could have loved each other once and made three children together, and now here he is trying to screw me over as if I had run off with Andy Garcia or something. I just can't understand how this all happened.

Alec senses my thoughts. "You will recover from this, you know."

"I will? When?"

"Five years."

"*Five* years?"

"That's about the normal amount of time."

I feel my stomach clenching. "What can I do?"

"Hang tight. I'll do what I can. But between you and me, you might start weighing your options."

"What do you mean?"

"I'm not a financial adviser, but I expect you'll need to anticipate making some changes in the future. But we've still got quite a bit of time before that happens. Sorry, I've got another call."

Changes?

I think about that for a moment. Haven't I had enough changes for one lifetime? My husband has dumped me, he has a new girlfriend, she's pregnant, my kids spend time with her, and I don't have enough money. That's quite a lot of change right there. Every night I am in bed alone, consumed with fear for the future and for my old age, dizzy with the pain of feeling abandoned and second-rate, unable to think about how to reinvent myself. Since Alec cannot mean changes to include feeding the kids bread and water or denying them summer camp, he must mean I should return to work. That's fine, but I'm fifty. I keep getting mail from AARP, for Christ's sake. Who hires old-timers like me?

Chapter 16

If you're going through hell, keep going.
—*Winston Churchill*

THE BLASPHEMY BOX

How do you prepare yourself for the inevitable: meeting your ex's new girlfriend? My friends at the support group advise against it. They think the whole thing is awful and awkward and just one more chance for humiliation by the ex of moi. But it's unavoidable, I suppose, and I need to be ready. I actually did a Google search for "Meeting your ex-husband's new girlfriend" and discovered there is quite a lot of advice on the subject. Most people said to smile a lot, not to laugh too loudly or talk too much, to make sure to include her in the conversation, to avoid sharing any of your ex's faults, and definitely, absolutely, one hundred percent to not reminisce with your ex about your life together. Oh, and look your best without overdressing.

Amanda's piano recital is today. Luckily, the space is so small that only immediate family can attend, which excludes grandparents.

Steven has his secretary call to inform me he will be going.

"Will he be attending by himself?"

"I'm afraid he didn't say, Mrs. Nelson."

That made me nervous. He always was particular about giving all the details to her. Seeing him won't be easy. Somehow I allow myself to hope that seeing our child perform will make him realize what he's giving up, what we have built—and come back. Somehow I know it won't.

I open my closet. What is appropriate wear for a mother whose husband has left her and who wants to remind him about what he's missing? I try on seven different outfits and toss them onto the floor in disgust, finally settling on a pair of black pants, a black T-shirt, and a short wool jacket in salmon pink. Now it's time for makeup. Last week, I read in some trashy magazine that cat's eye eyeliner is trendy again. I remember wearing it decades ago. I decide I'm going to go for it. However, I discover this is a far trickier proposition that I remembered. My hand won't stop shaking, and I can't see what I'm doing because I need my glasses. Try putting eyeliner on from inside your eyeglasses. Now if only Apple could solve *that* problem. (iLiner?)

The first three tries end in black smudges on my upper lid, bottom lid, hand, and cheek. Hmm. I try again, but this time I manage to poke the eyeliner wand into my right eye, causing it to sting like the blazes. I hurl the applicator onto the bathroom counter. I can't believe I'm doing at fifty all the things I did so much better at thirty, trying to attract the man I married all over again. I know it won't work. These things never do, and that just makes me feel even more pathetic. If he was attracted to me, he would be standing next to me shaving, filling the sink with those little black hairs that once were so annoying, but to which distance has now lent its storied enchantment.

I give up and settle on some kohl, powder, and blush, topped off with coral lipstick.

I look at myself in the mirror. Not too bad, I think. Especially now that I'm a bit thinner, thanks to the gym. I am still going religiously but can't afford Duane so I had to let him go. Not a bad thing. How much hectoring from a man in neon turquoise Lycra can a person take at eight in the morning, after all?

I marshal the kids together, and we dive into the car and drive the six blocks to the home of one of the twins' friends, where they will spend the evening eating too many M&Ms and watching too much television. Then it's off to the assembly hall.

"Don't worry, Mom. I'll be fine," Amanda says, seeing I'm in a state.

"I know, sweetie. I'm not worried." About *you*, I want to add.

Ten minutes later, Amanda and I approach the school's assembly hall. Parents and kids are milling around.

As we walk in, my head darts around in search of Steven. And his inamorata. Please make her not come, I pray. Please. My stomach is roiling like the English Channel, and I am relieved when Melanie Aston, the mother of one of Amanda's friends, Sydney, walks toward me.

"Maddy, how are you?" she says. I try not to see the mixture of pity and inquisitiveness in her hazel eyes.

"Fine. Looking forward to the big recital." My voice sounds high and nervous, and my mouth is so dry. "What's going on with you?"

"Not much," she says, a bit disappointed. "Sydney's been practicing for ages. I hope it goes well."

"I'm sure it will." I can't help looking over her shoulder for Steven.

"Listen, a few of us parents are going out for dinner after this recital. Do you want to join us?" Melanie says.

I can't think of anything worse. Being the fifth wheel is never comfortable. And all those questions.

"I don't think so, but thanks so much. I have to go pick up the twins from the Whitakers'." I look at Melanie, waiting for her to insist, but she's looking at the door. In the entryway stands Steven, and on his arm is a young woman, whom I am guessing is Girl Bambi. No makeup or exercise is going to make me look like that.

I want to shrink into the floor and disappear. I want to scream out choice curses. But instead, I just stand there, with Amanda at my side. Barely ten seconds later, Steven is standing in front of me, greeting me with all the enthusiasm of Lindsay Lohan for rehab. He gives Amanda a fatherly hug, and the smile on her face just kills me.

"Hi, Gabriela," Amanda says innocently.

"Hi, Amanda, nice to see you."

The ice broken, she slithers toward me then, like the snake she is, the woman who took my husband and won't give him back.

"Hi," she says, in that whispery way young sexpots have, and extends her hand. "You must be Madeleine." And then she smiles so warmly that I half expect her to ask me to Bikram yoga Saturday morning.

I don't know what to say, which for me is a bit unusual. My stomach is still roiling, and I feel dizzy. I had skin that dewy, once. I had arms that toned. I want to scream at her to leave me alone, to get her lithe, seductive, chopstick-thin body in its thigh-high raspberry sheath out of my face. But I don't. Steven is hovering.

"Madeleine," he says. "I should have properly introduced you. This is Gabriela Gilberto."

I hate this man's guts. I truly do. Nothing could be more humiliating than being forced to meet your husband's piece of crumpet in front of a host of fellow parents at a school function. I can see my friends looking my way in sympathy.

"Pleased to meet you," I say to Gabriela, shaking her hand briefly. I feel tears coming but will them away with as much strength as I can muster. I'm determined not to make a fool of myself in front of Steven, our daughter, and this young hussy.

At that moment, the music master asks the kids to take their places in the front row. All the mothers join up with their husbands except me. I am the only one there without a mate and sit down alone. I look around to see Steven and Girl Bambi sitting a few rows back. At least they're discreet, I think. I still am just so flabbergasted at the situation I'm in. Amanda looks around to smile at me, and I smile back. She is not one of those kids, thankfully, who is terrified at performing in public or fearful she will fail and be humiliated in front of all her peers. Lack of confidence has never been Amanda's problem. She seems to thrive on competition and the attention. I would have been a total wreck at her age.

Amanda's piece comes halfway through the program. She smiles brightly, makes a gracious bow, sits down on the piano stool, and focuses on the keys. When she launches into her performance, a well of pride swells inside me, and I look around to see other parents actually paying attention.

Suddenly, a cell phone goes off. Everyone sits up sharply and fumbles in their purses and pockets. The ringtone sounds like some disco song. I turn around to see Girl Bambi take out her cell phone with its rhinestone-encrusted case and press a button. The telephone goes silent. She doesn't appear the least bit mortified, merely giggling and whispering something into Steven's ear. He puts his arm around her and nuzzles her.

I feel sick.

Amanda finishes with a flourish and stands to strong applause.

An hour later, the last child finishes the program. The music teacher thanks everyone for coming and asks everyone to applaud his talented group, reminding people to stay for a small reception afterward. Everyone gets up and moves toward the back for cookies and punch.

I stand but don't follow the crowd. Amanda goes over to her father and Girl Bambi to say good-bye and hurries over to me. "Mom, can we go for ice cream? We can pick up Colin and Charlie from Andrew's house on the way."

Grateful for any excuse to escape, I agree readily. I look over to see Steven schmoozing with the principal and Girl Bambi nodding politely.

I hurry Amanda to the parking lot.

Once in the car, I say to her, "You did very well. How do you feel?"

"Oh, fine."

"I'm sorry Gabriela's cell phone interrupted your performance."

"Oh, I don't care. It was kind of funny, actually."

"Funny?" I say. "I don't think it was funny in the least."

"Well, you wouldn't, Mom."

We arrive at the Whitakers', where my boys fling themselves into the van, still in the heat of an argument over one of their silly video games. Andrew's mom, Carina, waves to me from her doorway. I mouth, "Thanks," and she comes over to Amanda's side of the car. I roll down the window.

"How did it go?" she asks her.

"Really well, I think," Amanda says. She is so calm and poised for only being fourteen.

"Did everyone applaud?"

"Yes," Amanda said, smiling.

"Good for you," Carina says and rumples her hair. Amanda smiles again.

The boys are still arguing as I take off.

"Now pipe down, you two," I say. "Or no ice cream for you."

After dropping the car off at home, we walk down Fillmore Street to Union Street and over to the kids' favorite ice cream place, which is fairly vibrating with Christina Aguilera. I promise myself I am going to be good and have the dietetic, no-sugar-added frozen yogurt, one scoop, no toppings. The kids get their favorites, with the works of course, and we find a table.

"Dad brought us here last week," Colin said, licking his ice cream with extravagant strokes of the tongue.

"He did?"

"Yeah. With Gabriela."

I hold my voice as steady as I can. "Really?"

"Yes," says Charlie. "She likes the mint chocolate chip."

That's my favorite, too, but I don't say that. "Is that right?"

Amanda is watching me carefully.

"Yup," says Charlie, "She's from Brazil and speaks four languages: Portuguese, French, Spanish, and English."

Yes, I think, she speaks four languages and probably can't say no in any of them.

"That must be nice for traveling," I offer politely.

"You know she's having a baby, right, Mom? A boy?" Colin says. His vanilla ice cream, smothered in caramel, is half in his mouth and half on his shirt.

"Of course I know."

"It'll be weird having a baby brother," Colin says.

"Well, dear, he'll be your half-brother."

"You mean he'll have no legs?"

Charlie laughs. "What a dumbo."

"Have you spent much time with Bam...Gabriela?" I ask, as nonchalantly as I can.

"Well, she's always there when we go to see Dad," Amanda says. "She helps with our French homework if we have any the nights we're there."

Note to attorney. She's not meant to be there overnight if the kids are.

"And she's nice to you?"

The kids all nod their heads. "And she knows all about Super Mario," Colin says.

Of course she does. She's a *child*.

"She's fine," Amanda says. "It's not like we're going to be best friends, but Dad seems happy."

I want to ask her if everything is fine just as long as Dad is happy. But I don't. I think about what it means to be a good mother, and I say nothing.

At home, I put the kids to bed and run to the computer to post my blog. I need to escape my life for a while. Half an hour after I'm done, I see I have a comment. So much fun!

Good for you for not freaking out or screaming at your ex's new sweetie. When my ex met his first girlfriend after me, she refused to acknowledge me or talk to me at school events and drop-offs and pickups. Just refused. My ex told me it was because she was jealous of the time I had spent with him and wanted to make it clear that that time had ended. (I think even I knew I was divorced at that point, but I guess the girlfriend just wanted to be sure.) I wanted to tell her I didn't think she should envy my marriage. It took her a while to figure that out. Anyway, I kept saying hi and hello every time I saw her, and finally, one day after a year or so, she actually answered me. She said, "Hi." That was it. A few months later, she said, "Bye." A year after that, we were friends, and she would come over to complain to me about her husband. My ex-husband.

Posted by JessieCan

Chapter 17

Growing old is like being increasingly penalized for a crime you haven't committed.
—Anthony Powell

THE BLASPHEMY BOX

Given the way HM is behaving, pretending poverty and all that, I should probably look for some kind of work, a job that will bring in a little money. Hopefully, I will get a settlement that will see me comfortable, but working will not only add to the bank balance but will more importantly provide some self-validation. Somehow I have this fantasy that my dream job is out there. I've still got a few contacts, but the problem is print media is laying journalists off, not hiring them. Advertisers, the lifeblood of newspapers and magazines, have gone online, leaving print dying a slow and sorry death. And what else could I do? Who knows if I even have the skills for journalism after fourteen years? Who says I am still suited to it? Or it to me?

BFF says looking for work is a brilliant idea and advises me to start networking. But the process is daunting at my age. Everyone I know is either a stay-at-home mom or a super achiever who stopped working only long enough to have their children and continue on. No one wants to hire someone who's over thirty-five. Fifty is supposed to be the new thirty-five, but don't believe it.

In the shower one day last week, I decided that I need to look for a job. Who knows how long this divorce process will take, and Steven will probably tighten the purse strings even more to make me give in to his demands. So, I thought, I need to try to bridge the gap. I got out, dried off, put on my robe, marched into the kitchen, sat down at the table, and made a list of former colleagues with whom I have kept in contact, along with their numbers and e-mail addresses. It was a short list. I have not been as diligent about staying in touch with them as I should have been. Most have made the transition to websites, single-market papers like *Catholic San Francisco,* and public relations. It would be a slog, to say the least.

Suzy said my new blog would help show I'm current. That, and my recent articles. All three of them. But, I needed to give it whirl. My former colleagues were very nice and supportive. They gave me tips about what places might be looking for freelancers, but didn't know about any full-time positions. Nobody's hiring in this economy. Blah, blah, blah. I made a few lunch dates, but nothing else. Exhausted, I took a break, had some granola and coffee, and then started checking out the job sites.

There were dozens of them, each one more complex than the next. The volume of listings was overwhelming, and you just knew everyone in the entire world was looking at them, too. There were masses of technical writing positions, but since I don't know MaaS platform from customer-facing documentation, they didn't really help. One job at a video game company asked for a writer who knows what SEO is. The ad said it was *not* Spleen Emergency Operation. (How kind of them to translate.)

A couple fit my experience. A job as an editor/writer at a San Francisco travel trade magazine in both print and online looked promising. I had the qualifications except for proficiency in Adobe InCopy. Maybe that's because I've never heard of it.

There was an ad for an associate editor for a home and design magazine, which directed you to apply to the "exectutive editor." (Should I have told them that what they really need is a good copy editor?) But most of the jobs had no contact numbers, no direct e-mail addresses, nothing. You don't know to whom you're applying. Worse still, most ads stated that they would only respond if they're interested. And the rest didn't say anything at all.

I tried to "age proof" my resume, but it looked silly. How can you cover a fourteen-year gap? Fudging dates won't help. I put together something that seemed appropriate. But the worst was yet to come: the dreaded cover letter. It was a task I truly did not feel up to, excruciating for someone like me who has been unemployed and fears she very might well be unemployable. Do I mention my past experience, or is it too far in the past? Do I mention my passionate interest in the job and exploring the great opportunity it affords? Or do I just say how desperate I am, because my husband dumped me? It's a nightmare.

I went on the net and tried to see what other people do. One site said I should address my relevant skills and experience that enable me to provide valuable work. In other words, concentrate on what you did, not what you didn't.

Fine, I thought. But how the heck do I do that?

I sat and sat in front of that computer, pondering my life and what value I could, without cringing, attribute to it. For fourteen years I'd been doing carpools and grocery shopping and homework and birthday parties. What did I truly have to offer? After all, if my husband didn't want me, why would anyone or anything else? Sometimes I didn't read the newspaper from one day to the next, I was so on the go. How could Mom turn into Maureen Dowd?

I sat thinking and agonizing until I was well and truly terrified and so fed up that all I was able to manage was a perfunctory sentence about all the experience, wisdom, and contacts I could bring to the job. And I signed off.

I applied for eleven writing jobs, including one as a practice question writer for an "adult site," whatever that meant. And then I waited for a response. It took a week to get one nibble. Some person named Pepper e-mailed me today on behalf of her boss and gave me a phone number.

I call. The young woman who answers the phone said both Pepper and her boss are in meetings, and she'd leave a message. That's the last I hear.

I call the travel magazine, where the young woman who answers the phone says she has no idea if Ms. So-and-So has received my application and to just wait until Ms. So-and-So responds. I ask if she has any idea when that would be, and she says, "No. She's traveling. We are a travel publication, after all."

I get very excited when the managing editor at a newswire I had applied to actually picks up his own phone and seems to have seen my application packet.

"Ah, yes, I did get your stuff. Quite impressive. But you are just way too over-qualified for this job. It's about proofreading and processing press releases for electronic distribution to the media and financial community. Entry level at best."

Even though it's not my dream job, I feel the need to pretend it is. "I'd be interested in learning a new position. I'm sure my experience will add value to the effort."

I hear him sigh. "This really is an entry-level position," he says. "Someone with your experience would be bored to tears. I'll keep you mind if something more appropriate comes up."

He hangs up so fast I don't even have time to thank him.

☙❧

Cameron's son, Kenny, is involved in some Internet startup, and she suggests I go see him. "Maybe he can use someone like you," she says.

"What kind of a startup is it, exactly?" I ask her.

"Some website to do with media," she says. "Here's his e-mail. I'll be sure to put in a good word."

I jot it down and send off a query. Kenny is friendly and sets up a meeting to see me the next day.

I put on some black slacks and a coral sweater and take myself over to some awful huge loft place in the former industrial area of San Francisco south of Market Street that is now a patchwork of old warehouses, hot nightspots, art spaces, indie stores, and Internet companies. When I walk into the place, a snippy little Generation Yer in a tartan kilt, Liverpool soccer jersey, and black fishnets looks up from her iPhone and says, "Yeah?"

"Hi, I'm Maddy Nelson. I'm here to see Kenny. I have an appointment."

The young girl sighs and pushes a button on the phone on her desk. "Your ten o'clock is here," she says. Then to me, she says, "Take a seat," and then goes back to her iPhone.

Minutes tick by until we're at 10:20. How busy can Kenny be? He's twenty-two. Then a young guy in cargo pants and a hoodie appears and beckons to me with a finger while blabbing away to someone on his Blackberry Torch.

He leads me into a fusty old office with one of those mid-century, modern steel desks in a pulsating orange. Like the stuff you see in all the stores, très downtown chic. If people really liked mid-century modern furniture, why is there so much of it for sale everywhere you go?

As he leaves, a person I assume to be Kenny looks up at me from his iPad. He's in khaki shorts and a rumpled Tommy Bahama floral shirt. His desk is covered with all kinds of office toys.

"Hi, Mrs. Nelson," he says. "Nice to see you again. My mom says you're looking for a job."

I smile sweetly. "Your mother is a dear friend. Yes, I'm looking to get back to work."

"That's great. We're an Internet start-up, devoted to local news," he says, and proceeds to regale me with all the details that are so far from news I need the Rosetta Stone to decipher what he's saying. He keeps on about chat rooms and podcasting, live streaming video and page views, online communities and open newsfeeds and algorithms and pinging and social media and leaderboard ads versus banner ads, and every incomprehensible tech acronym you could ever imagine.

I listen as if I'm interested.

"I thought you might like to look at my clips," I venture. I lay my portfolio out on his desk. He looks at it as if he were a vegan contemplating a juicy New York strip and doesn't even open it.

"Well, Mrs. Nelson, my mom said you had a lot of experience. That's great, but what we're looking for here are people who can do more than just write. People who are into social networking—you know, Facebook, YouTube, Twitter—who can do compilations and navigate through all the new media. Someone who can set aside the dated concepts and models of yesterday and embrace today and tomorrow—where, unfortunately, experience in traditional journalism is not enough."

"I just started a blog," I offer. "It's called The Blasphemy Box."

That registers. "Really? How many unique visitors do you get? Are you linked to any other sites?"

I give him a blank stare. "I'm a bit new to it."

Suddenly I hear a ping from his iPhone. He picks it up and scans it.

"I'm sorry, I need to answer this. I'll take a look at your blog and let my mom know if there's anything. Sorry I can't help more. I hope I haven't upset you."

I want to say, you've made me feel as old as Methuselah, as out of touch as the Amish, and as useless as a chocolate fireguard. But no, none of that has upset me at all.

But what I actually say is, "No, of course not."

Kenny smiles. "Well, good luck, and nice seeing you again."

I get up. He doesn't. "OK, well, say hi to your mom for me."

"I will," he says, already texting on his phone.

When I get home, I go over my comments from my blog readers.

I lost my "real job" in ad sales a year ago. I was unemployed for eight months and that was only because Sears hired me for the holidays (they'll take anyone, basically). I've already cashed in my 401k. Once that's gone, it'll be park benches and dumpster diving. I have an MA from a good university, and employers should be begging me to work for them, but there's nothing. A friend of mine said I should change my name to Singh. Then employers will think I'm Indian and hire me.
Posted by Anonymous in California

Chapter 18

For a list of all the ways technology has failed to improve the quality of life, please press three.
—Alice Kahn

THE BLASPHEMY BOX

Turning from a married mom into a single mom can be a challenge, in more ways than are obvious. I didn't know it would be so hard bringing kids up alone. Obviously Steven is nearby, and the kids are with him quite a bit, but I'm the custodial parent, and a lot of the time, when I need help with all kinds of things, there is none.

And it's not easy. Particularly in the technological age. That's always been Steven's bailiwick. HD TV, smartphones, Internet streaming. All I know is the names. How they work? Pff!

Now, however, I am more directly confronted with technology, the only parent in the room for much of the time. And the kids seem to know so much these days. When we were kids, we learned how to do Etch A Sketch. Today, they learn how to hack into Wells Fargo.

A group of parents at school were talking in the drop-off line today about how important it is to find out what kids are doing and saying online. Apparently there's a new language that parents need to learn.

When I get home, I go online and discover the idea is to misspell, abbreviate, and substitute words to save time and to create a language your parents cannot decode. Something like, "Do u no h 2 spel lik a freek?"

The people you're writing to will know what you mean, it says online. They will? I already have no idea what my kids are saying half the time. When Amanda first started blabbing on about the iPod a while back, I thought she said Izod and took her straight to Macy's. The whole online/Internet thing makes me feel like a portable antiquity.

I tiptoe into Amanda's room. I know she's not here, and I am invading her privacy. But she's fourteen, so it's moot as far as I'm concerned. A parent's life is often colored by some kind of ethical dilemma.

I sit down at her desk. Despite the fact that we are always saying to turn the computer off when not in use, it's on and luckily, she's signed in. I start by looking at her e-mails. They are completely unintelligible. I get online and try to find the meanings of the acronyms and letters in front of me. I find them in site after site of Internet slang, and it isn't that difficult. There's a string of e-mails between her and someone called HotBobby. That must be Bobby Patton from school. He's four grades above her. In fact, it has to be him. He *is* hot, but I was hoping Amanda wouldn't notice. One exchange in particular catches my eye:

HotBobby: "Heyy u, wadzup?"

Amanda: "NMU." (Not much, you?)

HotBobby: HK but CBFB. (Homework but can't be fucking bothered.)

Amanda: MOS, GTG. BRB. (Mom over shoulder, got to go, be right back.

HotBobby: Letz GNOC. (Let's get naked on camera.)

Amanda: PRW. (Parents are watching.)

HotBobby: LMIRL. (Let's meet in real life.)

Amanda: ABD. (Already been done.)

HotBobby: WHR? (Where?)

Amanda: Scool. (How the heck, I think, is she going to get into Stanford like this?)

HotBobby: WTHAY? (Who the hell are you?)

Amanda: WDYTIA. FIO. GTG. HK. (Who do you think I am? Figure it out, got to go, homework.)

HotBobby: WAFL. (What a fucking loser.) Wanafuk?

Amanda: P911. CUIC. (Parent emergency. See you in class.)

I gasp in horror and forward all the e-mails on to Steven.

We never did this kind of thing. Granted, when Suzy and I were twelve, we were at the cinema, and a boy we knew, Peter Ho from Hong Kong, was there, too, and I sent him a note saying, "Wanna do it?," and he ran out of the theater yelling, "Keep her away from me." But I didn't mean it, for Christ's sake. I was just talking big. (I always called him Peter No after that.) We didn't really know too much about sex when we were our kids' ages. I only thought about Laura Ashley dresses and Pink Floyd concerts. We snogged a bit with boys, I remember, but somehow it never turned into sex.

While I'm still sitting here in front of Amanda's computer, Steven rings up.

"Madeleine, I'm very busy here."

"I thought you might like to know what our daughter is doing."

He sighs. "Look, it's your choice to have the kids most of the time, so you need to deal with things like this."

"You're the tech expert, Steven. We both need to be involved."

"Fine. I'll speak with her," he says, and hangs up.

When Amanda gets home that afternoon, I don't say anything, thinking I'll chime in after Steven speaks with her. She goes up to her room and almost immediately comes down, seething.

"How dare you read my e-mail, Mom! And send them to Daddy. It's my private stuff!"

I am ready. "It isn't just me. All the other parents are talking about the stuff that goes on online. Is this Bobby Patton you're so crazy about? What happened to Nicholas? Bobby Patton's *eighteen*! You're *fourteen*, goddamn it. And you're grounded. You are not going to be corresponding with people like this. No computer or iPhone for a week, I don't care if school is over soon, and that's that. Your father will be calling you about it later. He is very concerned as well."

Amanda says nothing. She just looks at me with those steady eyes of hers and marches off. I march right along behind her and follow her into her room. The computer is on. "That's it, Amanda. Close your computer and do your homework."

"Well, how am I supposed to do my homework without a computer, Mom?"

Gotcha. "You can use mine for the time being. In the kitchen."

Dinner is quite a tense affair. The boys babble on about their games and who's winning and how school will be out soon, while Amanda picks at her food, sullen and quiet. It's all I can do to sit there without commenting.

After dinner, Steven calls and talks to Amanda on the phone, a conversation that ends with her banging down the handset in tears. Thank God he agreed with my punishment. I ring Mrs. Patton up, tell her everything, and forward the e-mails to her. She is shocked and upset and says she'll talk to Bobby. Nobody's happy.

The same thing happened to me. I was cleaning up Andrew's room while he was at school (he's fifteen), and his e-mail happened to be open on his computer. I know I should probably have walked out then and there, but I didn't. I only read the most recent one. He had sent "Diorable" an e-mail, and she had hit reply to send him one back. His read "wanna cu a3." I typed the phrase into Google and discovered it means I want to see you anyplace, anywhere, anytime. Not too bad. But listen to her answer! "Wtp? wanafuk?" meaning, "Where's the party?," and you can figure out the rest. It must be that precocious little number from school. Her mother wears nothing but Dior.

Posted by worriedmom

Chapter 19

Scratch a lover, and find a foe.
—Dorothy Parker

THE BLASPHEMY BOX

How strange it is to be dealing with attorneys working to free you from the person you have slept with and been married to for twenty years. Particularly when you didn't ask to be freed. For twenty years, I have lived with the same person in the same house with mostly the same life. Now I feel so adrift, so unmoored. I'm overwhelmed by confusion and chaos, and everything, it seems, is in the lap of the lawyers. Don't you hate that? Handing over control of your life to two lawyers who do not know you and probably don't give a damn?

My friend C had to sit in the courthouse corridor for hours while her lawyer and opposing counsel met with the judge, talking about her life, her future, with no chance for input from her.

Did her lawyer adequately argue her case with the judge? Did he let the judge know how mean and evil and totally unreasonable her third husband was?

Who knows?

We have the first meeting with the lawyers today at Steven's attorney's office. We should have had it much earlier, but he keeps stalling. The kids are out of school, and the babysitter, Gracie, from down the street, has arrived with pink hair and multiple lip piercings.

As I dress for the meeting, I think summer's here and we should be discussing where we're going to take the kids for vacation.

Instead, we're letting strangers help negotiate things like splitting IRAs and where said kids should live. All of a sudden, the person I thought was my life partner is now my sworn enemy and allowed to behave in the most egregious fashion with impunity. And he's not my only adversary. He has a lawyer who truly does have no sentimental tie to me and is there to crush and grind me into oblivion at $500 an hour.

I walk in, and there's my lawyer, Alec, and Steven's lawyer, John Harrison, who, even in an expensive suit, looks like an undertaker, sadly appropriate for the death of a marriage. Steven is not there yet. Figures. He's always late.

The secretary comes in to ask if I'd like some water or something. How about a gin and tonic instead, I think of asking, but don't. I settle for water.

Suddenly, Steven comes in through the door, accompanied by Girl Bambi. He sees me and quickly whispers to her to wait outside. She nods, waves at me, and goes to sit on the couch, closing the door behind her. I cannot believe he would bring his girlfriend here, the fucking bastard. Is he that insecure, or is she that greedy? I want to run out there and tell her listen, I was twenty-five once, and pretty and thin and accomplished. I had men after me. But she would not have believed it, and frankly, I hardly believe it myself anymore. I want to tell her to be careful, that when a man marries his mistress, he creates a vacancy. That she will be where I am now, and to have mercy. But that kind of person doesn't know what mercy is.

We sit down opposite each other, ready for the battle to come. Steven's lawyer calls the meeting to attention and starts talking about money, recession, debts, etc., handing out papers and graphs and lists I don't even look at.

Then Harrison lays it all out. He says Steven wants the house. He's offering a subsistence level of child support that won't even cover the kids' private school, let alone the household expenses, and a one-time cash settlement, which doesn't amount to much either. That's all he can afford, the lawyer says, with a straight face.

I burst out laughing. "You must be kidding," I say.

Alec cuts me off. "Mrs. Nelson stipulates that she wants to remain with the children in the house in which they were born and grew up," he says. "The children are happy there and comfortable. They each have their own rooms. Their friends are nearby, and it would be altogether injurious to move them from their primary caregiver and home for no good reason. Judges don't like to upset children's routines, particularly when it's by the person who moved out."

Steven looks like he might blow a gasket at any moment.

"Of course," Harrison counters, "my client would agree to pay all the expenses regarding the children if they lived with him in the house. Mrs. Nelson would receive alimony, of course."

"Unacceptable," I say with as much finality as I can muster, even though I feel my world slipping beyond my grasp.

"And Mr. Nelson wants the kids to spend the night with him when he has them."

"Unacceptable," I say again. "Not if his girlfriend is around. Period."

Steven sits up straight.

"We'll take this offer under advisement," Alec says, sensing another outburst. "Meanwhile, Mr. Nelson needs to pay appropriate support for his wife and children until a final settlement is reached. As you know, we have filed an order for support, stipulating the base amount that would cover all her expenses."

"Base amount?" Steven says, raising his voice. "It's way beyond what is necessary. I know how she wastes money and—" His lawyer stops him with a raised hand.

"Mr. Nelson can fight this if he cares to, but all it means is going to court and more attorneys' fees," Alec says. "Mrs. Nelson has no money. Her only source of income is her husband and their joint assets. Half of those go to her in a divorce, California being a community property state. We can get on the court calendar or not. I can at any time ask a judge to meet with all of us for a voluntary settlement conference, but in that instance, of course, Mr. Nelson will have to pay a lawyer/mediator, or a private judge. It is in all parties' interests to hammer this thing out among ourselves."

It's wonderful. Alec has become my champion.

"Mr. Nelson just doesn't have the resources at the present time to agree to this amount."

I look directly at Steven. "That's understandable, since he bought an estate in Napa just before we separated, without even touching his accounts overseas. It must all be very expensive."

Steven's head snaps up, and he looks at me with something approaching murderous contempt.

Harrison clears his throat. Alec goes in for the kill.

"Mrs. Nelson has brought up some good points. If these facts are introduced in court, we cannot predict what the judge will think of them."

Harrison looks surprised. "While we deny that these so-called facts have any bearing on the settlement, we will need to consider our options."

"Good. You do that, and let us know what you decide," Alec says. He stands, and I follow suit. "Let's speak tomorrow."

We leave the room.

I look back to the conference room. Steven is sitting at the table, the sparkling Bay behind him, the skyscrapers of the Embarcadero as backdrop. He is already engaged in conversation with his lawyer. Harrison stands quickly then and walks over to close the door. Girl Bambi's on the couch reading *Cosmo*. This time I wiggle my fingers at her in greeting. She looks up and smiles.

"Enjoy it while you can," I say as I walk by.

Her smile disappears, and she looks at the closed door in panic.

Chalk up one for the home team.

Chapter 20

If he was stupid enough to walk away, be smart enough to let him go.
—Anonymous

THE BLASPHEMY BOX

I've never been lucky in the finding-yourself-at-the-same-spot-as-your-ex department, you know, the kind of event where everyone is watching to see if you will stick a fork into each other. (A friend of BFF's "accidentally" dumped a piping-hot caramel latte over her ex's new love. What a waste.) But the idea of walking unprepared into an event or some coffee shop early on a Sunday with my hair sticking up only to come face to face with my ex-husband and his smooth-skinned sweetie scares me out of my gourd. Probably because despite all the misery he's caused, I miss him. I'm still reading his goddamn horoscope, for instance—and it's usually better than mine.

There is an army of advice on how to handle running into your ex at a party, in the street, or at some other function. First, you shouldn't leave abruptly, because he's probably seen you, and he'll think you're pathetic. Second, you should play it cool and keep it light—say hi pleasantly and move on fast. Third, you should be civil. Don't flip him off or tell him a carving knife in your kitchen has his name on it. Fourth, you should not flirt. Fifth, you should not divulge any personal information. And finally, you should look good whenever you go anyplace—just in case.

I don't know about all you out there, but my daughter Amanda has a social life to rival that of Kim Kardashian. It seems I am constantly ferrying her from birthday party to ice-skating party to swim party to popcorn-and-movies party. Of course she feels she needs a new outfit for each occasion. In the past, we have constantly been at the mall buying this dress and that skirt and this blouse and that bathing suit, and shoes, shoes, shoes. She has a fetish for them, like her mother. These days, if she wants to shop, she has to appeal to Steven, since he's got all the money.

It's Sunday, and Amanda's party du jour isn't until 1 p.m. It's ten, so that should give her just enough time to decide on an outfit. It's a pool party, and parents are invited. I know Steven won't be going, because he never liked Amanda's friend's father, and he never hesitated to say why: the guy beat him at chess on the first game, and Steven never played with him again. I think I'll just drop her off and go. I haven't bought a swim-suit in years and have no plans to do so. Shorts and cute sundresses are still out of the question. It's my usual: jeans and some kind of sporty top.

I drop the boys off at the Whitakers' again. Carina is happy to see them, and they're overjoyed to have a playdate with their mutual buddy, Andrew, who was born one day after they were.

Amanda and I then go on to her friend's house in St. Francis Wood, located in the southwestern portion of the city. The area is known for large, Italian Renaissance-revival style homes on spacious lots in a tree-studded, park-like setting. It's so lovely that I decide to hang around a bit.

The moment we get there, Hadley, one of the moms, comes wad-dling over to me. She's in a hot pink maternity dress. Hadley, who's forty-five, is always pregnant. I've never seen her not pregnant. A man has to just walk by her window, and she's pregnant. When she's preg-nant, she gets orca fat. But as soon as the baby comes, she's back to hav-ing a figure a Greek statue would envy.

"So sorry to hear about you and—" she says in my ear.

"Yes," I say, cutting her off.

"Bad luck."

I want to say that luck has nothing to do with it, you silly twit, but she's already on to the next subject.

"Are you coming to that fundraiser next weekend?"

"I'm not sure."

"But surely you will," she says, her eyebrows raised. "Everyone's coming."

I want to shake her again. Is she really this clueless?

"I'll be sure to let you know."

She looks at me questioningly. "He'll come back," she says. "They always do."

"I hope not," I say. But I am lying, and she knows I'm lying. Luckily, she waddles off to join her husband.

I look around in misery, the separation and divorce hitting me in a tidal wave as it often does. Suddenly, I notice Steven. I have not seen or spoken to him since the meeting with the lawyers. Why would our hostess invite him to the party? And why would he come? He never deigned to come before, preferring to play golf instead. Bad luck, I guess.

My heart is thudding against my ribs, and of course I break all the rules of engagement. First, I don't look as good as I would have if I'd known he would be there. Second, I turn on my heel and dash to the powder room, feeling nervous and sick. I keep wondering if Girl Bambi is out there, gliding around in some gold mesh bikini cover-up. I glance at myself in the mirror, where a disappointed Madonna stares back at me. I stay in the powder room for ten minutes, fluffing my hair, reapplying eye liner and lipstick, and trying desperately to muster the courage to come out.

When I emerge, Steven is standing there.

"Oh, hi," I say, trying to sound surprised and pleasant.

"Madeleine."

He's looking good in a rather attractive plaid shirt and khakis. Damn him.

"Can we talk?"

"That depends. Politics or the weather?"

"It's about the settlement."

"That's what the attorneys are for."

"Listen, you need to understand the situation. I had the house before we got married, you know. I think it would be better if you move out of it."

"Better for whom?"

"It would make it easier, financially, for everyone."

I feel bile rising up in my throat. "Listen, sonny Jim. No one asked you to set up two households. We're not moving out, so you'll need to find a way to make it work *financially.* Or the judge will. And now, excuse me, but I need a drink."

I'm proud of myself for just leaving him standing there with his mouth open.

I make for the nearest poolside bar. A curt bartender is busy mixing a drink for a man in Bermuda shorts. After taking his drink, he turns toward me.

"Hi. Maddy Nelson, right?" he says, smiling.

"Uh, yes. Have we met?"

He looks at me questioningly and then says, "I'm Jenny Dutton's dad, Mike."

"Oh, right," I say, a little sheepishly. "Sorry."

"No need to be. I don't think we've actually spoken before—except to confirm our daughters' playdates."

"Amanda just loves Jenny."

"The feeling is mutual," Mike says, taking a sip of his drink. "Hey, can I get you something?"

"White wine. Thanks."

"A white wine for the lady," he says to the bartender. "Jenny told me you are in the midst of a divorce," he says, handing me the glass.

I take a sip. "Yes."

Mike grimaces in sympathy. "I've been through it, and I know how difficult it can be."

Suddenly, I remember Amanda saying something about that a year or so back. At the time, I just wrote it off as something that happened to other people.

"I'm sorry. I didn't know." I'm a little stiff, assuming he is just another cheating husband who dumped his loving wife.

"It takes a long time to get over it," Mike says. "I had to take responsibility for my own part in the whole sorry mess."

OK, here it comes. My wife didn't understand me and...

"I was a jerk. Too distracted by work and my students and my own writing, and I just let the marriage slide."

I've never met a man so willing to share his feelings. Steven certainly never was.

"You're a writer?"

"I'm a professor of English at the University of San Francisco, and I do some writing on the side."

"I want to write a novel," I say.

"No, you don't."

"Pardon?"

"No, you don't. You want to have written a novel."

We both laugh then. It feels good.

The kids are still screaming incessantly as they leap in and out of the pool, so Mike picks up his gin and tonic and begins to usher me to the far end, away from all the action.

All of a sudden, seeing all the couples and their kids around me, I feel incredibly sad. A heaviness weighs me down, as if I am in a skin and life that is not mine. I want to feel normal again. I set my wine on the nearest table.

"I should probably get going," I tell Mike.

"Really? So soon? You only just got here."

"I can stay a bit longer, I suppose." We sit at the small table under an umbrella.

"You were telling me about your novel."

"No, I wasn't. You were telling me about your divorce."

"It had been a long time coming, I'm afraid," he says. "As Balzac said, 'Marriage must constantly fight against a monster which devours everything: routine.'"

I am impressed but don't say so. "As Balzac also said," I say, "'A lover always thinks of his mistress first and himself second; with a husband it runs the other way.'"

Mike smiles.

"My degree was in English and French," I say.

"No wonder we get along so well," he says mischievously. "Mine too."

We talk about books and authors then and the amazing power of words to move us.

"What's your novel about?" Mike asks.

"Love lost, love found. The usual, I guess."

"Ah, the universal theme."

"But I just started blogging also," I say, feeling myself flush a little at the admission.

"Really? Good for you. It's a whole new universe out there, and that's where things happen now."

He's so right and so spot on. I look at him admiringly.

"But you should also keep working on your novel," he adds.

"I know, but it's so hard."

"Fitzgerald said that all good writing is swimming under water and holding your breath. Hold your breath, Maddy, and swim."

Our eyes lock in understanding.

Amanda arrives right then, dripping cold water all over my jeans. "Hi, Mom."

"Hi, sweetie, this is Jenny's dad."

"Yes, Mom. I know. Hi, Mr. Dutton," Amanda says.

"You look like you're having fun."

"Yeah, I guess," Amanda says as nonchalantly as she can.

"If you want to get into some dry clothes, my tote's over there with your clothes."

"Maybe later." Amanda runs off. A few minutes later, we hear the kids singing "Happy Birthday."

"Would you like some cake?" Mike asks me.

"I would, but I can't. I'm trying to lose weight." I can feel myself blush.

"Really? You don't seem to need to, to me."

I smile.

On the way home, I think about what Mike said, the encouragement I felt, and how I wish I could have a week off, just one week, with no kids, no ex trying to screw me, no grocery shopping or cooking, no picking up or dropping off of children, no laundry, no house cleaning, no nothing—just to write again. Properly. To write and write and feel the words fall out of me and to craft a beautiful sentence and to have someone say I love the way you write. That's when I decide I'm going to focus on my novel more. Seriously. If Mike can do it with a full-time job, I should be able to do it too.

Chapter 21

We love to know that we are not alone.
—C. S. Lewis

THE BLASPHEMY BOX

Many women, when they're getting a divorce, swear off men com-
pletely. Bruised and battered by everything the divorce process entails,
they'd rather be boiled in oil than entertain even the slightest suggestion
they might consider another man.

I find myself in this category.

According to my divorced friends, the dating world is a cesspool
filled with nutcases who would do better to go to therapy than dinner
with someone they don't know. Despite what the myriad of dating ser-
vices tell you, dating is an exercise in arrant humiliation. It's high school
all over again. Not a pleasant prospect. But the real problem, truth to
tell, is to actually see myself as single again. I don't want to see myself
as single again. I don't much like it. To actually see that everything has
changed and that it has changed forever is bewildering, to say the least.

Mike Dutton rings and asks me out for coffee.

"You do know I'm still married, don't you?" I say.

And he says that as far as he knows, it is not illegal to drink coffee
while married.

"Very funny." I smile. This guy is pretty amusing.

"I'm actually calling because I see I am on the same committee at
school as you, to organize that fundraiser in November. I know it's only
July, but it won't hurt to start planning."

"Oh." Why do I feel a little disappointed? "What about your—"

"It's part of our arrangement. I do all the school stuff."

"That's practical."

"I'm trying to be," he says. There's a pause.

"You don't sound very enthusiastic about the idea of coffee."

"No, no, sorry. I'm just a bit distracted. I can only do mornings because of the kids."

We agree to meet at Starbucks the next day.

The moment I walk in, wearing jeans and a white shirt that don't look half bad, he comes over and leads the way to a nice little corner where two soft chairs face each other.

"What would you like?" he says. I hadn't heard that question in so long I had forgotten the requisite answer.

I ask for a decaf latte with nonfat milk.

"Won't be a minute," he says, smiling, before going off to stand in line.

Mike is in nicely pressed pants and a striped blue and white polo shirt. He looks attractive, with his hair short the way I like it. He doesn't have the chiseled, raw-boned look of Steven, but he's attractive anyway. I have to pretend to fumble in my bag just so as not to stare at him. His eyes are green sometimes, blue another, and he has this habit of fixing them on you as if you are the only person in the world.

When he sits down with his own coffee, he turns to me and says, "I'm very pleased you were able to make it."

I blush. "Not a problem. Thanks for the invitation."

"So," he says, "tell me about yourself."

"There's not really much to tell. I grew up in London. Father now teaches classics at Berkeley. Worked as a journalist. Met my husband when I was almost thirty. Moved here soon after, got married, worked at the *Chronicle*, had kids, got dumped."

"You're a journalist," he says, looking impressed. "

I know a reporter at the *Chronicle,* or she used to be, anyway," he says. "Elizabeth Langton. I know her from a writing group I used to lead."

"She's a good friend. She's still hanging on."

Then there is silence. "So, how's Jenny?" I ask.

"Oh, running me ragged," he says. "You know. You have a Jenny of your own."

"I do at that," I say, and we both laugh.

"So what are you going to do now?" he says. "Aside from take care of your family, I mean." It's amazing. He's actually interested in my life.

"I don't know," I say. "I've tried to find full-time work, but once they learn my age, it's all over. I still write an occasional article for small lifestyle publications, but that's about it." I tell him about the interview with Kenny. How he looked ten years old, had an ugly orange metal desk, didn't look at my portfolio, and checked his e-mail every five seconds. He laughs when he's meant to laugh and looks serious when he's meant to look serious, and I gain confidence, something I sorely need of late.

"You're funny," he says.

"I am?"

"Yes, very funny. Do you write all this stuff down?"

"Some of it."

"You should write all of it down. Never too much grist for the mill."

I smile.

We sit there companionably for an hour, chatting, surprising me. I thought I would want to leave after ten minutes, but I don't. It's such a pleasure to bask in the attention of someone who really cares what I think.

We talk about the fundraiser at the school, and then he tells me all about his ex-wife, whom I know vaguely, and her lunatic family. Then he tells me about his lunatic students. He says one of his former students was to get married last Saturday, and at the point in the service where the priest says if anyone knows of any impediment why this couple should not be joined in holy matrimony, some tiny little woman who Mike says resembled an Australian Shepherd puppy fur ball, hurled herself down the aisle and in between the couple and said, "Yes, I know of one. He's already married—to me."

He is droll and disarming, and I decide I quite like him. What was supposed to be a meeting seems to have turned into a sort of date. I can't believe how much I am enjoying it. And then I push *that* thought out of my head. What is the matter with me?

Then he mentions some French film they're showing on campus that weekend and asks me if I might want to go with him.

I blush fiercely. I don't know how to respond. I rummage through my bag for my car keys, and then look up. "Mike, you are a really nice guy. I appreciate the invitation, but I am just not ready yet."

He nods. "Yes, I know exactly how you feel. Maybe another time. Friends?" He reaches out to shake my hand.

"Friends," I smile, taking his hand.

And then I get up, thank him for coffee, and leave. And I have no idea why.

I loved your post on dating while going through a divorce. It's not easy. I've been divorced for three years, and I still have trouble viewing myself as single. It's a really hard mental gap you need to bridge. You don't want to date, of course; the whole thing is horrendous, but everyone says you must, so you do. The first time I did it, the guy I had been set up with said I must be a card-carrying member of the anti-proletariat bourgeoisie, because I get manicures. I told him his vocabulary was impressive, at which point he walked out.

Posted by EmilyP

Chapter 22

When we are well, we all have good advice for those who are ill.
—Seneca

THE BLASPHEMY BOX

Have you noticed how everyone always thinks they know if some-one or something is right for you?

No matter what you're going through, everyone instantly jumps in with advice, counsel, suggestions, recommendations. You need to lose weight. You need to date again. You need to not date again. You need to get out and about, join a softball league, take sensory analysis of wines classes at the Culinary Institute. You need to do yoga. You need therapy. You need a face lift. You need a job. Whatever. (I've been hearing a lot about getting a job lately).

Don't get me wrong. It's nice for people to offer caring advice. But sometimes, it gets a bit overwhelming.

I go to lunch with my old friend Elizabeth Langton, a features writer at the *Chronicle*, the one Mike knows. We go to Bistro Burger in the San Francisco Centre shopping mall, and it is so wonderful just to relax and catch up. We order salads and diet Cokes and grab the last two-seater table. Most of the other tables are filled with small, thin Asian girls in short skirts and teetering heels in colors designers would call Spanish Moss and Afghan Tan. Their fitted tops and skirts advertise their flat stomachs, something women of my age rarely see in the mirror anymore. The girls glance around the place expectantly, looking, I imagine, for something or someone of value, then flip their lustrous long black hair to one side and turn back to their two lettuce leaves and each other. We look around us and just shake our heads.

"So, how are you doing?" Elizabeth says, spearing a small tomato. "Annette tells me you're getting a divorce and that Steven's giving you trouble."

"Yup. He's being quite a prick about it all."

"Sorry to hear it. Can I do anything?"

"Well," I say, "I would like to get back into journalism."

"You don't mean full-time, do you?"

"If I could."

"It's not happening," Elizabeth says. "There are no full-time journalism jobs anymore."

"I know."

"Besides," Elizabeth says, "you'll be getting alimony and child support, won't you?"

"Yes," I say. "I guess I just want to get back to me, the person I was. I want to get back to the thing I truly love."

"Well, it's your lucky day," Elizabeth says.

"Why?"

"I was just in with my editor, Pamela, discussing upcoming stories, and she told me that as so many journalists have been let go, editors have been told to make up the deficit by using freelancers. The pay ain't great, but why don't you try to contact her and see if she likes any of your ideas?"

I want to say, "What ideas?," but I don't.

"I'll talk to her when I get back after lunch," Elizabeth says. "And clear the way."

"That's very nice of you," I say. "But I've been out of the fray. What kinds of things is she looking for?"

"She's into lifestyle, celebrity stuff, local color. You've always had a great nose for that. She'd be lucky to have you."

"Thanks," I say. Her solicitude and encouragement warm me. And then I remember. And I wonder why I remember.

"Hey, I met a friend of yours."

"You did?" Elizabeth says. "Who?"

"A guy named Mike Dutton."

"Oh yes, he led the writing group I was in for a while."

"That's what he told me," I say.

"And?"

I feel myself flush a bit. "And nothing. He's the father of one of Amanda's schoolmates, that's all."

She looks like she might argue that point but thankfully doesn't. "Well, he's a very good guy."

"Yeah, seems like he is," I say. And trying to sound as casual as I can, I say, "So what's his story?"

"He's a well-liked professor whose writing classes always fill up fast. Good writer as well. He knows a lot of people in New York."

That's impressive. "Yes, he seems like a real pro."

We chat for a little while longer, and then Elizabeth has to get back. "Be sure to call Pamela later today."

"Thanks. I will." We hug. Good friends make life so much easier.

After the kids are home and settled, I give Pamela a ring. I'm impressed that she picks up her own phone.

"Yes, Elizabeth mentioned you," she says, her tone less than enthusiastic. "I'm going off to a conference and then on vacation. Why don't you give me a call in two weeks? You can come in, and we'll see if we can work something out."

"That's fine," I say. "I'll call you then. Have a good trip."

She's a bit like Alec, not too warm and fuzzy. But at least it's a lead.

Chapter 23

Don't cry for a man who's left you. The next one may fall for your smile.
—*Mae West*

THE BLASPHEMY BOX

One of the worst things about getting a divorce is having to continue to deal with your ex because of the children. It's like the difference between stopping smoking and being on a diet. Stopping smoking is obviously easier, because you can withdraw from it completely. Dieting is harder. After all, you have to eat to live. If I didn't have to see my ex picking up and dropping off the kids every week, withdrawal would be easier. But this constant barrage of negative emotions that rises up each time he's around only injures me further. The ties that bind still bind if you regularly have to interact with the person to whom you have been bound for so long.

Today, Steven arrives to drop the kids off, and as they enter the house, he tries to follow them inside. I stop him at the door.

He nods at me and says, "Can we talk?"

"What do you want? It's not about the house again, is it?" I say, finally letting him into the foyer. It's so strange to see him standing there with his keys in his hand instead of slipping them onto the hook above the demilune table like he used to.

"It's been in my family for two generations. I can't give it up."

I sigh. "No one is asking you to give it up. We just need to live in it."

He seems somewhat relieved, but remains cold.

"Now," I say. "If you're through, I've got children to look after."

We stand there facing off. The Bay is gleaming in the distance, the little houses of Cow Hollow and the Marina bright white in the sun, and sadness overtakes me. I still can't believe the entire situation is truly real.

"What happened? What did I do?" I ask him.

Steven rolls his eyes. "Nothing, Madeleine: you did nothing wrong. It's just life."

"You mean mid-life. As in crisis. Yours. We've been together for twenty years. Doesn't any of that count?"

He looks at the floor, the Bay, and then, finally, at me. There is something like sadness in his eyes. "I don't know," he says.

He turns to leave, and then stops. "Mind if take my golf clubs from the garage?"

"Only if you take half of them," I say, tapping into a new well of pettiness.

"You are insufferable."

⁂

After the kids are bathed and fed and in bed, I collapse onto the sofa. The lights of the city are shimmering below me, and I am looking forward to getting back to my Henry James novel. I am rereading all of them and am now on *The Golden Bowl*, one of my all-time favorites. As I lie on the couch, letting the words overtake me, I think for a moment how comfortable it is, just to lie there undisturbed, the television silent and Steven not belittling my obsession with books. I think about how I don't have to make those gourmet dinners anymore. The kids and I eat simply. I can tweeze my eyebrows in bed, and I have much more room in the walk-in closet for my shoes. I love the hushed stillness of the house, the inky night invading every corner of the room.

Then the phone rings. I reach over to the side table and pick up the receiver.

"Hello?"

"Hi, it's Mike."

I sit up smartly on the sofa, feeling a rush of excitement and then awkwardness. "Oh, hi," I say. "How are you?"

"Exhausted, actually."

I relax. He's so normal.

"Why?"

"Oh, I had a full load today, and then there was an interminable faculty meeting, during which I could have written an entire PhD dissertation."

I laugh. "All those big egos blathering away."

"Exactly," Mike says. "Everyone jockeying for space, everyone blowing his own horn instead of working on how we can improve the education students are getting for all this money they are paying."

"So, how are the students this semester? Any brilliant ones?"

"There is one," Mike says. "She's going places. But the rest…Anyway, I was calling to let you know I got Andy Hartman to buy two tables at our fundraiser."

"Wow," I say, "Impressive."

Mike sounds pleased. "All in a day's work," he says. "So what are you up to?"

"I'm just lying on the sofa reading Henry James," I say.

"Ah. Which one are you reading?"

"*The Golden Bowl.* I'm actually rereading it."

"Which do you like the best?" he asks.

"Gosh," I say, "that's an impossible question to answer. I love them all."

I sit there in the meager light of the table lamp, happy to be asked the question and thrilled that a man is interested to discover my answer. Steven rarely talked about concepts and ideas. He was always for the black and white, the basic, the nitty-gritty of life. "Pseudo-intellectualism," he called it, when any debate of ideas started up.

"Hmm…I like James, but I have some issues with him," Mike says.

"You do?" I say, surprise in my voice. "How can that be?"

"His writing is so loping and flowery and ornate, it's often impenetrable. The grammar is so convoluted, the prose so dense, the language so florid." Someone to discuss Henry James with who knows what he's talking about, I think.

"I agree. So many of his sentences go on for a paragraph," I say. "But I love the language and all the subtleties below it."

"We will agree to differ on this point, I guess," Mike says with a chuckle.

"If we must."

"What else is going on?" Mike says. "Wanna go for lunch this weekend?"

"I'd like to," I say, "but I have the kids." I feel myself wishing that I didn't have the kids.

"Oh, of course. Got it. Anything else happening?"

"Nothing much. More hassles with lawyers. It's still all very painful and horrible."

"It will be for quite some time," Mike says, his voice full of concern. "As my father used to say, 'This too shall pass.'"

I feel so comforted by these simple words. I almost even believe them.

Chapter 24

There is a time for departure even when there's no certain place to go.
—Tennessee Williams

THE BLASPHEMY BOX

It's been my experience that people will do anything but be alone. A while back I was reading an article in some newspaper that stated that one of the things people most regret is divorcing their first spouses, because it forced them to confront loneliness. It's sad but all too true.

Even if you want to rethink the breakup, however, after the papers have been signed and the property divided, you can't regain your marriage. They say the overwhelming majority of marriages can be saved with counseling. Perhaps that's true, before they get to the lawyers. I don't know. But when someone else is already in the picture, I don't think any amount of counseling could work. Sometimes the only way out is out.

The awful thing is that many people believe, incorrectly, I think, that divorce will relieve them of their unhappiness, only to discover it has only created a whole bunch of new problems.

"Darling."

Mother is at the door. It's 10:00 on Saturday morning.

"Is something wrong?" I say. "It's a bit early for you."

"Oh darling, so sorry, I thought you would be up, perhaps on your way to the gym."

"Not quite yet, Mother."

"I just wanted to see you, darling," she says, sweeping in with a cashmere wrap over her slacks and sweater. "See how you're doing. And I wondered if you wanted to go shopping."

"I don't think so, Mother. I don't have a lot of extra cash right now."

"Well, I could always get you something, darling."

"That's kind of you, Mother, but I think not. I'll make some tea."

"Where are the kids?"

"Steven took them to ballet and soccer practice." I pour boiling water into my Blue Italian Spode teapot, put it on a tray along with two matching teacups and a creamer of milk, and make my way over to Mother.

"Don't forget I'm meant to take them to Cirque du Soleil soon."

"No, I haven't forgotten," I say. "They're all really looking forward to it."

"Me too. So how are you, darling?" she says, sinking into the sofa in the family room, her legs crossed at the ankle in the ladylike way she tried to teach me.

"Well, I'm OK, I guess," I say. "Things aren't great."

"Have you talked to Steven?"

"Well, yes, as a matter of fact, I have." I pour the tea and hand her a cup. "All he cares about is this damn house."

"I see. Can't blame him, I suppose. It is a lovely home."

"Yes, and that's why I'm fighting to keep it."

"Quite right, dear," Mother says, sipping her tea with her little finger daintily in the air. "But don't worry so much about all this, darling. I'm going to help you. I'm going to have a little chat with him."

I feel panic rising in me. "Please, Mother, I prefer you didn't."

Mother sniffs but says nothing more. She turns on the television, where SpongeBob Squarepants is playing, and flips to Fox News. I instantly change the channel.

"Now why did you do that, darling?" Mother says.

"Because no Republicans are allowed in my house, Mother."

"Really, darling, just because Republicans are better dressed than everyone else, is that any reason to despise them?"

I don't bother to answer. You should never talk religion or politics with anyone.

"Now, darling, don't you think a little word from me might do some good with Steven? You really must trust me." Mother looks as if she is truly listening and cares. "I know how all this is very upsetting, but you know, in times like this, you must be strong and go for what you want. I mean, how can you stand the loneliness? I go crazy if your father's not at home. Actually, I go crazy when he is, but you know what I mean."

I say nothing.

"Have you told him you want him back?" Mother says in a wheedling tone.

"Yes."

"And what was his reaction?"

"He ignored me."

"Ah," Mother says, frowning. "Not optimum."

"No. And there's his pregnant fiancée."

"Pregnant? Fiancée? " Mother's voice rises several octaves in alarm. "When did you find that out?"

"A while back. I would have thought the kids would have told you."

"I make sure never to talk to them about this situation," Mother says. "That's your job, and I don't want to remind them of anything unpleasant."

She sits in obvious consternation for a while. "Well, that does change things a bit, doesn't it? What a shame. I always thought you two were quite good together."

"So did I."

"Hmm," Mother says, frowning some more. "Well, you know, darling, men are volatile. Something could happen to change things."

"What something?" I say. A nuclear meltdown? I think. "And you think that I should want that to happen, Mother?"

"Of course, darling. I mean, I know it would be hard to forgive and forget, but you've been together for so many years and have these three children together and just for their sakes, it might be better for you two to reunite."

"I don't think I can agree, Mother," I say. "Getting back together with your husband is not always the best idea, it really isn't. And do you think I could be at all happy in that situation? Too much irrevocable damage has been done. Too much hurt, too much trust broken. Things could never be the same."

And for the first time since Steven left, I actually find myself believing it. And it makes me sad and glad. Sad that I am beginning to let go. Glad that I'm beginning to let go.

Chapter 25

Youth is a disease from which we all recover.
—Dorothy Fuldheim

THE BLASPHEMY BOX

Have you noticed how men look right through you when you get to be a certain age? (Which age that is, exactly, would be useful to know; then you could prepare yourself for all those blank stares.) All of a sudden, it's as if you're invisible. That guy at the Hertz rental car counter—who would have upgraded you with a smile and a proposition when you were thirty—now barely turns his head from the computer to say, "All we have is the Chevy Aveo, take it or leave it." The maître d' at that trendy new restaurant says he doesn't have a table until 10:30 p.m. and that they close at eleven.

Your face and mincing ways won't let you cut to the front of the line at Safeway anymore (ahead of that man who's shopping for the entire state of California). And you sure as hell won't get that interview with Robert De Niro you might once have landed when you were young and thin and pretty and the PR person susceptible to all three.

Even your children treat you differently, like some burdensome old crank who's constantly nagging at them to do their homework and no longer able to race them up San Francisco's famous 288 Lyon Street stairs, even for those breathtaking views of the Bay.

And the maintenance and upkeep of your person! I have to have my roots tinted every three weeks now. Very expensive. And yesterday, I thought I saw some wrinkles hovering around my eyes. Then when I *moved a bit to the right, I saw, no, those weren't wrinkles, they were just sun rays reflecting onto my face through the bathroom mirror. Whew!*

And the health issues that all of a sudden jump out of whichever box they've been hiding in and wake you from your dream of eternal youth and beauty! Not to mention menopause, which has brought me hot flashes and dry everything.

When you're married, there's someone to complain to. When you're single...well...who cares?

I'm at the gym this morning, and they have the music blaring. It's the worst. Something they call electronic rock.

I try to ignore the racket, but can't, so I ask the guy next to me if he knows how I can turn the music down a bit. He immediately walks to a closet, and after a moment the music stops. Heaven. When he emerges, I thank him. Another man near us who's doing bench presses (a guy who, I've noticed, always interrupts people on their machines, asking them if he can alternate sets with them, and, when they say yes, changes all the weights and adjustments so that they then have to change all the weights and adjustments back to complete their three sets) says, "What, you don't like music?"

The guy who helped me kind of shrugs, but I say nothing. I don't need to get into it with some obnoxious guy who obviously gets everything in life he wants when he wants it.

And then he says, "Must be an age thing."

I want to haul off and send a three-pound free weight at his head, but I say nothing. Yet it just brings home in alarmingly clear bas relief the sad notion that even though I may feel the same as when I was twenty, I most assuredly do not look the same, and that if I ever need a little reminder to that effect, then there's this jerk right here to give it.

Then, Alec, my lawyer calls, and suddenly, as I'm talking to him, a nebbishy little manager-type person appears by my side. His head is bobbing up and down like a Pez dispenser, and he looks suspiciously like he might be wearing eyeliner. He tells me I can't use a cell phone in the building and that my talking is interfering with other exercisers' enjoyment of their workouts.

"You mean people actually enjoy working out?" I say. "Isn't that amazing? From a sociological point of view, I mean."

He glares at me and walks off.

When I get home and into the shower, I decide to wash my hair but I can't read the writing on the shampoo, conditioner, and gel bottles. I peer as expertly as I can, but I just can't tell them apart. I step out of the shower, pick up my glasses, and go back in. But I still can't read the lettering, because my glasses are now fogged up. I open up each bottle and smell its contents but still can't figure out which is which. So I step out of the shower again, taking the bottles with me, wipe my glasses down, and find the shampoo.

After I am dressed and my hair dry, I leave the house and drive to McDonald's to pick up some coffee. The kid taking my order says, "That'll be sixty-five cents."

I say, "What? I thought it was $1.09 for a small decaf."

And he says, "The senior rate is sixty-five cents."

I am not kidding.

Then I go to see Nadya, a stout, no-nonsense Russian woman with brawny arms, to find out why I have suddenly grown sideburns and why whiskers seem to be sprouting from my chin like the yellow Lab next door. I feel like Hairy Maclary From Donaldson's Dairy or Cousin It, for Christ's sake. When I told my friend Cameron about my situation, she said, "Everyone grows hair on their face; it's due to our past cousins, the gorillas."

So helpful.

Anyway, I hate going to see Nadya, because her Chihuahua, Kissy, yaps relentlessly and insists on biting my ankles. But she's cheap, and that's what I need right now. As soon as I ring the bell, the yapping starts. Yap, yap, yappity yap. When Nadya opens the door, the yapping intensifies. Kissy, the six-pound monster, is behind her, jumping up and down, waiting to bite me or bark me to death.

Nadya gestures to enter, and I move gingerly inside and into the small room where she makes her clients beautiful, all the while with Kissy yapping. Then he bites my ankle.

"Oh!" I say, hoping Nadya will put Kissy outside. Fat chance.

She closes the door, and I take off my jacket and shoes and lie down on the bed, trying to inhale the scent of cinnamon candles while Kissy yaps and jumps at the bed like a Pogo stick.

"Nadya," I say, "what's going on? Why do I have sideburns and hair all over my face?"

Nadya does not immediately reply. She's never been much of a talker. (Probably can't hear herself over Kissy's incessant yapping.) She puts on her magnifying glasses and then runs her fingers across the peaks and valleys of my face and chin, humming and tut-tutting as she goes.

"Hmm…" she says as she pulls at the thick growth of my sideburns, "Tut-tut," she says, as she tugs on excess hair around my temple, over my face, and across the chin.

I wait for her to say something, but she still doesn't. Kissy yaps.

"Nadya?"

"You menopause?" she asks. She has an accent right out of Dr. Zhivago.

"Yes, just going into, I think."

"Pff!" she says. "That's it!"

"That's what?"

"That's it! Estrogen less, testosterone more."

OK, as we age, we get sideburns like Elvis? Hardly seems fair, now does it?

"So what do I do?" I say.

"I do for you," Nadya says quickly. "No problem; I do for you."

I lie there for a moment, listening to Kissy yapping, and then all of a sudden, she's slathering my sideburns with what I presume to be steaming hot wax. I want to scream out loud, "No!" I had a leg and bikini wax once, and I swore it would be the last time.

But it's too late. I hear her ripping up some kind of material, and the next thing I know a strip of that material is on one of my sideburns, and Nadya is ripping it off my face with a ferocity more suitable to a gladiator in the ring than an esthetician who's meant to make you feel all nice and relaxed.

"Ouch!" I scream. I'm blinded by stinging, searing pain. Nadya hums to herself and takes no notice. Kissy yaps.

OK, my vision is returning. But now it's time for the other sideburn.

"Ouch!" I scream again.

"Stop!" Nadya says. "Breathe!"

I try to breathe, but between you, me, and the gatepost, breathing isn't so easy when your face is being torn off. And when a certain annoying, noisy, unbearable canine won't shut up.

Now it's my upper lip area, chin, and temples. Ouch, ouch, ouch.

"Is nearly over," Nadya says, surprising me with her fulsome conversation.

But of course, it's not nearly over. She strips the sides of my face bare of hair with military precision and zero mercy. I've had broken limbs that hurt less than this. Who knew hairless, silky skin came at such a price?

"If wax regular, hair no come back," Nadya says.

But what would I do for fun, then?

After, I dash across the street for an appointment with my internist, Dr. Casey. My left shoulder has been acting up from an old hockey injury, my sciatica is back with a vengeance, and the bunion on my left foot is red and burning.

"Why is all this stuff happening?" I ask Dr. Casey. He is an older man with snowy hair and a wry smile.

"It's called aging," he says as he presses into my shoulder. I yelp.

"Why does no one tell you about it?"

"What can they tell you?" he says. "That you'll have arthritis in every bone you broke, and maybe some you didn't? That years of wearing high heels will cripple you into nurse shoes? That your body breaks down whether you like it or not? That you can't smoke and drink and play cards all night and be ready for work the next morning? That none of that is going to get any better? Who's going to want to hear that?"

He presses into my shoulder again. I yelp again. "Hmm, good point," I say.

Dr. Casey grins.

"I think I'm going into menopause," I say. "I just have no patience with getting old. Everything is so dry, and I mean everything."

He laughs. "Go see your gynecologist for that problem. He or she will fix you up."

"I don't want to be fixed up. I want all this stuff to go away."

"Let me know how that works for you," the doctor says, grinning. "OK, look, obviously you have osteoarthritis, and I can either send you to Dr. Margolin to get this shoulder operated on, or you will have to manage it with meds, exercise, and physical therapy."

"What do you advise?"

"Only you know how painful it is on an ongoing basis," he says. "Surgery might be an option if you can barely move it, but there is movement here. Is it impacting your life all the time, or just now and then? If it's not all the time, I'd try to manage it, because surgery is drastic, the recovery time is long, you have to undergo months of physical therapy, and you still won't be able to move your shoulder the way you once did. But it will help with the pain."

"Hmm…" I say. "Neither choice is great."

"Right."

"Well!" I say. "This is all very discouraging."

"Not at all," Dr. Casey says. "There are therapies."

"But no real remedies."

"No long-term, pain-will-never-come-back-again remedies, no. You just have to moderate your expectations."

"I do?"

"You do," he says, typing notes of our visit into his computer.

"Because?"

"As I said, it's called aging. No one can fight it forever. At some point, you just have to accept it."

I've had to accept so much lately, I don't think I'm up to accepting much more right now.

I have so much less energy than I used to, and by the time I leave Dr. Casey, I'm dragging. I decide to get some coffee and duck into Starbucks at the same time as a guy in his thirties who looks like George Peppard. He smiles at me and politely stands to one side to let me enter first, and I smile back. Perhaps I haven't lost it, I think to myself happily, just before he says, "Age before beauty."

Aging sucks.

When I get home, I decide to give myself a pedicure and manicure. I don't want to spend money on something I can do myself—or at least, *used* to do myself, before marriage allowed me to pay someone else do it.

I soak my feet and get my clippers out to cut my nails, but when I try to bend to do exactly that, I can't! I can't reach them. Jeez, with all this exercise, you'd think I'd loosened up a bit, but I've never been too flexible and haven't really exercised until recently.

Cameron calls then to suggest we go to dinner.

"Do you have the kids?"

"Yes, but maybe Gracie will come over," I say.

"Great. Wanna go to that new Italian place in North Beach?" she says, mentioning the name of San Francisco's current cloister for the *beau monde*.

"Isn't it a bit expensive?" I say. "I don't think I can."

"It's my treat," Cameron says. She has lots of money, because she's had lots of husbands.

"That's very kind of you, but I'm already in major debt to you."

"Hush," she says. "We are friends. Friends help friends out. I have some dough, and I am happy to spread it around when it comes to you."

And then I think how happy and grateful I am to have a friend like this.

"OK, let's go, but you know there's nowhere to park down there."

"We'll just go to that lot and pay," she says. "I hear the cannelloni's divine. And all my friends have already been."

When we get there, the place is fairly busy, and an Italian love song is on the sound system. I approach the host, a tall drink of water with thick, wavy hair. I can tell he's Italian, because he isn't wearing any socks with his shoes. (And because he's gorgeous.)

"Yes?" he says, looking up from his reservation book. I can see he is one of those well-trained despots of dining so prevalent in San Francisco's world of *haute cuisine*.

Yes? I think.

"A table for two," I say, smiling brightly.

His cobalt eyes flicker over me briefly and then move on. Not a crack in his hauteur, not a softening in his arrogance. I used to be able to get a table at a restaurant pretty much as soon as I walked in. But this Moses ain't going to part the Red Sea for me now—or ever, I think.

"You have a reservation?"

"Uh, no, we don't. But we won't be here long."

He looks at me as if I had spilled red wine on his white shirt. "This is not McDonald's," he snarls. "Here, one does *not* eat and run."

"Could I put our name down on the list?"

He sighs. "Si," he says, and dutifully writes down *Maddy/2*.

"How long is the wait, do you think?" I am still being pleasant and polite, but his eyes are behind me now, on two latter-day Elke Sommers types each carrying the latest Vuitton purse. His face breaks into a wide smile.

"Ah, signore..."

They smile back.

"Reservations?"

One of the blondes makes a moue.

"Right this way, please," he says, and sweeps them off to a table near the entrance.

I look at Cameron, and she at me. Her eyes tacitly beg me not to make a fuss. I stay quiet. After twenty minutes more of waiting, however, our eyes glazed with ennui and our stomachs rumbling noisily, I approach the throne and wait for Mussolini to get off the phone, into which he is pouring a rather large mouthful of vitriol.

"Another poor customer wanting a table?" I say sweetly when he rings off.

He says nothing.

I lean toward him. "Look, we have been waiting quite some time. The two blonde girls got in before us with no reservations, and they arrived after us."

He shrugs. A Roman shrug, a don't-be-in-such-a-hurry-life-is-too-short shrug, a what-do-you-want-from-me? shrug.

"I don't have any tables right now."

"When will you?" I say.

"Perhaps fifteen minutes?"

I turn around to Cameron and run my finger across my throat. She demurs. "I want the cannelloni."

"Fine," I say and sit back down on the bench.

Twenty minutes later, we are ensconced at a table the size of a quarter near the restroom. I want to complain, but for Cameron's sake, I don't. It's just so uncomfortable to be treated as if you are of no importance. I'm not used to it.

Cameron orders a salad and the cannelloni, and I order salad and *frutti di mare* with penne. All the food arrives together in thirty minutes. By this time, we are pale with hunger and demolish our salads in short order. As I finish my salad and begin on my pasta, I drop my fork. I look around, thinking our waiter, another waiter, the omnipresent busboy with bad breath, will pick it up and offer me a clean one. Nothing doing. And though the restaurant is filled with attractive men dining stag, not one sends over any drinks or propositions to our table, like in the good young days.

"Do you notice how men don't notice you anymore?" I ask Cameron.

She grimaces. "Of course. Why? Haven't you?"

"Oh yes, I notice it all the time. Twenty years ago, those guys at that table by the bar would have been sending us mai tais by the minute."

Cameron laughs. "It only gets worse," she says.

I laugh then, too. But frankly, I don't like it. The whole thing is so baffling—and bruising. I've lost weight, and my arms are more buffed, but it doesn't seem to make a difference. In how men notice me, that is. I noticed this problem a little before Steven left. All the whistles and whooping were dying down at an alarming rate. Now, on the street, where men would have once said hi and winked, there's nothing. Everyone looks right through you. Even women. (You're no longer competition.) In fact, I am certain I could walk naked down Van Ness Avenue, and nobody would bat an eye.

And there's no one to talk to about it when you get home. No one to tell you everything is fine, you look great and not to worry.

So I worry.

When I read some comments from readers of my blog, I worry more.

I know exactly what you mean. At this age, we women are invisible. Where once I got more attention than I wanted, frankly, it would now take a nuclear bomb to alert men to my presence. I went to Rome last year with a friend, and I didn't get my butt pinched once.

Posted by usedtobehot in Georgia

Chapter 26

WEEK 31 OF SEPARATION

Death will be a great relief. No more interviews.
—Katharine Hepburn

THE BLASPHEMY BOX

Going on job interviews is never easy. There's a definite skill set for that kind of thing, and mine, I'm afraid, has never been great, and might now be a bit rusty. And things only get harder later in life. You have to project the vim and vigor of a Gen-Xer half your age, even though the interviewer can well see you're more of the "I Love Lucy" era. (And don't you just hate that "What's your greatest strength, what's your greatest weakness" question? I mean, really. Like you're going to be truthful.) Job interviewing is like going on a first date, essentially. There's the forced chitchat without a gin and tonic to steel your nerves, the awful knowledge that you are being sized up and may very well be found wanting. And how do you convincingly explain why you haven't worked since the kids were born, since so many women with children do, in fact, work? They have to. Even for part-time or freelance work, you have to make the right impression, exude confidence you don't have. And there's all this conflicting advice, as usual. Be outgoing and tell the interviewer what you can do for her or him and the company; but don't be full of yourself. Arrive a little early; don't arrive early, because the interviewer is busy and will feel rushed with you sitting out there in the lobby. All very SCARY!

Today was my interview with Pamela, the *Chronicle* editor.

I pull out some very ordinary black pants, a white blouse, and a burgundy jacket and shrug them all on. Professional, I say to myself. Nice.

I head over to the paper, arriving five minutes early, and sign in with the guard, who calls up to Pamela. When he hangs up, he gestures me toward the elevator.

"Third floor," he says.

I swiftly rise up to the third floor, where all the paper's editorial offices are, and when I get out, I get that thrilling frisson I always get walking into a newsroom.

I survey the splendid squalor about me: the dingy gray carpets striped in red and mottled with the stains of cheap company coffee; the red rickety chairs; the six-foot-by-six-foot cubicles in which reporters worked, their desks laden with newspaper and magazine clips and expensive, glossy press kits that would never be read and would be tossed unopened into rubbish bins by people who do not have the luxury of time to spend on the inessential. TV monitors are hanging from the ceiling are blaring, telephones are ringing, and reporters and editors are talking. Everyone's online, stuck to their computer screens. I barely notice the cacophony. I have missed it so much.

I wander around looking for Pamela's office. Things have changed quite a bit since the last time I was here. Sports is now where Business used to be, I notice, and the Art Department is gone, probably to another floor.

I walk past what used to be my boss, Russell's, office. It sits empty, he having had a heart attack and gone to meet his maker. He was the one who had said, when I informed him I had made it through my three months of probation to full-reporter status and that he could no longer fire me unless I got drunk or danced naked on my desk, "If you dance naked on your desk, it's a promotion."

Right next to it, I see a door with an imposing sign attached: Pamela Day, Assistant Managing Editor, Features. In my day, editors didn't have their names on their office doors.

I'm biting the inside of my mouth from nervousness, and my portfolio seems very heavy all of a sudden. This is only the second work interview I've been on in over twenty years, and that first one with my boy Kenny didn't go too well. I knock on the door and immediately hear a peremptory, "Come in."

I go in.

A woman swings around on her seat to face me and gestures to a chair piled high with features pages from the *New York Times* and the *Wall Street Journal*.

"I'm Pamela Day. You must be Madeleine Nelson. Have a seat." She is a large, lumbering kind of person with wiry salt-and-pepper hair and in dire need of a manicure. I immediately relax, move the newspapers to one side and sit down opposite her.

"Now," Pamela says, "Elizabeth tells me you used to be a reporter here."

"Yes, a little while back. Russell Jackson was my immediate boss."

"Yes, I worked with him for a couple of years. Piece of work. I think he moved to Florida or something" she says.

"Actually, he just died."

"Oh," Pamela says, unperturbed. Then she fixes her eyes on me. "What kind of areas do you cover?"

I don't know what to say. "Uh, I've done fashion, lifestyle, travel, food, a little bit of local news, arts, books, celebrities, business where it intersects with apparel retail and manufacturing."

"Well, let me have a look at your work, then." She leafs through my portfolio, giving nothing away, and then says, "Have you done anything more recently?"

"Well, no, not really. A small piece for a local magazine from time to time. Nothing regular."

"Nothing online?"

"Well, I did just start a blog. The Blasphemy Box."

"Interesting title. I'll check it out. Never hurts to be out there."

"That's what I've heard."

Pamela smiles, getting my irony.

"OK, here's how it works," she said, closing my portfolio. "This is not a job, nor will it ever be. You know that, right? And there are no benefits."

I nod my head.

"When you have an idea for story, just e-mail me the hook. If it works, I'll put you on it and give you a deadline. If we use it, the fee is $200. No kill fee, unfortunately, if we don't."

"That sounds fine."

"Got any ideas right now before you leave?"

Again, I draw a blank. "I was hoping you'd have a story to start me off."

Pamela doesn't miss a beat and begins to rifle through files on her desk. "I do have a story for you, actually. It's for a collectibles issue to coincide with the vintage show on Labor Day weekend at the Moscone Convention Center next month."

I'm excited. I love vintage.

"OK. Tell me about it."

Pamela draws out a piece of paper and hands it to me. "Some woman called Kitty McGee has collected pigs and everything to do with pigs almost all her life and has apparently amassed one of the largest collections of pig collectibles in the world. She has porcelain pigs, crystal pigs, plastic pigs, hand-painted enamel over metal pigs, vintage Hummel pigs, and it goes on and on. She's the best-known collector of pig paraphernalia in the country. Here's the overview. I'll e-mail you her particulars. Good human interest story."

I try to drum up some enthusiasm. "Say no more," I say. (Are you kidding? I think. What a stupid-assed story.) "I'm on it. How many inches do you want?"

"About fifteen with photos. You do have a good digital camera, right? You know how to take good pictures, right?"

"Of course," I lie.

"OK," Pamela says, consulting her editorial calendar. "You need to have this to me in two weeks. And be sure to e-mail any other ideas you might have."

After I leave Pamela's office, I wander around the newsroom looking for Elizabeth. She used to have a desk by the window on the left side of the newsroom, but now a young man with floppy bangs occupies the seat there. Finally, I ask someone on the copy desk where Elizabeth's cubicle is.

"Last aisle, three back," says the young, harried woman.

When I reach Elizabeth, she is talking on the telephone and taking notes frantically. I remember how that was. When *Basic Instinct* came out, I had requested an interview with Sharon Stone, never expecting it to be granted. A few days later, my phone had rung, and a voice had asked for me. When I said, "This is Maddy Nelson," the voice had said, "Sharon Stone."

I was so taken aback I forgot all my questions. I frantically rummaged through my notes and found them just in time. It was tough, but I made my deadline.

Elizabeth signals me to wait, and I sit down on a nearby chair. After five minutes, she winds up her interview and puts the phone down. "Oh, thank God I got him," she says of her source. "Without him I wouldn't have been able to run the story. So how did it go?"

"Fine. She gave me an assignment and told me to e-mail her with story ideas."

"Great," Elizabeth says. "If she likes your work, she will use you steadily. That's what she's doing with all the freelancers. But it's harder to find a good feature writer than a news writer, so you have something going for you there. Not as much competition."

I smile. "Do you have time for lunch?"

"I'd love to, but I just don't have an extra second today. Rain check? I'm looking forward to seeing you in print regularly again."

"Me too." I kiss her good-bye and leave the paper with somewhat of a spring in my step.

When I check my blog, I'm elated to keep finding responses.

Good for you for going on the job interview! What happened? Will I be reading you online and—offline too? Sure hope so. You are a great writer.
Posted by SereneCoreen

I reply:

Coreen, did my BFF pay you to say these things? If so, it's money well spent! You are my cheering section. Thanks for reading me.

Chapter 27

Work spares us from three evils:
boredom, vice and need.
—Voltaire

THE BLASPHEMY BOX

Going back to work for a mainstream newspaper after all this time is exciting—and a little scary. You want to do a good job. In fact, you want to do a great job, so you can get more work in the future. But in journalism, like everything else, you have to prove yourself all over again, and at fifty, it's not as easy as it was at twenty-five. Still, the idea that you might be part of a large, powerful organization again, with the gravitas that that implies, and that you might get a regular gig, and that you might even get paid for it, is still the thrill it was. Not to mention, in my case, seeing my name in print. That's the great thing—and irony—about divorce. In losing something you love, you have time to get back to something else you love.

Today was my interview with the pig lady. I still cannot believe a major metro daily newspaper would requisition and publish a story about a woman and her pig collection, but there it is.

The house, in the Sunset District, is a typical mid-1920s stucco row house, with a barrel front over a garage and open stairs leading up to the front door. I ring the bell, and almost immediately the door opens. A small, voluptuous woman of a certain age, with hair too blonde, lips too red, and jeans too tight appears before me.

"Kitty? I'm Maddy Nelson with the *Chronicle*," I say, sticking out my hand. She takes it and shakes it and smiles.

"Pleased to meet you. Come in." Her voice is soft and soothing.

I have been expecting the place to be cluttered, and I am not disappointed. Every conceivable surface is covered with pig-related memorabilia.

"Where shall we start?" she says.

"Right here, in the living room, maybe?" I say, getting out my notebook.

"Sure."

We pick our way through the vestiges of hardwood floor that are not inhabited by pigs over to the mantelpiece, where she starts a recitation of each item in front of, behind, and around us, her mind an encyclopedia of date, place, and provenance.

"That's a copper pig with peridot eyes circa 1906 that I found in London," she says gaily. "I just fell madly in love with the guy who sold it to me, too. I also found this blue and white spatterware pig figurine there. Isn't it adorable?"

There are teapots and cork stoppers, ashtrays, coffee mugs, pitchers, cookie jars, bowls, jardinières, salt and pepper cellars, and even prizes from cereal boxes. There are pig-imprinted tea towels and aprons, pig needlepoint cushions, and pig paintings. Even fictional pigs are not forgotten: there is a talking pig (Babe), a fortune-telling pig (Hen-Wen), a television-watching pig (Arnold), and a singing and tap-dancing pig (Miss Piggy).

Kitty knows her stuff. She points out a "Paws at the Kerb" piggy bank, produced by the English company Wade around 1955 and seldom offered for sale, and a grouping of exuberant hand-painted floral piggy banks from England's Arthur Wood Company.

"Some of these pigs are really valuable," Kitty says. "My collection has been valued at upward of half a million dollars, partly because I only collect perfect or almost-perfect pieces, and partly because some of my pieces are really rare, like this gold-trimmed and pink-hoofed 1942 Shawnee Smiley Pig, now worth around six thousand dollars!"

Kitty's eyes are veritably shining. "This Tithe Pig Group figurine by the English company Old Crown Derby Bocage is from between 1806 and 1825. Can you believe that? I have pieces from all the great makers. And just look at this gorgeous glass pig that I found in a flea market in Paris!"

We tour the entire house this way, me scribbling away and interjecting occasional questions as I walk.

As we wander through the house's six small rooms, they begin to contract in size, every wall lined with bookshelf after glass cabinet after Welsh dresser, displaying pig figurines, pig cookie jars, pig everything. Kitty's voice is high with animation and pride, and her enthusiasm eventually draws me in.

We sit down finally in the kitchen, which is decorated in white laminate everything, home to the only table in the house that is not covered with pigs, and I begin the formal interview.

"How many do you have?"

"About twenty-five thousand," she says.

I look at her questioningly.

"Oh, they're not all here," she says. "I've run out of room for them here."

She offers me a diet Coke, then pours herself one and talks languidly about her obsession and its roots.

"Where are you from originally?"

"Smyrna, Georgia," she says, adding coyly, "You know, like Julia Roberts."

"Why this passion for all things porcine?" I ask her.

"Well, my mom told me they were good luck, and really, why not?" she says. "Everybody's obsessed with something, aren't they? Why not be obsessed with the cleverest domesticated creature in the world?"

I don't quite know what to say to this, so I say nothing.

"People have it all wrong about pigs," says Kitty. "They're extremely intelligent. They pick up tricks faster than dogs and are better at video games than a young child. And they don't smell, because they have no sweat glands. That's why they roll in mud. To cool down. They never go to the bathroom near their living or eating areas, so they're not dirty. They have just gotten bad press."

"How do you decide which pigs to buy?"

"I buy any pig that takes my fancy. I wipe them down, dust and polish them all regularly. It takes me half a day, at least. I like to see them twinkle on their glass shelves," she says.

"Do you have children?" I say.

"No," Kitty says, her head to one side. "The pigs are my children."

I'm not sure how to ask my next question, so I hope for the best and just ask it. "How do you live like this, I mean, with pigs vying for space everywhere?"

"It's about collecting, not decorating," Kitty says firmly. "Pigs are sweet, intelligent creatures, and I love living with them."

I am still frantically taking notes, and frankly, my hand hurts a little. "Do you have a day job?" I ask her.

"I'm an administrative assistant at a law firm downtown."

"Have you done that long?"

"Around ten years."

"Have you ever been married?"

"Yes, once," she says, grimacing.

"As bad as that?"

She grins.

"Me too," I say. She smiles at me warmly, and we sit quietly for a moment in the stillness of the kitchen.

I smile. "Can I take a few pictures?"

"Of course," Kitty says. She jumps to the mirror, smears some color on her lips, and fluffs her hair.

I take several photos of her at her mantelpiece and then standing in front of various cabinets. Then I take a few close-ups of pig collectibles.

"When will this article appear?" Kitty asks then, her voice tremulous. "I'm so excited about it."

I smile. "At the end of this week."

She leans over to me and whispers conspiratorially, "You won't make fun of me, will you?"

I sit up straight in my chair. "Of course not," I say, knowing that that's exactly how many reporters, even I, might be inclined to treat a story like this.

"Because so many do, you know." Her voice is breathy now, like Jackie Kennedy's. "It's hurtful."

"I know. And don't worry."

She smiles sweetly at me as she sips her Coke. "I am doing something worthwhile with it all, you know. I won't sell it. And I could. I've been offered huge bucks for it, but I'll be donating the entire collection. Kids will see it and enjoy it. Adults too. That's worth something, isn't it?"

"Of course it is."

When I get home from my interview, I sit down at the computer and read through my notes. I have to get the story done.

I struggle with the lead for a time but finally come up with: *"When it comes to pigs, Kitty McGee goes whole hog."*

In an hour, I have finished the story. I e-mail it to Pamela and sit back in my chair, looking at the glittering Bay. What a nice day I've had, I think. And then I think, that's the first time I've said that to myself in eons. And I smile.

Chapter 28

A divorce is like an amputation; you survive, but there's less of you.
—Margaret Atwood

THE BLASPHEMY BOX

In a divorce, you not only lose your husband, but, to some degree, your children too. It's especially hard on holidays, when everyone is with his or her family—everyone except you. Most divorced parents work out some ad hoc arrangement, switching off each holiday or getting the kids for the minor holidays one year and the major holidays the next. HM and I are doing the former, but it ain't easy. Divorce changes everything, but our need to connect and to stay connected with our family is an unassailable human instinct, and it's just damn difficult when it can't be satisfied.

"Amanda Lesley Nelson, pack your things now!"

The Labor Day weekend getaway is underway, and Amanda has done no packing, as usual. The twins' *Harry Potter and the Deathly Hallows: Part 1* black tote bags are packed and ready at the door.

For the past fifteen or so years, we have gone with three other families from school up to Lake Tahoe for the holiday, where we rent a house on the lake for a large sum of money. I thought Steven might pay for me and the kids to continue the tradition, but my e-mail to that effect went unanswered. Because he had the kids for July 4th, it was my turn to have them for the next holiday. I had planned on surprising the kids by taking them to Tahoe so we could spend the weekend with the other families as we had in the past. A friend of Cameron's had even offered us her timeshare, and I just imagined Steven would do his own thing with Girl Bambi.

That, however, was not to be. Yesterday, the boys come crashing through the front door shrieking, "We're going to Disneyland! We're going to Disneyland!"

"What do you mean?" I say, as Colin rushes at me for a kiss.

"Dad's taking us to Disneyland tomorrow."

That bastard. "He is? How did that happen?" I say.

"He was keeping it a secret till the last minute," Charlie says. (I bet he was.) "To surprise us." (To surprise me, more like it.)

"But it's my turn to have you guys," I say. "I had planned for us to go to Tahoe like before."

"But Disneyland is fun, and we get to go on a plane and everything!" Amanda says. "We want to do something different, Mom."

She's right. But I can pick out the traces of Steven's sabotage so clearly, the bribery he employed to leave me alone on the holiday with no remedy and bring the kids closer into his camp. Divorce is a dirty game.

Amanda dashes to her room. "Mom! I can't find my bathing suit." She can never find anything.

"In the third drawer."

"Mom! I can't find my polka-dot shorts."

"In the second drawer."

Finally, Amanda is packed and ready to go. Her cell phone rings. "Dad's here."

I look outside and see Steven's car idling in the driveway.

"OK, you lot," I say, "kisses and hugs."

I envelop all three of my babies in my arms, inhale their smell, and try to bind them to me. But they are struggling to get away and on to their weekend of fun.

"Bye, Mom."

"Bye, Mom."

"Bye, Mom."

"Bye! Call me!"

They are already out of the door and heading down the steps. I watch them tumble into the car and crane my neck to see if I can see Girl

Bambi in the front seat. Why do we torture ourselves? There are so many other people around who can do it so much better. A piece of teal fabric is visible, and I realize she is there. I shut the door after they drive away.

It's really hard to not have the kids around on the long holiday weekend, and tears threaten to overtake me. I steel myself against them and take a gulp of coffee from my I Love You Mom mug. Truth to tell, I find I'm relieved not to go to Tahoe this year. Spending the time on my own up there with three other happy couples would have been torture. Being the only dumped housewife and now single person in that federation of families is not something I have been looking forward to. And I know that as soon as I would have been in close vicinity to mine and Steven's usual room with that huge king-sized mahogany bed mocking me, I would have broken down and had a good cry.

I sink into the couch, feeling very sorry for myself. I haven't felt this lonely in a while. Holidays are the worst. I know loneliness comes with the territory in a separation, but it's so damn hard to deal with. If I still had Steven, I could have been in Tahoe right now with him, and our kids, having a great time. Or I could have been in Disneyland right now with him, and our kids, having a great time.

But I don't, and I'm not, and it sucks. On the other hand, I remind myself, I have lots to celebrate. I got countless calls and e-mails on my pig lady story, for instance. So encouraging and cheering, I cannot even tell you. A nice feeling of accomplishment, which was sorely needed.

I walk into the kitchen and look around for something to do. I clear up the breakfast things, wipe down the counters, and wander into the bedroom to get my Henry James novel. But after half an hour of reading the same paragraph five times, I fling the book onto the bed and head for the shower. When I get into the bathroom, I remember I've already taken one and return to the bedroom to dress. I pull on a pair of old grungy sweats, turn on the TV, settle down on the couch with the remote in hand, and start flipping through the channels. Some man with a bad rug and bushy eyebrows is proselytizing at the top of his voice on the religion channel. QVC is hawking the most dreadful fake diamond rings on another, and I've already seen all the Golden Girls reruns they're showing on yet another. I hit the power button, and the house goes silent once more.

Since the pig lady article was a success, Pam gave me a couple of other assignments that I should start pulling together, but I just can't bear the idea of it. I walk into my room, throw myself on the bed, pull my pillow toward me, and pummel it with my fists. My head hurts, and I am just plain miserable. I wish my divorce group was around, but there's no meeting this week because of the holiday. At least there I can cry and complain to the other over-fifty divorcées, and they won't throw an ear of corn at me or tell me to quit sniveling. We're all sniveling, all of the time. It's so comforting.

I try to shake myself out of my lethargy and self-pity and go over to my walk-in closet. I will clean and rearrange it, I think, and gather up a bunch of stuff I no longer wear and take it down to Goodwill. Then I will go for a jog, make gingerbread for when the kids come home, and work on my novel. I feel better.

I spend the next two hours clearing everything out of my closet, throwing away old shoe boxes, piling up clothes I never wear, and vacuuming and dusting the entire place. When I'm done I feel a real sense of accomplishment. I have cottage cheese and blueberries for lunch, then take a nap. Around three in the afternoon, I sit down at my laptop and pull up my novel. I stare at the screen for some time. I'm at the point where I have to write a love/sex scene, and it isn't easy. Why should my female protagonist have a better love life than me?

I tap out a few paragraphs, but reading them back to myself, they only sound ridiculous. There really are only a few different words you can use to describe sex and the human anatomy and how it works—what goes where and why. And after a while, you've used them all up. Why can't I just bang this thing out, like a newspaper article, I think. As Nathaniel Hawthorne said, easy reading is damn hard writing.

I return to my novel. After struggling with it for another hour, I slam my laptop shut in frustration, pull on my exercise capris, an old T-shirt, and some socks and tennis shoes and head for the door. Outside the summer fog is coming in (in San Francisco, summer can be colder than winter), and I start a slow jog down Steiner. When I reach the Marina, a freighter is steaming by on the Bay, gulls are screeching, and the Golden Gate Bridge hangs before me suspended in the air, enigmatic, beguiling. I put on my headphones to the strains of Steely Dan and stretch my calves.

The air is fresh and, as a succession of muscled men run past me, their faces red from exertion, I take off. To my left is a line of spectacular Mediterranean-style houses sitting just steps from the Bay, once fishermen's cottages, now the homes of the city's ultra-wealthy. To my right is a stretch of grass along the water, busy every day of the week, teeming with bike riders and runners and Rollerbladers.

I run to the Bridge and then back and stop at the Marina to catch my breath before walking up Divisadero back to Pacific Heights. I feel so much better, cheered by the signs of life around me, not so isolated. As soon as I get back to the house, the phone rings.

"Mom!"

"Hi, Charlie sweetie, how are you?"

"Fine, Mom."

"When did you get there?"

"A few hours ago, but we already went on some rides." Charlie's voice is an octave higher than it normally is. He is excited.

"You did? Which ones?"

"We did the Buzz Lightyear Astro Blasters ride."

"And what is that all about?" I say.

"You're a space ranger for Buzz Lightyear and the Galactic Alliance." Colin is speaking now. "You ride through and shoot at enemy targets!"

Then it's Charlie again. "Yeah, they want you to destroy Zurg's army."

"Oh my goodness, be careful. Can I talk to Amanda?" There's a tussle, and I can hear the crowds in the background.

"Hi, Mom."

"How's it going?"

"Fine," she says. "The boys are out of control, but Dad's trying to calm them down."

"Well, you remember how it was the first time you went to Disneyland."

"Yeah. It's still loads of fun. We're getting ready to go to a parade. Gabby's holding our spot."

I am silent. Gabby? That sounds too cozy for my taste.

I take a deep breath to calm myself. "Well, that sounds great. Remember when—"

"Sorry, Mom, got to go now."

"OK, have fun."

But Amanda has already hung up.

Loneliness invades me again, but I will not give into it. I am happy to have heard from my babies, and I'm going to concentrate on that. I shower, eat a large bowl of Cheerios for dinner, and decide to go to bed and read. I pull the covers over me and pick up my Henry James.

I read a bit and then feel my eyes closing. My first day of being absolutely alone is over. And it sucked.

Chapter 29

I prefer a pleasant vice to an annoying virtue.
—Moliere

THE BLASPHEMY BOX

Have you noticed just how many annoying people there are in your life? In anyone's life? In everyone's life?

I thought being a grown up meant you could cut out the most irritating of them. I now find you can't. Especially when you're separated, getting a divorce, and have children. There is no shortage of well-meaning but troublesome people. Like that Peruvian woman down the street who lectures every woman in her orbit who is getting a divorce to remain friends with her ex-spouse for the sake of their children. And then asks the women for their ex-spouses' numbers. No wonder they call her "The Lima Lay."

I've just got off the phone with my friend Cameron when Candy Mendelsohn from down the street arrives, thumping at my door. She's the one who complains she can't wear her mink coat, because every time she gets it out of the closet, the dog humps it. She's also the one with a trout pout from too many injections in her lips. Her daughter, Emily, goes to school with Amanda, and Candy is the kind of knows-what-she-wants, let's-have-it-direct, do-it-all person I admire, traits her daughter shares. One day when Emily was two and I was picking her up for a playdate with Amanda, she jumped in the car, then immediately hopped out and ran to her front door, yelling back at me, "Shit, I forgot my purse."

"How *are* you, Maddy?" she says when I let her in. Air kisses and Chanel. She is a very attractive woman who always displays her considerable assets in tight sweaters and T-shirts. She was attending Wheaton when she met her husband, Ken, who told Steven that when you go out with a Wheaton girl, be sure to make her take her cross off first. Candy never finished Wheaton. She got married instead. Steven doesn't like either of them much, but loves Ken's considerable portfolio, which he manages.

"Fine," I say, beckoning her inside.

"Very brave of you to pretend so," she says, plopping herself down on one of the stools at my kitchen counter. "Now I must tell you."

"Coffee?" I offer, heading for the espresso machine.

"Decaf espresso, thanks." She continues, "Ken and I were at the opening of the opera last night."

The kids are back to school and San Francisco's social season has begun.

"You were? What was on?"

"That God-awful *Ring* thing," Candy says with a huge sigh. "Ken's parents are big donors, and we simply had to go along."

"Did you stay the whole time?"

"God, no. I'd have killed myself. I told Ken I had the most frightful headache and that I would see him later. A lot of people left early. I mean, if anyone wants to see the last act of that opera, it must mean the bar ran out of decent champagne. That's where I went, to the bar. After all, I didn't drop ten grand on that Valentino gown to sit in the dark all night!"

We laugh. Candy is very funny and sharp, but in small doses only.

"Steven was there last night."

I pause for second in front of the espresso machine. "He was?"

"Yes, and he was with his fiancée or whatever she is, in the cutest maternity gown I've ever seen. Low-cut and everything."

"Oh," I say. Bitch.

"Steven even had the nerve to approach Ken and me before the opera started," she adds. "Anyway, you will be pleased to know that I gave him and his paramour the cold shoulder. But Ken chatted with them. You know how men are."

I try to control myself.

"So are you *really* OK, Maddy, about all this?" Candy says. She leans into me and puts her hand on my shoulder. "Is there anything I can do?"

"No, Candy, there isn't, but thanks for asking."

"I just don't know how you're coping with all this. It's just so horrible, your whole situation," she says.

I feel humiliated, an object of pity in front of everyone, someone who is gossiped about and watched cautiously for signs of impending lunacy.

"It's really not as bad as I thought it would be," I say. I hand her the espresso.

"Thanks," she says and then prattles on about her upcoming vacation to the Four Seasons in Hawaii, her new kitchen, and a dozen other items I have no interest in hearing about.

Luckily, her cell phone pings then. She looks at it and stands up.

"I'd love to stay longer, but Ken just texted me about a wine auction we have to get to. I'll see you soon."

More air kisses, and she's gone.

Thank God.

I sit down with another cup of coffee and gaze out at the Bay. Half an hour passes most pleasantly like this until the doorbell rings again.

It's Mother.

"So sorry to barge in on you like this, darling, but I just had breakfast with Sabrina Channing, you know, she's married to your father's colleague at Cal. The restaurant's on Union Street, and I thought I'd buzz by and look in on you all, but somehow I left the house without my cell phone. So I couldn't call ahead. Did you know there are no public phones anymore, darling? Well, anyway, Sabrina has this most wonderful son, darling, Andrew. At least I think that's his name. Anyway, he just moved back to the Bay Area from LA. Very successful. Something about real estate. Anyhow, she thought you might like to meet him."

"I think you mean *you* thought I might like to meet him."

Mother flushes a bit. "Now darling, I'm just trying to be helpful and supportive."

"I know," I say, putting my arm around her. "But these things never work out, do they? And things are so awkward afterward."

"Really, Madeleine," she says. "You have to try, at least. You can't just give up, now can you? I hope I didn't teach you to give up."

"Mother, don't worry so much. Things will work out."

"But darling, you can't be so laissez-faire about things. At your age. You have to make your own luck, now. I mean it's not as easy to meet the right man when you're…"

"When I'm what, Mother?"

"Oh, you know what I mean. Things are more complicated now. You have three kids. You're not twenty with no responsibilities."

"Mother, I appreciate your concern, but meeting new men is really not at the top of my list right now."

"Well, darling, it should be. After all…" And she carries on and on, blah blah blah, until I finally yell, "Mother, enough! Go put the kettle up and stop rabbiting on."

She stops then and looks injured, but I smile at her, and we both laugh and soon are drinking PG Tips and looking at the view.

"Where are the kids?"

I walk to the back of the house. "Kids! Granny's here." Three sets of feet clomp down the stairs and then along the hallway. Three voices say, "Granny! Granny! Granny!"

"They're going to be with Anita much of the day," I say. "I've held her off as long as I could."

Mother sniffs audibly at the mention of Anita, but then holds out her arms as the kids barrel toward her. "Ah, here are my little angels," Mother says, engulfing each child in a large hug. "And what are we up to today, then?"

"Homework, and then Nana is taking us to the Academy of Sciences, then to Mel's for burgers," Amanda says.

"Hmm…" Mother says. "Sounds like a wonderful outing. Do remember to bring your jackets in case the Academy is cold."

"We will," Amanda says.

"OK, kids, off you go and finish your homework. Nana will be here any minute," I say.

Mother kisses each grandchild fiercely and lets them all go. The kitchen is peaceful again. We sit quietly for some time, sipping tea and gazing at the cobalt blue Bay, the ferries and liners gliding across it.

"So, do you think, darling, that you could talk to Steven again?" Mother says, her tone cajoling.

"Mother, please. That boat has sailed. I just don't see us reconciling. Both parties must want it."

"Well, darling, of course you're right, but both parties could be *made* to want it, don't you think?"

"No, Mother, I don't. It's really hard for me to accept this, but I just don't think there's any way out but divorce."

At that moment, the doorbell sounds yet again. I am sick of this damn doorbell and the annoying people who ring it.

"Who is it, darling?" Mother says.

"Probably Anita."

I can feel Mother bristling. "I should go."

"No, Mother, you don't have to go. She's just here to pick up the kids."

I go to the door. There is Anita in an extravagant camel-colored cape more suited to a Siberian winter than a San Francisco Indian summer, but I saw it in *Vogue* last month, and so, apparently, did she.

"Good morning, Anita. The children will be ready soon. Can I get you some tea?"

"No, thank you."

Mother has followed me to the door. Anita and Mother nod their heads.

"Edna."

"Anita."

There is silence. They have never gotten along. Mother thinks Anita is a great pretender and a cold fish. Anita thinks Mother is just not up to snuff, married to a university professor instead of a *grand financier*.

"Good-bye, darling. I'll call you later," Mother says and is gone.

"We really should be going as well," Anita says.

"I'll go rout them."

When I get back, Anita is still standing awkwardly in the foyer, engulfed by wool and disapproval, her mottled, veined hands clutching her purse. Her blonde hair is set and sprayed so an earthquake couldn't move it.

"You know," she says. "I picked up the kids from school yesterday, because Steven couldn't, and you, apparently, wouldn't, and when I brought them home, they asked for cookies with their drinks."

I say nothing, waiting for the onslaught of criticism she usually delivers as soon as she arrives, taking me to task for my parenting skills, which, she has always maintained, do not involve discipline. But this time, I am not scared to confront her.

"Madeleine," she said, "I really don't think you should allow the children to have cookies before dinner—"

And I say, "Let me stop you right there, Anita. First, I couldn't pick the children up from school because I had a doctor's appointment, and your paragon of a son knew that, and he should have done it instead of asking you to. God knows he doesn't do much else. Second, if you or Steven think that I am going to continue to allow you to interfere in the way I raise my children, you have another think coming."

Anita sputters. "I am not staying in this house a minute longer! Tell the children I'm waiting outside." And she marches out back to her car.

"Yes," I call after her. "And you have a nice day as well."

Chapter 30

I've been on so many blind dates, I should get a free dog.
—Wendy Liebman

THE BLASPHEMY BOX

Midlife divorce and dating for women are such terrifying concepts it's a wonder anyone ever gets into another relationship, let alone gets married again. Particularly women. You've been ejected from a long association like the loser you now feel you are, you're completely clueless, and you're dealing with men who are far better at this game than you. Along with the normal worries of too many unrealistic expectations (I'll meet a wonderful, loving, rich man and live happily ever after), and how the heck, if you even get the chance, you're going to be able to take your clothes off with the lights on again and not frighten the man waiting to see you, you can add the difficult notion of "being" with someone else, someone new, an experience you might not have had for more than a quarter of a century. And which seems rather daunting. Frankly, when I think about some new man's hands all over me...well...

A thousand people can tell you the divorce is not about your failings but his shortcomings, and it doesn't help. It truly doesn't. The fact still remains that your very own His Majesty has left you for his chickadee, and you now have to go through the relentless, nightmarish rituals of dating and mating (does he like me? will he call?) all over again while contemplating another man's hands all over you—or be alone for life. It's not that I don't like sex. It's just not easy to find someone you want to have sex with. And we've all heard the horror stories about the men you can meet who make you want to reach for Germ-X pronto.

The members of my support group tell me I need to seriously consider dating again. When I tell them I could never feel about another guy the way I once felt about Steven, Rachel takes on the firm tone she uses when she thinks any of us is whining. Ever the practical optimist, she will not take no for answer. After suggesting all the usual dating sites and regaling me with the success stories she's heard from her friends, I agree to consider it seriously. I shiver at the thought.

Cameron offers her solution to the dating problem: a blind date with someone she actually knows. Thinking that a personal recommendation from a close friend is better than some generic dating site, I ask to hear more. His name is Gary, and he's an eligible oral surgeon she has known for a while. Smart, outgoing, and of course, very well off. She says it'll be fine, but since this is my first date in twenty years, I imagine the learning curve still might be steep. I'm terrified but agree to have her set it up.

There are so many rules to consider about dating again in middle age that I'm not sure I'm even ready. I get all kinds of advice from the women in my divorce group. It's confusing to say the least.

"Keep it short, Maddy," Myla says. "Have an exit strategy."

Good.

"Don't talk about your ex, his ex, or sex," says Rachel.

That sounds easy.

"Avoid politics, current events, money, kids, and religion. Don't complain about how dating sucks," says Lillian.

What's left? I wonder. The weather, sports, health care?

"Just be yourself," says Sally.

And how do I do that without being able to talk about my kids or career or my marriage or my concerns about the world? It's all so complex.

The day of the date with Gary the Oral Surgeon, Cameron comes over to help me with the most pressing question at hand: what to wear.

"What do people wear on a blind date these days?" I ask her.

"Well, it depends on how you want to look: sexy, classically attractive, or nice and casual. I'm thinking sexy."

"Hmm," I say. "I don't even know if I *can* look sexy anymore."

"Oh, stop. You're fifty, not dead."

"No, what I mean is I certainly don't *feel* sexy."

"You will."

We head upstairs to my closet and begin looking for options.

"How about this black dress?" she says, pulling out a strapless black dress with an illusion lace bodice.

"It's a bit short, isn't it?" I say. "I don't want to look like Madonna."

"Put it on so I can see," Cameron says. "It's always better to be overdressed than underdressed."

I pull the dress over my head and smooth it down on the hips.

"Too formal for a first date, I think, unless you're going to a club," Cameron decides.

We continue rifling through the closet, Cameron flicking hangers back and forth in her search to find something suitable. "What's this?" she says, pulling out a floral dress.

"That's my Diane von Furstenberg wrap dress."

"Well, why not wear that?"

"I guess I could, but wrap dresses never seem to stay wrapped on me. I'm constantly tying and retying them, and this one is no different. I'm just not comfortable in them."

"Yes, but they're so flattering," Cameron says with a sigh. "Anyway, how about these black pants with something?"

"I'm afraid they are too tight for me right now. I've had them for years. Why don't I just wear these black drawstring ones?"

"They look like yoga pants."

"They are yoga pants."

"Oh."

"I could pair them with some really pretty blouse," I say reassuringly.

"What kind of a pretty blouse?" Cameron says in a suspicious tone.

"How about this one?" I draw out my favorite pleated white shirt with jeweled buttons from Nordstrom.

"Hmm," she says, unconvinced. "I guess it's OK."

"It's really pretty on," I say.

"Fine," Cameron says. "Now what about shoes?" She picks up a pair of towering black sling-backs that look like instruments of torture. "These Manolos are nice."

"Cameron," I say, "this guy won't know Manolo from Mossimo, and those shoes are the most uncomfortable shoes I've ever worn. They just kill my bunions."

"You have bunions?" Cameron says.

"Sure. Don't you?"

"Of course, but I don't let them stop me from wearing my favorite shoes. I bet those Manolos look great on you."

I ignore her.

Cameron returns to my closet.

"I thought we'd decided what I'm wearing," I say.

Cameron doesn't answer. She's flicking through my clothes again. Finally, she alights on a filmy black Emporio Armani blouse with a ruffled front.

"Why didn't you show me this?" she says in an aggrieved tone.

"I'd forgotten about it."

"Try it on."

"It's a bit much, don't you think?"

"Maddy, there might not be a lot of dates in your immediate future, so you have to make the most of the ones you have."

"Charming!" I say.

"Oh, just try it on."

I pull the top over my head.

"Very nice, much better than a boring old white blouse," Cameron says with a sigh of relief. "I just want things to go well and for you to have a good time."

I hug her. "I know."

After she's gone, I shower and blow-dry my hair. Then I apply my makeup carefully to make sure what should be minimized, is. The result is not so bad. Hopefully I won't frighten any animals or small children.

I'm to meet Gary at Balboa Café, affectionately known as "The Balb." It's a bistro kind of place with a long wooden bar and shiny brass fixtures. I am a few minutes late, and when I walk in, I see a man who fits the description Cameron gave me. He's at the bar surrounded by several waitresses. So that's what Cameron meant when she said he was outgoing. He is very good looking, in that preppy kind of way, with a full head of hair to boot, which at this age, by the way, is no minor consideration.

"Are you Gary?" I ask, sliding in between two of the waitresses. Drink in hand, he wheels around to face me. "Jeez," he says. "Yes, hi, you must be Maggie. Cameron didn't tell me you were so tall."

I want to say, "Cameron didn't tell me you were so short." But I actually say, "It's Maddy."

"Well," he says, knocking back his drink, "Cameron said it was Maggie."

I smile, wanting to tell him that a woman whom I have known for several years probably knows my name better than a lush who doesn't know me at all, but I restrain myself. This is going south already, but I soldier on.

"Shall we sit over there, then?" he says. I nod. We sit down at a marble-topped bistro table in the bar area. The waitress comes over quickly.

"What are you drinking, hon?"

"Actually, Gary, I don't really drink."

He looks puzzled. "At all?"

"Rarely."

"Hmm," he says and looks up at the waitress. "A screwdriver for me, then, and...?"

"Orange juice is fine."

The waitress heads off.

Just then, two twenty-something women walk in, dressed in tighter-than-right jeans and with midriffs flatter than Florida. Gary's eyes bug out, but he tries to stifle the urge and turns sharply back toward me.

"So you're getting divorced," he says.

"Yes."

"Bummer."

"Cameron says you are newly divorced," I say.

"Yep. My bitch of an ex-wife, who already took all my money, now wants more, if you can believe that."

"I'm sorry," I say. "The money part of divorce is very frustrating."

"You bet it is."

The waitress returns with the drinks. He quickly slurps his and starts listing everything he's frustrated with in his life: his Presidio Heights neighbor, who is the reason Gary has crab grass and dandelions on his front lawn; his huge alimony payments; President Obama, who should go back to where he came from, which Gary seems to be suggesting is the Gorilla Age; and his patients, who balk at paying his huge fees.

"I went to school for years so I could charge those prices," he says petulantly. "It's unfair for people to complain about them."

I sit there looking at him, smiling politely, wondering if he will show any semblance of knowing he is on a date with a person other than himself.

"I imagine being an oral surgeon must be very interesting," I say.

"I guess," he says. "But you have to deal with so many crazy people."

"Like who?"

"Well, one patient called last week and said she couldn't come in, because her tooth hurt so bad she couldn't get out of bed."

Gary laughs, and so do I. "And then there was the model."

"What happened with her?"

"Well, she came in recently for some work, but I needed to finish up with her, and she had an appointment for last week. Then she calls and says she can't make it in, because she'd been bitten by a lion on a fashion shoot."

"Was she all right? I mean, how bad was the bite?"

"Oh, probably nothing serious, I think. Shame really, because she was so hot. And I think she really liked me."

"Ah," I say.

"So," Gary says then, "why don't you drink?"

"I don't really like the taste of alcohol too much, and it makes me sleepy."

He looks skeptical.

"I'd rather have a piece of chocolate cake."

Gary frowns. "You know sugar's really bad for your teeth, don't you? But no, really, are you in rehab or AA or something? Do you not drink because you're an alcoholic?"

"No," I say, "would you please excuse me?," and I get up and run as fast as I can toward the bathroom. Once in, I flatten myself against the wall and breathe deeply. How could Cameron fix me up with this cretin?

When I get back, Gary is chatting up our waitress, who is flicking her long blonde hair from side to side. I say, "I hope you will excuse me. I just got a text from the babysitter, and she said one of my twin boys is feeling poorly."

"But if the babysitter's there, why do you need to go home?" he asks. He's slurring his words a bit from all that vodka.

"Because I am a mother and..."

"OK," he says grudgingly.

I hold out my hand to shake his. "Thanks for the drink, and nice to meet you."

"Same here," he says. "I'll call you."

I just smile and leave as quickly as I can.

Soon after I get home, Cameron calls. "How did it go? He's really good-looking, right? And rich!"

"Well, yes, all that is true, but he's really not my type. We didn't hit it off. " I can feel Cameron reproaching me down the telephone line. "Too short?"

"No. Too drunk."

"Too bad. He's such a catch."

Yes, I think. I'd have to catch him as he fell off his barstool.

I sign onto my blog just for some light relief.

When I was newly single, I went on a blind date. He was the brother of a friend, and he seemed all right at first, but after dinner at this strange hippie place, he pulled out a lime-green box of Trojan Twisted Pleasure condoms and said, "Shall we?"

Posted by AvaG

Chapter 31

WEEK 36 OF SEPARATION

Grandparents are there to help the child get into mischief they haven't thought of yet.
—Gene Perret

THE BLASPHEMY BOX

When you're suddenly a single parent, any help you can get with the kids is welcome. And any time the help comes from family members, it's even more so. You already feel immeasurably guilty and terrified your kids will be permanently damaged by the split of their parents, so continuing their lives as normally as possible with their extended family becomes the most important thing in the world. If you are an only child, like me, the presence of grandparents in your children's lives is vital.

This being said, although some grandparents take instantly to caring for their grandkids, others don't, at least not as much. For all her faults, Anita seems to take good care of my three kids, even though she hates their mother. But when it comes to my own mother, well, that's another story.

I am on deadline for an article on local boutiques, so I ask Mother to come take the boys out for the afternoon. Amanda's with a friend, and I just need a few hours to finish the piece up and send it to Pamela.

At 1 p.m. sharp, Mother is standing at my door, carrying a large leather satchel, the San Francisco wind behind her.

Despite the blustery weather, Mother looks, as always, as if she's going to lunch with the Queen. Today, she's in camel pants and a brown turtleneck, on which lies an extravagant gold chain.

"Mother," I say. "What, pray, do you have in that huge bag?"

"Now, Madeleine, you're not going to start talking like Shakespeare again, are you?" Mother says in an indulgent tone. "It was bad enough when you did it in upper fourth. I just brought a few snacks for the kids for our little jaunt, that's all. And now, darling, why don't you call the boys down?"

I grumble to myself as I climb the stairs to the boys' rooms. I just know how this is going to go. The children love having her around, of course. To them, she's just a dotty person in nice clothes who makes them laugh, if not for the reasons she thinks. But to me, she's a bit overwhelming.

I wrap the boys up in their jackets and scarves and bring them with me into the kitchen.

"Oh, here are my baby boys," Mother says, opening her arms for their hugs.

Colin and Charlie run to embrace her. "Where are we going, Granny?" Charlie says.

"Well, I thought the zoo might be fun. They don't get enough biology in American schools," she says to me in a confiding tone.

"I think you mean zoology, Mother."

"Now don't correct your mother, darling," she says. "It's impolite."

"It's my favorite, the zoo," says Charlie, jumping up and down.

"Me too," says Colin.

It takes ten more minutes to get Mother and the boys out of the door. The kids are ready, but Mother is determined that a thick cloud of my hairspray will prevent the wind from wreaking any havoc on her hair. When the hair is firmly in place, Charlie says, "Let's go, Granny."

"Going, darling, going," she says and flutters toward the door with the boys.

"Have fun and keep your jackets buttoned!" I call to them.

After they've gone, I inhale the silence around me and sit down at my laptop. Instead of getting to work on my article, I open my blog, which, in the mysterious ways of the Internet, has somehow garnered me a bit of a following. More people have been posting comments. One woman quotes the French writer Colette, who said not to eat too many almonds because they add weight to the breasts. Wouldn't that be a reason to eat almonds?

Another woman from Canton, Ohio, says her husband moved for a job, and she had no idea that job consisted of a pretty young thing. He has never sent support, and even though he and the woman are not divorced, he and his girlfriend wear matching wedding rings. He canceled all her credit cards and health and car insurance, and she has no money to pay for anything.

The moral of this story is that there are always people much worse off than you, and you'd be smart to remember it. I do remember it, I think to myself, and I am grateful. And then I think, God, I really meant that.

Thirty minutes later I have finished my blog entry, and I start in on my article on fabulous boutiques in San Francisco that only the true insider has heard of. I have been writing for two heavenly, uninterrupted hours when the phone rings.

"Darling?"

"Mother? How's it going?"

"Oh darling, poor Charlie." Mother's voice is shaking, rather unusual for a take-charge, can-do, British matron such as she.

Panic surges through me like a tsunami. "What do you mean? What's happened?"

"Oh darling, he's only gone and broken his arm, hasn't he?"

I nearly drop the phone. "Is he OK?"

I hear a scuffle in the background and then Charlie's voice. "Mom, I broke my arm."

"So I understand," I say, trying not to sound panicked with him. "Where are you?"

"At the emergency room. It really hurts."

"Of course it does, sweetie. But it will heal really fast because you're a kid, so don't worry. How did it happen?"

I hear some scratching and then Mother. "Darling?"

"What the hell happened?" I say. I am trying not to raise my voice.

"Now, Madeleine, don't raise your voice. He was simply hanging upside down on some bars near the penguin exhibit, which, by the way darling, stunk to high heaven of urine, and some hooligan in a green uniform came over and ordered him off. He fell to the ground like a stone."

"You mean a zoo ranger? How could you let him climb the bars? There are signs everywhere. I have had this child for ten years, and he has never broken anything. And you have him for two hours, and one of his limbs is broken. What hospital is it? I'm coming right now."

"Darling, I can't believe you're blaming me. Boys will be boys, and you know how they like to swing on bars and shove each other around. And that's what happened. I only turned away for a moment. No need to come. The doctors are through, and we'll be home soon. Mother has it covered."

Soon after, in they shuffle: Colin, red cheeked, and Charlie, face pale and drawn, arm in a cast. Charlie heaves himself onto the kitchen stool with his unbroken arm and looks at me.

"Here we are, then," Mother says cheerfully. "Darling, I could murder a cup of tea."

"Would it be all right if I ministered to my child for a short while?" I say.

"Of course, darling," Mother says. "Put the kettle on, sweetie, there's a love."

"Do you want something, Charlie?" I say.

"Maybe a Sprite? And some of that cake Mrs. Whitaker sent over?"

I am about to tell him both those items are only for special occasions but realize that this is a special occasion, so I tell him to take himself off to bed, and I will bring everything to him on a tray.

When I have settled him in bed with Sprite and cake, I return to the kitchen to see Mother collapsed at the table, the kettle screaming.

"I'm exhausted, darling, I truly am. I had forgotten how much work it is raising children. Could you make the tea?"

"Mother, you've only been gone a few hours," I say, shutting off the gas and pouring the hot water into the teapot.

"I know, darling. Now just come and sit down here with me. Don't worry, Charlie will be fine. He's a kid. Part of this is fun for him. All the attention. And Sprite and cake, which you shouldn't be giving him, by the way, darling. And I hope you're not having any cake, darling."

I sigh heavily. "No, Mother, I am not having cake. I have lost a lot of weight."

"Really, darling?"

"Can't you tell? I've lost twenty-five pounds, for Christ's sake."

"Now, Madeleine, don't start with the swearing. You really have to give that up."

"How the bloody hell am I going to stop swearing?" I say. "It's not like there's a fucking pill for it like Chantix for smokers, is there? I mean, me giving up swearing is like the Pope giving up his catamite."

"Really, Madeleine, there's no need to get blasphemous. All those catechism and confirmation classes we sent you to. And all for naught. The Pope giving up his catamite, indeed."

I collapse onto a stool.

"Listen, darling," Mother says. "Why don't you go back to that computer of yours you love so much, and Colin and I will make dinner?"

She prances into the kitchen, a place in which she has never been overly adept. In fact, one time she told Father that she wanted to go somewhere different that year, and he said why not try the kitchen.

I almost beg her not to make dinner. Or anything else. Mother is good at many things, but cooking is not one of them. She always said cooking was just making food hotter. She's a terrific hostess, decorates superbly, makes a mean G&T, puts together beautiful flower arrangements, can discourse about everything from anteaters to the correct temperature at which to grow coffee beans, and dresses like a dream. And she has always made sure to stay slim. (This is the talent I most admire. No headline there.) She put on lovely birthday parties for me (someone else made the cake, of course) and generally ran the ship beautifully. The only thing she can't do is cook. Soufflés didn't rise, crème caramels didn't set, and she always somehow managed to leave out key ingredients—like sugar for the cookies. (When she discovered that she could find cookie and cake mix at Waitrose, and all she had to do was add some eggs, you'd have thought she'd solved the legend of King Arthur.) "Darling," she once told me, "as I always say, anyone who believes that the way to a man's heart is through his stomach flunked geography."

"No, that's fine," I say. "I was just going to do spaghetti. It's really easy."

"OK, darling," Mother says in obvious relief. "Now you know I don't eat meat. And can you find me the remote?"

I hand her the remote, and she falls onto the sofa and starts searching for *CSI*. In the kitchen, I start making the sauce and browning the ground beef when Charlie wanders in.

"Sweetie, shouldn't you be in bed, resting?" I say. "You've had a nasty shock. You've still got all those books we got at the library the other day."

"I can't hold a book with one hand, Mom." He is cranky, but he looks like something out of the Vienna Boys' Choir. Mother said the doctor said the break is not too bad and will heal quickly, but he's ten and hates being in a cast.

"How long am I going to have to wear this thing?"

"Not too long, sweetie. Maybe a few weeks."

"A few weeks?" he says. "How the heck can I do that? What about my softball league?"

"You'll have to sit out the games until the cast comes off."

"I can't do that. I'll get dropped."

"I'll speak to the coach. He'll understand. Now why don't you go to your room and read sitting up, and dinner will be ready soon."

Charlie trudges off to his room. Right then, Amanda bounds up the stairs.

"I'm starving," she says.

"I'm just making spaghetti. Did you have fun?"

"It was OK. We went to the mall and then watched videos. Where are Colin and Charlie?"

"They're in their rooms. Charlie broke his arm at the zoo."

She looks concerned. "Is he OK? Why was he at the zoo?"

"He's got a cast, but he's fine. Granny took him and Colin. Dinner will be ready in half an hour."

At dinner, everyone gobbles up the spaghetti I've made except Mother, who eats plain pasta with a little pesto sauce I had in the fridge. I have made broccoli on the side, something the kids are trying to ignore. When I tell them to eat some, Charlie says, "You know, Mom, everyone knows that sick kids should be able to eat what they want, like Mars bars and M&Ms and Oreos."

"Nice try. Sick kids need their veggies even more."

When dinner is over, Mother kisses the kids and me and says, "Well, that was lovely, darling. And now I should get home. Glad I could lend a hand today."

I am relieved beyond mention. "Yes, Mother. You have been a great help."

Chapter 32

WEEK 36 OF SEPARATION

The bonds that unite another person to ourself exist only in our mind.
—Marcel Proust

THE BLASPHEMY BOX

When you're going through a divorce, you (hopefully) have a law-yer who (hopefully) takes all the necessary steps without you having to do much more than pay him and curse the gods above who tied you to your brute of a husband in the first place. But soon, at least in some divorce cases, you will find yourself in a courtroom or something like it being grilled by a judge who has infinite power over your life and you. And let me tell you, it isn't fun. The whole idea of a courtroom and the law it exists to uphold makes me feel like a vegan at the House of Prime Rib.

Suzy's divorce from her gay husband is amicable. Completely. A textbook example of a friendly parting. The boys will go back and forth from Suzy to Rex and Craig, and everyone will have Sunday lunch together once a month. (Yes, that's in the divorce settlement.) It is all very civilized.

I wish my divorce was like that. It isn't. It's acrimonious. And every interaction feels like I'm walking on crushed glass.

The other day, we have another meeting with the lawyers. We sit two across from two, a position that still seems so odd to me. For the last twenty years, I have grown used to sitting next to my husband, not oppo-site him. Things are so different now. But I think I've finally realized I must accept it and move on.

I just sit there as I listen to the attorneys go over old ground. Steven chimes in once in a while with comments about how unreasonable the whole thing is. I know enough to keep quiet and just let Alec do the talking.

Finally, the conversation stops, and there is a pregnant (excuse the pun) pause. Alec finally breaks the silence. "As we still are unable to come to terms, we are going to put the case on the court calendar."

That gets their attention in a hurry.

"That is totally premature."

"After months of meeting with no resolution, I don't see any alternative. Unless, of course, we can agree to our terms." Silence. "I guess not. Since Mrs. Nelson has no significant income of her own, she will not be able to bear the burden of any attorneys' fees for the court appearance. Those will be allocated to the settlement costs as well."

Steven is beyond angry. I sit back and gloat.

"We'll see about that," Steven's attorney says.

"And, we'll see you in court," Alec says. And with that, he rises from his chair, and I follow suit.

∽∾

The battle continues, this time in court. Since Steven has not been willing to settle the matter of proper support, either spousal or child, we're sitting with our attorneys in a stark, cavernous court room, awaiting the judge. Steven sits stiffly, scowling and ignoring me. How can two people who have been married for twenty years end up like this?

"These hearings are usually very short," Alec says as we sit down on opposite sides of the courtroom from Steven and his lawyer. "The judge may want you to speak," he adds.

I turn to him in shock. "Are you kidding me? You wait until now to tell me?"

"Don't be nervous," he says. "Just tell her your situation as you have told me. Judge Enright is usually nice."

I'm relieved to have a female judge. "I wish I had time to prepare."

"Mrs. Nelson," Alec says. He still doesn't call me Maddy. "Don't fret. Everything will be fine."

I look away and immediately see the side door at the front of the court open and a smidgen of a black robe moving toward the judge's bench. Below it I see black patent stiletto-heeled shoes with fire-engine-red soles. They look like Louboutins. The judge is strikingly attractive, tall with blonde hair pulled back into a ponytail and a face carved by the angels. A pair of tortoiseshell glasses, which must be Gucci, rest on her head. And then I remember. This is Judge Amanda Enright, known for her litigation chops and for her glamour quotient, the highest in the San Francisco legal community—or at least that's what *San Francisco Life* proclaimed last year.

Judge Enright looks up from the bench. "I've reviewed the income and expense forms in this matter and would now like to hear from the principals involved," she says.

My stomach caves in a little, and my mouth is suddenly very dry.

"Shall we start with Mrs. Nelson?"

I feel dizzy but somehow manage to stand up.

I grip the side of the table. "Your Honor, my situation is I've been married for twenty years and have three children, one fourteen-year-old daughter and ten-year-old twin boys. My husband wants a divorce because he has a girlfriend who is pregnant, and I am prepared to give him one, but he is not sending enough money for us to live on. He also wants the house."

The judge's expression is one of fierce concentration. "Go on."

"Your Honor, I'm finding it very difficult to subsist on what my husband is sending, and I would just like enough money to get along. I am not asking to live in high style. Divorce is difficult for everyone in a variety of ways, and I certainly don't expect to continue to live at the same standard as I have up until now."

"Are you the Maddy Nelson who used to write regularly for the *Chronicle*?" the judge asks me then.

"I am, Your Honor, but please don't hold that against me."

A smile bubbles at Judge Enright's lips. "Right, let's hear from Mr. Nelson now."

Steven rises from his chair. His face is red. He is not a man who ever discusses personal matters with or in front of other people, and this hearing is testing the limits of his endurance.

"Your Honor," he says, "I am not fabulously wealthy, and I am running two households right now. I pay all the essential costs of my family's life— car, home and health insurance, food, clothing, school fees—and when all those are paid, there is very little left. My wife has returned to her career as a journalist and can well earn her own living. She has already published two articles in the last month or so."

Judge Enright's eyebrows go up. "Are you suggesting that Mrs. Nelson has a full-time position and needs no support?"

"Well—" Steven starts his answer, but the judge interrupts him.

She turns to me. "Mrs. Nelson, are you once again on staff at the *Chronicle*?"

"No, Your Honor. I do an occasional article on a freelance basis."

"How much are you paid for these articles?"

"Two hundred dollars each."

She turns to Steven. "Freelance articles paying no more than two hundred dollars each can hardly be taken as enough income to support your wife and children."

Steven frowns.

The judge makes some notes, removes her glasses, and gives Steven a look that would wither a field of daffodils. "It has always been my experience," she says, "that a man only leaves his wife when he has someone else to go to, and it appears to hardly be fair that a wife who has lost her husband should also lose her house and adequate funds to run it and her life," she says. "Any man who has to be ordered to pay *sufficient* support instead of doing so willingly is not the kind of man it is my inclination to look upon with favor. The court finds that the support requests are reasonable and should be paid immediately and retroactively from the date of filing."

The whole thing has taken no more than twenty minutes.

My heart leaps. Finally, something has gone my way.

Let me tell you about an acrimonious divorce. My best friend caught her hubby cheating with the au pair from Poland. She threw them both out and filed for divorce. Her hubby wanted the house, because he had put down the original down payment. My friend was so furious at him, she called in bulldozers to raze it. In the judgment of divorce, the hubby got everything but the house. The house, she got.

Posted by LizClaire

Chapter 33

My computer dating bureau came up with a perfect gentleman; still I've got another three goes.
—Sally Poplin

THE BLASPHEMY BOX

The idea of Internet dating just horrifies me. It makes of us products to be sold to anyone who thinks the product has value, kind of like buying a turquoise bracelet ("Absolutely stunning! An instant classic!") on the Home Shopping Network. The only difference is that you don't have some perky spokesperson/model doing the selling.

To put yourself out there in the ether, where resides some of the strangest specimens of homo sapiens, most of whom you would wish never to meet even at the best of times, suddenly becomes imperative if you don't want to spend the rest of your life winning prizes for the best rose or going on singles boat cruises in the San Francisco Bay. Because, let's face it, we all *are looking for love, someone to share our lives with, someone who gives a damn about us. Not an easy task.*

And writing a dating profile! I'm no clearer how to write it now than I was before I went online, and everyone there put their two cents in and muddied the waters so horribly. One of my problems is I don't have a job and haven't had one a while, so I can't write about that. And I don't want to say I'm getting a divorce. As BFF says, everybody's getting a divorce.

And it's so hard to describe oneself. Particularly for someone who has spent her entire professional life describing everyone else. Add to that the extra complication that self-esteem is at a record low right now and fear at a record high, and it just makes me want to throw the baby out with the bath water. Your dating profile can't sound like a Hallmark card or therapy session with cringe-worthy sentiments like, "I am looking to share life and love." It has to be your virtual ambassador, sparking an inferno of irresistible attraction to capture all those wonderful men who, everyone keeps telling you, are all out there just waiting to read it and pounce.

After having gone on three blind dates: one with the oral surgeon; another with a lawyer, who spent the entire time crying into his Campari about how he still loves his ex-wife; and a third, set up for me by my newspaper friend Elizabeth with one of her colleagues from the office, who made me pay my share of lunch and then asked if he could keep the receipt so he could write it off on his taxes, I thanked my support group for their terrible advice and told them I was quitting the dating world.

No, no, *no,* everyone said in unison. You have to date, and the best way to do that, they said, is online. (Thirty-five million people have done it, if you can believe that.) And so I have given in. The whole thing is quite horrible and gives me a tummy ache.

I sign up with "the Internet's first and best" dating website, which apparently allows me to order up the perfect man like a pizza Margherita. The site, which says that online dating is no longer seen as the last hurrah of old-maid solitary singles, lets me see pictures and profiles of potentially compatible boyfriends for free, but if I want to contact them, I have to pay. And if I want to contact them, but they haven't paid for contact, only for browsing profiles, they can't receive my e-mails, which puts me back to square one. Oh dear.

As part of the process to sign up, I'm presented with a form to search for singles, where I must enter simple details like if I'm a man or woman looking for a man or woman, and in which age group I'm interested. I enter "woman seeking man" and "between fifty and fifty-seven," click the "View Photos" icon, and up comes a bunch of small photos of men meeting my basic parameters. One looks like he's been dragged through a hedge backward, and another has a cobra tattoo on a bulging neck. Another is just plain unattractive. Perhaps he's smart, I think to myself. Women will date an ugly guy if he's smart and interesting, because they think they're getting a good deal, like 20 percent off at Macy's. And because they think he'll be grateful for the attention and treat them well. It doesn't always work that way, however, but when it does, it's nice. Even if he does weigh as much as a small SUV, he is so grateful for regular sex that he'll tell you that you're beautiful a hundred times a day. And that's all right by me. (And many other women.)

I survey some of the other pictures. Some of the men look like they're a hundred years old, others look gay, and some just don't bear looking at, at all. Does it make sense to be gay and registered on the site as a man looking for a woman? And as for the profile names they have chosen for themselves! One guy's tag is "justloookn." Great. Right off the bat, someone who can't spell. And you should see the man who calls himself "LuckyYou!" Does that smolder in his eyes mean he's sexy or just in pain?

A screen suddenly appears in which I must fill in my e-mail, password, and birth date. Then a screen comes up to subscribe to the service, which is very confusing, because you think you have to pay to look at profiles and search, but you don't. I subscribe to the free part of the service, and now I have to create a dating profile. I fill out the questionnaire part of the profile relating to me, which consists of general basic lifestyle compatibility questions like what I look like (options are slender, about average, athletic and toned, heavyset, a few extra pounds, or stocky), my religious and educational background, my occupation, my ethnicity, and whether I smoke or drink and how much. The questions then get more specific like eye color and how much money I make and...you get the picture. Then I fill in the form about what type of person I'm looking for.

I proofread carefully. I don't want typos to detract from the magic, now do I?

Now I have to write the dating profile's "About Me" section, a capsulized look at me and why a man might want to date me. And it's not as easy as you think. Apparently you can't just say, "I love skydiving, sex on the beach, and mascarpone with my Sunday brunch pancakes." No, the online advice says, it has to be much more detailed than that (sex on *which* beach, for instance) and reflect every single thought you have ever had about every single thing for the entire time you have been alive. And do you know there are people who actually write these for a living?

Some woman in New York is making a killing creating dating profiles that highlight her clients' "most positive and unique traits." What other kind of profiles are there? Is anyone going to write a profile that says, "I'm a fat cow with hair growing out of my toes"?

Anyway, I go online to get tips, and boy, are there plenty of them. If everyone out there practiced what they preach on the Internet, there would be no need for even one dating site. The rather pedestrian advice runs from don't write anything negative or serious to think up a good catchy headline that truly describes you like "Pepsodent smile with a Mensa brain," or "Blondes tease, brunettes please." (Actually, whoever wrote those is quite clever.)

Be specific, the online advisors say: don't write, "I like all kinds of music," or "I like to stay in, and I like to go out," because that could describe anyone. But others say if you're too specific and exclude every-one who does X or Y, you'll cut out half your dating pool. One site advises prospective members to, above all, be friendly and approach-able. Start your profiles with captions like, "Hi there," or "I'm friendly, truly I am; e-mail me and find out."

Another site says, "Don't forget to spell check."

I just want to hit the off button on the computer, but I resist. I feel like I'm in an episode of "The Twilight Zone." And everyone contradicts everyone else. This person says don't be forthright or opinionated and the other person says *do* be forthright and opinionated, so you stand out. Some people say write a lot, and some say just enough—if one can ever gauge what "enough" is.

I decide to read over some male profiles and find tears rolling down my cheeks. I had a husband and now I don't, and I'm searching for the next one on a computer, for Christ's sake.

The first profile I see is from a younger guy who describes him-self as a "sensitive misanthrope" who's looking for a woman between forty and fifty. Such a woman should only contact him, he writes, if she finds him interesting and not, he adds, "in the sense that snake-headed Medusa is interesting." He says he's six feet tall (which means he's not), wants to teach "wrting" (which means he's unemployed), and that "I have moved to San Francisco just two years ago" (which means he's illiterate.)

Things go downhill from there. A good-looking vet in Sausalito says he's a "total movie slut," that his DNA has given him "a charmed life," and that he has been compared to Arnold Schwarzenegger (once) and The Marlboro Man (twice.) Why doesn't he just say he was married to Christie Brinkley, who has a PhD in aerospace engineering from MIT?

I wonder how Steven's profile would be and whether I would cringe as much reading it as I am looking at all this rubbish. Then I look up some female profiles to get ideas on how to write my own. One dating site gives an A to a woman who writes that she doesn't like most guys, which makes the guys she does like unique. She is "antsy," has strong opinions, and welcomes sarcasm, which, she says, guys really like. Then there's the usual rubbish about liking old movies and walks in the moonlight and a question about pet peeves. And it's right about then that I again consider shutting down my computer and/or throwing it out of the window into the Allens' garden alongside their myriad of topiaries of Disney characters.

Again, I resist. I troll through site after site after site from link to link to link in search of sample profiles to see if I can get any ideas for my own. The website iVillage.com says that for people searching for love on the web, the key to online dating success is an excellent profile. In my day, the key to dating was eyeliner, a short skirt, and "Boogie Oogie Oogie" on the stereo. One woman's profile says she disapproves of cults and cover bands and pedophiles, but approves of photographs and fistfights. Is she nuts?

Everyone says you must post photos, and someone advises to post pictures of your entire body, not just the face, arguing that that will cut down on any disappointment you may encounter once your date actually meets you in person. ("You need at least one photo! No exceptions!") Many others say you have to be original, otherwise you won't stand out. Like the woman who likes fistfights?

On one website, they tell you to choose a clever tagline. In journalism they're called "subheads," and they're important for giving extra information. You should present yourself in a way that attracts the right kind of person, not everyone out there in the dating ether. The goal is to define yourself in a way that people can figure out whether you're a good match for them.

You must apparently think about what you want and who you are to write a good, exciting, fun tagline. You can even use quotes from your favorite author, the site says, like this one by Dorothy Parker: "Way down deep, I'm very shallow." The website simplified-dating.com has some amusing taglines, to wit: "Since light travels faster than sound, is that why some people appear bright until they speak?"

This website also suggests writing a short tagline or finding a site that displays long ones in their entirety, because if you write a long tagline for a site that only displays the first few words of it, things can get dodgy. "Please help me get off this site by being my match" became "Please help me get off."

And that's what gets me off my computer.

∾

And now I'm back on. I read online that someone did a study to see which words occur more frequently in women's profiles as opposed to men's profiles. Women used the words "movies, "music," "beach," "friends," and "dancing" the most, and men used "sports," "fishing," "movies," "music, "camping," and "outdoors" the most. Well, at least they agree on two things.

After many arduous hours of writing and rewriting, here's the profile I came up with. Tell me what you think:

"Compulsive/neurotic, over the hill expat British female who loves to shop at K-Mart and camp in cemeteries seeks man with similar interests. A bonus for the lucky one who clips his toenails while watching 'Law & Order.' I am obedient and trustworthy."

Just kidding.

Here's what I really wrote under the tag browneyedgirl: "word-loving expat British journalist, 5' 8", brown/brown, fit, N/S, N/D, three kids, seeking same in male version. Anyone interested?"

Reading over my favorite movies, I see they look too pretentious. I had put down *The Golden Bowl, The Wings of the Dove, The Age of Innocence, Ryan's Daughter, Brokeback Mountain,* and *Angels and Insects.* Then I excise all of those except *Ryan's Daughter* and add *The English Patient* (everyone loved that), *Dial M for Murder, The Illusionist, Guess Who's Coming to Dinner, My Best Friend's Wedding, Driving Miss Daisy,* and *Gone, Baby, Gone.* Then I see some of those movies aren't as mainstream as perhaps they should be, so I take *The Illusionist* out and replace it with *Pretty Woman*, and in order to pander to the man reading my profile, add in a good violent choice, *Unforgiven*.

Then I go crazy trying to find a photo of myself I don't mind the whole world seeing. I rummage through drawers and closets and drag out albums and envelopes of pictures from every corner of the house, studying every photo for what it will and will not say about me. I want a flattering photo that's a study in nonchalance, but all I can find are pictures that look a bit like my driver's license photo, as if I am a recently escaped convict from San Quentin. I've never taken great photos. I just haven't. I consider posting a picture of our erstwhile yellow Lab, who went to dog heaven five years ago. Perhaps not. I find some skiing pictures, which all look great because everything's covered up, even my face. But that would rather defeat the purpose of the exercise, wouldn't it? I finally find a photo from a recent visit to the ballet that isn't too horrible and upload it and my profile onto the dating site, praying I don't attract any rapists, murderers, first cousins, or Homeland Security personnel setting up a sting.

Chapter 34

Online dating is just as murky and full of lemons as finding a used car in the classifieds. Once you learn the lingo, it's easier to spot the models with high mileage and no warranty.
—Laurie Perry

THE BLASPHEMY BOX

This online dating thing is crazy. People can say whatever they like: you think you're meeting Paul Newman, and along comes Friar Tuck. (You can't believe how many men our age have that balding pattern.) The process has all the romance of ordering a dishwasher from the Home Depot. And the out-and-out lies! They say their names are Ashton and Chase and Errol and Fabio, when you just know they're called Al and Ernie and Frank, and then they post pictures from that one day twenty years ago when they didn't look like serial killers who drink too much beer.

The first bright spark I communicate with is an attorney, Henry, who I "speak" to through a flurry of e-mails. He sounds like the perfect suitor. He has an undergraduate degree in English literature and is a copyright lawyer. Not bad-looking either, from his picture. But when we meet at a restaurant near my house, I am sad to see that the picture does him too much justice. He's been in the sun too much, is a lot shorter than he said he was in his profile, has a bald patch he cleverly hid in his online picture, and an expanding middle over which his Brooks Brothers shirt buttons are straining. Even before the waitress brings us some cloudy tap water, he says, "So, are you on divorce number two or three?"

I think, jeez, "hi, how are you, and what grade are your kids in?" might be a better opener.

"One, actually," I say, waiting to see if he will ask me what I want to drink.

"It's my third," he says. "Hope that doesn't put you off or anything."

"Of course not." But it does.

"I guess you're wondering about my hair," he says.

"No."

"I know the photo online makes me look as if I have a lot of hair, and I do, but not in front, in the back," he says, and he turns around to show me.

"I hadn't noticed," I say. "Not something to worry about, anyway."

He smiles. "You're nice."

I can see him relax a bit and then he starts talking. And never stops. (The waitress has to ask me what I want to drink.) He talks about high school and college and law school and his family and his girlfriends and his three wives, two of whom left him and the most recent one, who died. He must have talked her to death.

I run over in my mind what I could have achieved in the forty-eight minutes this guy has blathered on and on: I could have got a manicure, picked up the dry cleaning, and made a run for some fat-free milk. When he stops—I had been waiting for him to breathe at some point—I do the whole "I just got a text about my little boy who's not feeling well" trick again.

"I'll call you," he says.

I hope not.

A few days after that, I meet a guy named Tom to go for a walk (my idea) along the Bay through Crissy Field. The sun is out even though it is a little breezy, and the Golden Gate Bridge is doing its daily striptease, shedding its cloak of fog.

I find Tom easily. He told me he would be standing outside the St. Francis Yacht Club. He also told me he's in retail, and I imagine he's some bigwig at Saks or Neiman's, a world I know a lot about.

He's on time and pleasant-enough looking—tall and slim with short blond hair and brown eyes. He is wearing a T-shirt imprinted with the Gucci crest, neatly pressed lavender pants with razor-edge creases, and what look like real Gucci loafers. (To go on a walk?) But he smiles nicely and shakes my hand politely.

"I love your highlights!" is the first thing he says. (I should have had a clue when I saw every sentence in his e-mails ended with an exclamation point.)

"Oh, thanks. I have a really good colorist."

"Will you give me his or her name?" Tom says. "I haven't been able to find a good one."

I digest this as we start walking toward Fort Point under the bridge. "So you said in your e-mails that you are in retail."

Tom looks a bit puzzled. "Yes. I work at Gucci."

Gee, I think, aren't most men in sales at fashion stores…well…gay?

"I used to write fashion for the *Chronicle*," I said.

"You go, sister! Really?" Tom says, smoothing down his hair against the wind.

"Yes, but I quit work when I had my first child."

"When was that?"

"Amanda's fourteen now, so about fourteen years ago, I guess."

"I only just moved here," Tom said. "A year ago. Tell me about your job."

"Well, it was a long time ago," I say. "Anyway, it was fun. Hard work, but fun."

"Who did you meet?"

"Everyone."

And then we talk fashion for the next half hour, dissecting trends and their meanings and comparing notes and gossip on designers. It's all very pleasant and nice, but it doesn't feel like a date.

"So you're divorced, are you?" he says.

"In the middle of."

"I don't understand why people get divorced."

"Have you ever been married?" I ask him.

"No."

"That's why you don't understand why people divorce."

He is talking now, but I don't hear. I am thinking maybe I should go north, to Vancouver, or south, to Mexico, and take some of their men.

"Do you want to go get something to eat?" Tom asks as we return to the marina.

"That's a great idea, but my kids get off from school early today, and I have to do the whole homework thing and then make dinner. I'll call you."

I don't.

When I get home, there are several e-mails from potential suitors. I nearly hit delete, but as Mother always says, live in hope, die in despair.

The first e-mail is from a guy whose handle is "Me'n'you." He writes that he's an overnight stocker at the Marina Safeway and offers the woman of his dreams great deals on durable goods.

The second is from a guy who says I sound like his soul mate, a little more promising. But the note ends there.

As I keep opening the responses, I expect, I hope, I pray I will find just one normal, nice, genuine someone interested in romance. One e-mail reads, "Hi, where are you from?" (That's in the original profile, isn't it?)

One photo catches my interest. I open the response up and see a picture of Andy Garcia. Good thing I know what Andy Garcia looks like. I might have actually corresponded with this nutcase.

Another e-mail asks, "How your day is going?"

The next eleven e-mails have "Hi" as their subject line, a real grabber, don't you think? I hit the delete button on all eleven. Then there are five e-mails from the same person. Whoa, stalker land. I e-mail him to stop e-mailing me. He e-mails back, saying his brother, recently released from a mental institution, got a hold of his computer and had e-mailed everyone. Creepy. Of course, there are creeps all over; they just shine brighter on dating sites.

By this time, I have a headache.

Whoever invented Internet dating should be shot at dawn. Why wait until dawn, actually?

Chapter 35

Many women long for what eludes them, and like not what is offered them.
—Ovid

THE BLASPHEMY BOX

You think you know about relationships, having been in one successfully—or so you thought—for many years. But after the separation, all of a sudden you find you're as stupid as you once were and making the same mistakes you made at twenty. I guess you revert back to the time when you dated regularly.

Marriage makes you feel smug, as if you've finally figured out this whole romance/mating conundrum and how good you are it. You relax a bit. You don't try as hard, or learn as much as you once did. You have a husband, don't you? It's not like you're going to have to go to some cheesy nightclub so you can find someone just to talk to, now is it? Now that you feel safe and secure, you can be yourself, and there's someone nearby who pretty much has to put up with you and your flaws or insecurities. Someone to talk to, someone to eat with, someone to do most everything with.

So when you find yourself suddenly single, you tell yourself not to worry too much, that you're now a more mature, wiser person who can successfully navigate relationships and all that they entail with aplomb and certainty. That you can recognize more easily what is good and what isn't. And then you realize you're completely delusional and go to a meeting of your therapy group.

The kids were with Steven on Saturday, and I had read my book and worked on my novel and played Spider Solitaire for so long I had a headache and my wrist hurt. So, when Mike rang me up and asked me out, I said yes.

He picks me up around three in the afternoon in his silver Honda. I am wearing a brown sheath dress from Ann Taylor and ballet flats and look pretty good, if I say so myself.

"Is there anything in particular you want to do?" Mike asks. I'm a little surprised to find he has no plan.

"Wherever you like is fine," I say. "Surprise me."

He looks at me and smiles. "OK," he says, "but don't say I didn't warn you." He is maneuvering up and down San Francisco's perilous hills. It's San Francisco's Indian summer. The sun is out, the entire city is bathed in a warm glow, and I feel wonderful. The last time someone asked me out was when Reagan was president.

Eventually we pull into the lot behind the De Young Museum. Mike gets out and opens the door for me.

"I thought you might like to see the Impressionist exhibit."

I am pleased and excited. "I've been reading about it. It sounds wonderful."

The paintings are glorious: Van Gogh, Gauguin, Cézanne, Monet, Renoir, and Degas. It takes me back decades, when Suzy and I enjoyed a similar exhibition at the Jeu de Paume in Paris as students, the one week in Paris there wasn't a strike. Steven never took me an art exhibit. He didn't like art all that much. I feel wistful and a little sad. After we have walked through the entire exhibit, Mike takes me for jasmine tea at the Museum Café, a large, light-filled conservatory-type place with windows on three sides. We sit and sip our tea and munch on a fresh fruit plate.

"What a pity it is that all these hugely interesting and talented people are dead," I say. "How I wish death were not so irrevocable."

"It wouldn't be death if it wasn't," he says with a smile.

"How true." I find I am more relaxed than I thought I would be.

He smiles. "By the way, you look great. I love your new highlights, and that dress really suits you."

"You noticed my highlights?" Steven never noticed my highlights. If he did, he never mentioned it.

"I notice everything about you, Maddy."

My face flushed, I look down at my empty cup. He takes up the small porcelain teapot and fills it.

"What shall we do now?"

All of a sudden, everything seems too much for me. I'm no longer comfortable. I have to go. Now. "Actually, it's probably time for me to get home. Steven's meant to drops the kids back before dinner."

"Really?" Mike says. "On a Saturday? It's still so early. I thought we could grab a bite and watch the sunset over Baker Beach. It's gorgeous. Maybe next time."

Mike really is a sweet man.

"Yes. I'd like that."

"I'll get the check."

Next time. Now that sounded nice.

Chapter 36

Prosperity makes friends, adversity tries them.
—Publilius Syrus

THE BLASPHEMY BOX

In a divorce, along with your husband, you sometimes lose friends. People often don't know how to navigate the awkward waters of split-updum, and frankly, your divorce makes them question their own marriages. Quel horreur! Marrieds always wince at the word "divorce." They think it's the epitome of failure—and may even be catching. They don't want the concept too near to home for fear it will infect their house and their spouse. (One woman I told looked at me as if I had forgotten to shave my legs.) And it's always a huge shock to discover this—to confront what you would normally never confront: friends who make choices—and not in your favor. And based on things other than friendship.

A divorce judgment can divide assets like the house, the cars, the furniture, the Beatles collection: he gets the dog, you get the budgerigar; he gets the pressure washer, you get the clothes washer; he gets the smoked salmon, you get the air miles. It can divide the kids' time spent with each parent: you have them every other week, he has them every other week. It can even iron out who'll get the IRA and who'll be able to sell on eBay the laminated copy of the front page of the New York Times the morning after Obama was elected. (One couple, I read online, who jointly owned a prize stallion, fought over horse semen. I kid you not.) You might not love the ruling, but that is what the law allows for.

But no law on any books allows for any judge to determine which of your friends you'll get and which he'll get.

Today I go to a meeting of a charity I volunteer for. It awards school and college scholarships in the arts to underprivileged kids. I've been involved in it for many years, because I truly believe in it. I'm not overly enthused about the meeting or the lunch. I'm still not in the mood for all the sympathetic looks and people huddled in the corner talking about me, people I know but don't see too often.

As a result of working on behalf of this charity, I have become friendly with some of the women who also volunteer, but the only one I know well is Dana, the woman who's engaged to Steven's friend Mark. I stopped hearing from her after Steven left.

I pick out something to wear from the designer section of my closet, because you'd better be in a well-known label in front of *this* bunch of cut-glass women. And carrying the right bag and wearing the latest heel—strappy platforms this season; Louis and kitten, so last year. I hope my simple Michael Kors crepe sheath, in a color the saleswoman told me is called Melon of Troy, and Coach bag will pass muster. When I get there, I see they will not. It's like a fashion show, with everything once on the skinny models now on the backs of the skinny audience. The women look me up and down and smile indulgently, as if losing weight is not enough, only losing *more* weight would be, and when they start mentioning Steven and the divorce and how sorry they are, I nearly throw an orchid at them. I excuse myself and go to get some Perrier.

I guess losing twenty-five pounds doesn't make much difference when you've been 160, at least not to these ladies. When I come back, the women are parading into the dining room in a flutter of chatter and silk. The place grows larger with noise as everyone mills around looking for their tables. I don't see Dana anywhere, which is strange.

I find my seat next to Anne, the wife of a vice president at Bank of America who's in the middle of telling our table that Demi and Johnny Levitan bought the Horowitzes' house for $13,000,000.

"You're kidding, right?" I say.

Anne frowns. "No, I'm not."

"What street is that house on again?" a woman called Marci asks.

"Washington," Anne says. "And they're gutting it to make room for Johnny's art collection."

"Do you know if they have a view?" Marci says.

My mouth falls open. I know a few super-rich people, but I am always a bit shocked when I find out how rich they really are. Or how rich they really *think* they are. One thing I have always respected Steven for was his donations to charities that I felt needed supporting. He never once argued with me on that point, which is amazing, actually, considering how he's behaving now. Maybe because donations are tax deductible, and ex-wives aren't?

My tablemates talk on, but I sit there silently, not hearing their chatter, their laughter. I know most will go home to husbands and I won't, and I suddenly feel lost and alone.

We eat our salads, and our chairwoman rises to give a nice approbation of our efforts and camaraderie. Polite applause follows. I excuse myself and head for the ladies' room. When I walk in, Sandy Warren is there, being consoled by a woman I don't know. She's crying as usual, probably over her husband's extramarital activities, and who can blame her. But I must say, Sandy seems to breed drama wherever she goes. After fixing her makeup, she and her friend leave.

Just as I've gotten into a stall and shut the door, I hear two other women come in. Peering through an opening in the door, I recognize them as Emma and Samantha, women I know through working on charity events. They don't know I am there, and they are talking about my friend Dana's wedding.

"When's Dana getting married again?" Emma says.

"Late November," Samantha says.

They babble on about what sounds like a very posh affair.

Why didn't I know this? I haven't heard anything about a specific wedding date, but these women, apparently, have and have received invitations. I have not. I can't believe Dana would not invite me to her wedding.

I open the stall door and walk over to the sink. As soon as they see me, the two women stop talking and look at me as if I'd just told them their husbands are cross-dressers.

"Oh," Emma stammers. "Hi, Maddy."

"Hi, Maddy," says Samantha. "Didn't know you were coming today."

I smile. "Wouldn't miss it for the world."

"How are the little ones?" Samantha asks.

"Fine. Busy. How about yours?"

"Same. You know."

Emma chimes in as well.

My eyes are stinging, so head down, I busy myself washing and drying my hands and then pick up my purse to leave.

"Love your necklace, Maddy," Emma says. "You look good."

"Thanks, Emma; you too."

The rest of the lunch is a bit of a blur. I am so hurt and embarrassed. Probably everyone at this luncheon knows about the wedding except me.

It's about dinner time when the phone rings. It's Dana. Someone at the luncheon must have tipped her off.

"How are you? I'm so sorry I haven't called, I've been so busy."

"Yes, I heard, planning your wedding. I overheard about it at the luncheon today."

There is a long silence. "Yes, well, you understand. Mark and Steven are college buddies. It's a bit awkward."

"I thought we were friends, Dana. I was surprised you didn't tell me sooner."

Another long silence. "It would just be too complicated, Maddy. What with the separation and Gabriela and all. I'm sorry. I should have called."

"Well, I'm sorry too, Dana. But I wish you all the best. I know you and Mark will be very happy together." And I hang up.

I go on my blog where one person has left a comment.

When I got a divorce, a lot of friends chose to remain close to my ex. Losing them was as hard as losing my husband, which surprised me. One dinner at an Italian restaurant with neighborhood friends, I remember, I was put opposite a woman I had known for years. She had been to dinner at my house numerous times, and when she saw me sitting across from her, she got up and moved. You have to tell yourself that you did nothing to deserve this treatment and go forward.

Posted by RonyaD

Chapter 37

The greatest happiness of life is the conviction that we are loved.
—Victor Hugo

THE BLASPHEMY BOX

When you're suddenly made redundant in the marriage arena, you stop feeling normal. Everything feels different: how you pick up just one latte from Starbucks on a Saturday morning, instead of two; how the silence of the house echoes all around you. You feel like a part of you has gone missing, that you are living a life manqué somehow. Intellectually, you know that things will settle down to the new normal, and you'll get on with your life, but that always takes time. Developing interests and relationships that weren't part of your married life helps. A lot.

In response to my "losing friends in a divorce" post the other day, a reader with the tag "AllyBoop" wrote to say that the great about thing about losing friends is that it gives you time to make new ones. And those new friends will make you feel, well, new again. Here's her experience: when she was going through her divorce, her husband refused to move out of the house, so they lived for two years in separate bedrooms and tried to avoid each other as much as possible while home.

One day, AllyBoop was giving a little dinner party for a few of her work friends, and when she arrived home at five and walked into the house, she noticed that all her dining chairs were gone. Her husband came home then, and she asked him where the chairs were. He said in his locked room, and that's where they were going to stay; he bought them. Trying to control her rage, AllyBoop went into the kitchen to start preparing dinner and found that all her silverware was gone. When she banged on the door of her husband's room, she learned that the same silverware was in his room, too. This time she went out of the front door and screamed several times very loudly on the sidewalk. The lawyer across the street came running over to see who was being murdered.

AllyBoop told him what had happened, and he carried his own six Louis Seize-style dining chairs over to her house. When she took him an orchid the next day to thank him, they sat and chatted for an hour. A week later, he invited her over to meet his sister, Jane, a divorcée, and his brother, Alan, also divorced. The lawyer asked her to go to dinner with them. She did, and Jane became the best friend she ever had. And so did Alan, whom AllyBoop married.

Anyway, her point, she said, was that I will feel normal again, and I will be happy again. I will? When exactly will I feel normal and happy again? By the time the latest version of Anna Karenina *comes out? When the firemen down at the local firehouse have their next pancake breakfast? By the time Amanda is married and screaming in her hospital room for an epidural or else?*

The divorce progresses slowly. Steven stalls and delays as much as possible. He certainly doesn't want any quick judgments that will cost him any more money than he has to pay. I live in limbo.

Mike Dutton rings and invites me out for lunch. It is gratifying to hear his calm, assured voice expressing interest in spending time with me, a real balm to my poor, bruised ego. I tell him I have the kids and can't go but am free the next day.

"I loved your shopping piece," he says.

"I can't believe you read that. It was…girlie."

"Well," he says, laughing, "where to find silk ribbon from Paris is not the number-one goal in my life, but I enjoy your writing."

"Thank you, kind sir."

"And I just loved that you included Lefty's San Francisco, the store with all that stuff for the left-handed person," he continues. "Even though it's down at the Embarcadero and not chic. I adore that place. I'm left-handed myself."

"The most intelligent people are, you know," I say, laughing. "I've been searching for a notepad that opens backward for a thousand years."

Mike picks me up, and we glide over the Golden Gate Bridge, which hangs there right in front of us like some huge valance, and over into Marin. Mount Tam stands inviolate ahead of us, and everything looks clean and fresh and feels suburban.

"I thought we'd go do a little wine tasting before lunch," he offers.

Not my favorite thing. Steven was such a wine snob I grew to hate all the pretension at tastings.

"Isn't there anything else to do in wine country?" I ask him. "The landscape is so lovely up here."

"There's a ten-mile hike up Mount Helena that has terrific views, or biking up Howell Mountain."

Panic rises in my throat.

"Given the alternatives, wine tasting is fine," I say, keeping my voice light.

Mike smiles. "Seriously, we could skip it and just fine some nice little place for lunch if you like."

"Thanks, but it is wine country after all, so why not sample a bit? Do you know a lot about wine?"

"A little." And then he regales me with all kinds of interesting information on grapes and vineyards and acetaldehyde and bouquet and demi-sec and carbonic maceration.

"I thought you said you only know a little. You're a walking encyclopedia."

"I took a few courses up at the Culinary Institute," he says. "I love to learn new things."

I smile inside. I feel the same way. That's why I have always loved journalism: you have to get up to speed on a new subject for every article and have it in by five.

We stop at a couple of pretty wineries. We meet all kinds of people, some more intent on drinking instead of tasting. At one place, a rather unkempt sort of man, who has drunk so much he has knocked over the "We're Open" sign, winds up sitting on the floor, looking bewildered. At another, a tall woman with a bad bleach job is so drunk she puts the tip in the jar used for spitting out wine after tasting.

It's more amusing than I remember from the stuffy, formal tastings I attended with Steven.

"Why don't I show you my favorite winery?" Mike offers when we're back in the car.

When we arrive, I see an Italianate building sitting amid acres of gorgeous gardens that make my heart want to sing. We wander alongside the flowerbeds, still bursting with summer color and nectar for honeybees to do their jobs, and then make our way into the tasting room. Greeting us is an impressive curving teak and black granite tasting bar set against large, arched windows overlooking the vineyard and surrounding mountains. We are the only ones in the entire place.

Just then, a slight, fair man in his late fifties appears. He is wearing a blue shirt and bow tie, puzzling for someone in casual viticulture. He announces himself as the manager. After we nod hello, he recognizes Mike. "Ah, Michael, how lovely to see you again. How are you?"

"Fine, just fine, Jim. How are you?"

"Wonderful. Appreciate so much your help on that project."

"No problem," Mike says. "This is a friend of mine, Maddy."

Jim turns and looks at me quizzically.

"Nice to meet you. Do you know much about our wine?"

"Not too much," I say.

The man smiles sweetly. "No problem. I am here to help."

We spend an hour, tasting and chatting, and it's all extremely interesting and pleasant. I had no idea wine tasting could be so relaxing and fun.

Finally, Mike gets up from his stool and turns to the vintner. "Thanks, Jim, as always. I will take a case of my usual."

"My pleasure. Nice to meet you, Maddy."

"What a delightful man," I say as we walk to the car.

"Yes, and his wine is superb," Mike says, handing me one of the bottles from the case. "Enjoy this as a memento."

I am touched. "Thank you. I will."

We drive to La Campagna, a pretty little place with a stone patio overlooking the surrounding vineyard. We sit at a long, pitted wooden refectory table shrouded by whispery-looking trees and gorge on a wonderful dish of little rice balls in a tangy tomato meat sauce. I refuse to follow my diet and even eat some of the restaurant's crunchy peasant bread.

"What project did you help Jim with?" I ask him.

"Oh, nothing major—he just wanted some written materials done, and I did them."

"That's very kind of you."

Mike ignores my comment and says, "So, are you having a good time?"

"Yes," I say. And I am. I feel almost normal for the first time in a long time. Like that thing nagging at me in the back of my head—that thing that keeps telling me I'm a dumped housewife of fifty with a miserable future—is taking a nap, at least for now.

On the drive back, we sit without talking, listening to the Sinatra channel, which has more singers than just Sinatra singing the old standards I love. I sing along to "P.S. I Love You," and then both of us sing along to "A Nightingale Sang in Berkeley Square." I realize it's nice to be with someone who likes to sing along to the radio. Steven would just turn it off.

Chapter 38

Like the measles, love is most dangerous when it comes late in life.
—Lord Byron

THE BLASPHEMY BOX

Once in a while in the fog of divorce, things do become clear, if only temporarily. The brain works as it should, and a clarity is sparked, even though you fight it. You realize your choices so far have been rather uninformed. And you promise to do better.

And then, of course, you don't.

You know a potential relationship currently staring you in the face is pretty good, but you're so mixed up emotionally, so discombobulated and terrified by misery, so damn sure you are unlovable, you're just too afraid to entertain it. You just resist it.

Mike calls. He hasn't called in a week, and I am happy to hear from him. Every time I think of him, something tightens in my chest and a little frisson of thrill and then unadulterated fear rises up in me. Despite all the months that have passed and my first victory in court, I'm still so unsure of myself. I'm so unsure of everything. And the whole dating thing feels so strange, even with a wonderful man like Mike.

We chat desultorily and then, without even meaning to, I ask him over to dinner. I can't believe I'm doing something that intimate.

"That sounds great," he says. "Tonight?"

"Oh, I'd love that," I say. "But I have the kids."

Silence.

"Tomorrow?"

"Yes, tomorrow is fine."

"OK, what shall I bring?"

"Just yourself. Shall we say 6:00?"

He arrives with tulips—somehow he knows they're my favorite flower—and an Italian pinot grigio. The first thing he says when he walks into the family room is "You look great."

I smile. I still am not used to someone saying that.

"Shall I open this wine, or do you want a cocktail?" I ask him.

"The wine is fine."

While I'm in the kitchen, I hear him call from the living room, "You have books on so many different subjects."

"Yes," I answer, joining him. "My husband called me the Pac Man of books, because I just devour them. He also always said they cluttered the house, but I love to have them around."

"Me too," he says. "I can't live without them. I got a Kindle and it's fine, but I just like the feeling of paper in my hands."

"I know what you mean." I uncork the wine, pour it into a glass, and hand it to him.

"What an incredible view you have here," he says, wandering toward the window. This is the first time he has been inside my home, and I can tell he is nervous. So am I. The setting is so intimate, so personal.

"Yes," I say, "it really is one of the best ones I've seen. I could watch the water and the skyline for hours."

"How do you get any work done?" he says.

"It's not easy, that's for sure."

"I love your blog, by the way," he says. "It's so smart and…insightful."

"It is?" I say, a little embarrassed, given the nature of the posts.

"Of course it is. It's just like you are."

"Thanks. I'm just going to get going on the dinner, but we can chat while I work."

"What are we having?"

"Something healthy. Do you like salmon?"

"Love it. Can I help?"

"No need, but thanks for offering."

Mike is still drinking in the view while working his way through my bookshelves.

"See anything of interest?"

"Quite a few, actually. I envy that you have the time to read so much."

"It's my great passion."

I prepare the simple meal of salmon and veggies with brown rice. When it's ready, Mike joins me at the small kitchen eat-in nook.

"This is the best salmon I've ever had," Mike says, tucking into the food with gusto. "This pesto butter is unbelievable. How did you come up with it?"

I realize I feel happy at that moment, happy to have a man around to cook for, who loves what I've made. "I just have always loved pesto, and even though people always use dill with salmon, I thought basil would work as well."

"Well, it does. It's delicious."

"So glad you like it."

There's silence then, but not an awkward kind of silence, a more companionable kind of silence—the sort you have with someone you don't have to worry about or impress or flatter or please. With someone you feel comfortable.

When we have finished our meal, Mike stands up to clear the plates, but I try to wave him away. "I'll do it; you're a guest." Steven barely cleared the dinner plates once in twenty years of marriage.

"Guests can help load the dishwasher. Not a problem."

After he's done, I bring a crystal bowl of blueberries and raspberries to the table along with some vanilla low-fat frozen yogurt and two matching bowls.

"Voilà," I say and serve us both.

"This is all delicious," Mike says. "And there's no guilt."

"Exactly," I say.

When we get up from the table, I change the music to Frank Sinatra. "Would you like some tea or cappuccino? Or a dessert wine?"

"A cappuccino sounds great, if you have decaf coffee, that is."

"I do, and I think I'll have one too."

As the cappuccino machine hisses and steams, Mike sits down at the kitchen counter watching me. "You really are a woman of many talents," he says.

"I am?"

"Of course you are. Look at you, a journalist, aspiring novelist, a wonderful mother, a great cook. All that and gorgeous to boot."

I flush bright red and smile. "I'll have to serve that pinot more often."

We both laugh.

We take our coffee to the living room just as the sun is setting, bathing the room with a warm glow.

"Well, that was a real treat," Mike says after draining his cup. "Feel like playing a game?"

"That depends on the game."

"You have to close your eyes."

"It's not anything kinky, is it?"

Mike chuckles. "Not at all. Each of us has to take a turn going up to the bookshelves, pick out a book, and describe what we were doing when we first read it."

"OK," I say happily. "You first."

Mike closes his eyes and stretches his hand out to me to lead him to the bookshelves, which line the back wall. He spends a long time running his hands up and down all the books. He settles on one and pulls it out.

"*The Bridges of Madison County.*" He frowns briefly. "I certainly remember what I was doing when I first read this," he says, leafing through it.

The house is completely silent, and I sit down on the sofa opposite him.

"I was going on my annual fly fishing trip with my colleague, Doug, and when we got to the motel, I opened my overnight bag, and for some reason this was in it," he says.

"When was this?" I ask.

"Three years ago."

"Go on."

Mike runs his hand across his head. "We go fly fishing for trout on the Fall River, which starts near Mount Shasta and flows southeast through the Fall River Valley to and through the town of Fall River Mills. Only about twenty-five hundred people live there."

"Sounds remote."

"It's special, because it's one of the few rivers that have natural rainbow trout. Anyway, we got there kind of late, we had lingered over lunch, and when we arrived, there was a light rain. We met up with our local guide, Bob, who's really knowledgeable about fly fishing and the characteristics of each of the local rivers and streams, and then we checked in to our usual fishing lodge, which is very Spartan but does have a restaurant, which is useful."

Mike is not looking at me now. He is gazing ahead to the Bay.

"Go on."

"Well, the rain kept coming overnight, but we got up early on the Saturday morning to start fishing. It was just a bust. Driving rain all morning. Finally, Bob said it just wasn't worth carrying on, so we went back to the fishing lodge and had showers and lunch. Doug and I decided to spend the night and see if we could get a break Sunday morning. There was no television or anything in the rooms, so that afternoon and evening we just amused ourselves with reading. The only thing I had was this book. I had expected it to be so soppy and plebian, the worst kind of supermarket trash, but the more I read, the more I was drawn in. I read the whole thing that night and found the denouement really quite affecting. I kept wanting her to go with him. I kept thinking, the kids are in their teens, it's OK for you to be happy, so just go."

"So did the weather clear the next day?" I say.

"No, it stormed all night, so we decided just to wrap it up and got up at five and started driving home. I had a lot of work to do and so did he, and off we went."

Mike stops talking and takes a deep breath.

"So?" I say.

"Well, I drove fast and we got home in five hours. It was about 10:30 when we reached the city. I dropped Doug off and went home. Jenny was off on a sleepover with a friend. As soon as I got into the house, I called Liz's name."

Mike pauses. Then, he says, "When she didn't answer, I called out again, and I walked through the kitchen toward our bedroom. I imagined she was still sleeping. But when I got there..." He stops.

"When you got there, what?"

"There she was, wrapped in a sheet, and a man I had never seen before was pulling on his clothes."

"Oh my God," I say. "How dreadful."

"It was dreadful. And it was more the shock than anything else. I just didn't expect it. I truly didn't."

Mike is silent then, his head lowered, and I can tell he is fighting the awful knowledge even now.

"What did she say? What did you say?"

"Nothing. She said nothing. I said nothing. I just left. I walked out of the house and went to my brother's place. A couple of days later, I went and rented an apartment, and when she was at work, I packed up all my stuff and moved out and told Jenny."

"Liz never called you or tried to?"

"No. She got herself a divorce lawyer and made things as difficult as she could."

"But why? You were the injured party, not her."

"That's not what she said. She's a lawyer. What do you expect?"

"Do you talk now?"

"Very little. Mostly by e-mail and only about Jenny."

"Did you ever find out who the guy was?"

"Yes, another lawyer from her firm. He dumped her six months later."

"Karma."

"Yes. But the strangest part of the story is that I think she planted this book in my bag, a message of some sort. I'll never know for sure."

"I'm so sorry, Mike."

"Well, as miserable as it was, I've come to realize that betrayal takes many forms, and cheating is only one of them." He gets up and returns the book to the shelf. "Your turn."

I close my eyes and step gingerly to the shelves. It takes me forever to choose a book. I'm afraid the book I choose will have a story around it I do not want to tell. I end up taking one with a smooth spine, not too big, just big enough for a nice, solid story.

It's *The Greengage Summer*, a story of young love and deceit.

We sit back down on the couches.

"Well? What's the story around your first reading of this book?" Mike asks.

"It was the summer holidays, and my best friend Suzy and I were fourteen," I begin. "Our parents took us to the South of France—not to the Riviera, of course, where we wanted to sunbathe topless across from the Carlton Hotel to attract boys with names like Jean-Jacques and Loic—but to Champagne country near all those boring old battlefields.

"Julia, one of our classmates, said, 'Oh, if you're going there, you just have to read that book *The Greengage Summer*.' She said it took place there and was a bit racy.

"Well, of course we wanted it immediately, but we were a bit embarrassed to get it from the library. So Suzy got Julia to take it out for us. We took turns reading it in the days leading up to the trip. I remember we loved it from that very first sentence."

I open up the book and read the first sentence: "On and off, all that hot French August, we made ourselves ill from eating the greengages...

"After we landed, I remember we drove in a long black car in suffocating heat to the villa our parents had rented, and Suzy immediately flopped down on her bed, next to mine in one of the bedrooms, but I ran outside and saw the river, the Marne, just like in the book. And I flew down the fresh green lawn and put my feet in cool, soft water.

"Anyway, we went to see the battlefields and vineyards in the Marne region and all those old rare timber-framed churches around Troyes, like Bailly-le-Franc. Suzy hated it. She kept saying, 'We've got enough old churches in England to look at, where are the boys?' Everywhere we went that summer, we looked for romance and intrigue just like in the novel and couldn't find it anywhere except back at the villa one day, when Suzy and I came back early from town because of the heat, and we walked into the stone house covered in fuchsia bougainvillea, and saw Suzy's father and one of the femmes de ménage in all their white nakedness."

Mike's eyes are fixed on mine.

"Suzy screamed bloody murder, and I said, 'What the bloody hell do you think *you two* are doing?,' and they jumped up, trying desperately to cover those limp, blue-veined bodies. The next day, we were packed and back on the plane to London, our vacation cut short. The excuse was a sudden family calamity, but we knew the truth. No one ever mentioned it ever again."

It's ten thirty, the fire in the fireplace has died, and Mike is still looking at me, his sandy hair falling into his eyes. He's been looking at me most of the evening, I remember.

"Quite a story. I'm sorry you were so young and had to witness that."

I nod. "It was a shock."

"Too bad. Betrayal is the only thing truth that sticks."

"Shaw?"

"Arthur Miller." Mikes stands. "I suppose I should go. It's late."

He takes his time picking up his jacket, straightening his shirt collar, and then asks for a glass of water. I know he's waiting, wondering, wishing I would say, "Stay, don't go, stay." But I don't, I can't, and when he's sure I won't, he takes my hands in his.

"Thanks for a wonderful evening. I hope it didn't get a bit too heavy there toward the end. That game is usually more whimsical."

I smile and squeeze his hands. "I had a wonderful time."

In an instant, he's gone. And I regret it.

Chapter 39

It's so easy to fall in love but hard to find someone who will catch you.
—Anonymous

THE BLASPHEMY BOX

You know how everyone always says the pain of heartbreak abates over time and soon you wonder why you ever loved the bastard? They're right. It's not that I don't feel sad and I don't have regrets, but I'm beginning not to imagine His Majesty in my life anymore. I still see him in my mind, of course, but he's no longer standing next to me by the Christmas tree. I find I don't even hate him anymore, which feels odd, by the way. Hating him gave me something to do, and now I'm wondering if I should take up knitting again to fill the time. I don't feel the need to respond to his calls or e-mails in three seconds flat or hope we will get back together. It's such a relief.

Steven calls and asks if he can come over. Even though I no longer want him, I still hope he's back to wanting me. That would feel good. To have him come on bended knee to recapture and repair my broken heart, all for the inordinate pleasure of saying forget it.

The kids are upstairs, meant to be reading, but last I looked, Amanda was tapping away on her iPhone, and the boys were listening to music on their iPods. Mike is meant to be picking me up later to go out, and Gracie the babysitter should be here any moment. I'm not sure I want Steven and Mike to meet, so I'm hoping Steven won't stay too long.

I dress with care, knowing I must look my very best. A pair of black stretch boot-cut pants with a white ruffled blouse makes me look nice and trim. But he arrives still in his business suit, looking tired.

"Can I have a Scotch?"

I want to say, "Get it yourself, you know where everything is." But I don't. I pour him a Scotch.

"Thanks," he says, collapsing onto the sofa. He looks at me quizzically. "You look good, Maddy."

"Thanks. You look tired."

"I know. I'm just beat. Work has just been all-out hectic, I've been having to entertain clients every night this whole week, and parenting the kids alone…I never knew how much energy they had."

"They are a handful."

Steven nods. "And it's not easy keeping up with someone in their twenties."

Music to my ears, but I say nothing.

"Nothing to say, Maddy?" Steven is looking at me questioningly.

"What is there to say?"

"I thought you'd be happy to hear that things aren't all flowers and roses on my end."

"Why should I be happy to hear that? You are the father of my children. I wish you well." And I can't believe I mean it. But I do.

Steven looks surprised. I sit down on the chair opposite him, bewildered again that my marriage has reached a point where I feel so distant toward a man who, until a few months ago, I had seen every day for more than twenty years.

"Really? Don't you see me roasting on some spit somewhere?"

"Sometimes."

Steven chuckles. "Are you…are you seeing anyone?" he says with a slight hesitation in his voice.

I ignore his question. "Why don't you tell me what you want to talk about?"

Steven downs his Scotch. "I know I've asked you this, but before we go for the mandatory settlement conference in a couple of weeks, I'm wondering if you would reconsider the house situation."

I sigh. "This is the only home I've ever known in the States. This is the only home the children have ever known. I can't reconsider."

I wait for him to erupt. But he doesn't.

"Life never turns out the way you think it will, does it?" he muses, running his finger around the rim of his glass.

"I don't know, Steven. Life is life. We all make our choices. Sometimes with no idea of how they will pan out, but then we're stuck with them. It is what it is."

"And I suppose you think my choices are all wrong, that I'm to blame entirely for this divorce."

"Absolutely."

He laughs.

How many times, I think to myself, have we sat in this position—he on the sofa, me in the tufted armchair across from it—talking, interacting, living? And how at the beginning of this whole nightmare, I had hoped and prayed that it could happen again, and now that it is, it just feels strange, not right, as if he shouldn't be there, as if the house no longer has a place for him.

"Well, I guess I should go. I'll come get the kids in the morning."

He heaves himself off the sofa and walks to the foyer to pick up his car keys. I go over to the kitchen stool and retrieve his jacket for him. I wait for him to pull it on so I can help him straighten the collar on his shirt like I always have, but then I stop mid-move, remembering. This is not my life anymore. He is not my life anymore.

"OK, well, drive safely. See you at the next handover."

He turns, as if to say something, but stops himself. He waves and is gone.

I feel numb.

As soon as he leaves, Gracie arrives. This time her hair is dyed Crayola blue. I guess she's channeling Katy Perry. I give her my instructions and put my earrings on and at that moment, the doorbell rings and Mike is bounding up my stairs much like my kids do.

We're going to a reading and book signing of someone he knows at a small bookstore in Marin.

We glide along Lombard, onto Doyle Drive, and over the Golden Gate Bridge, fogged in from all sides so only the tips of its towers are showing.

"How was your day?" he asks with a warm smile.

"Just fine," I say. "My blog is going well, and I've made all kinds of nice cyber friends, though of course I have no real idea who they are. I've got a new assignment on the vital issue of pet grooming, so I'm OK." Of course, I don't tell him about my meeting with Steven. What's to tell anyway?

Mike laughs. "I'm glad your writing is going so well."

We drive up 101 and take the Corte Madera exit. Soon we're in the bookstore parking lot, which is studded with those annoying bumps that force you to slow down.

"Why do they put all these sleeping policemen in a small parking lot like this?" I ask Mike.

"What the heck is a sleeping policeman?"

"You know, those things on the ground you have to drive over that ruin your alignment."

Mike bursts into laughter. "You mean speed bumps?"

"Yes, that's right, but in England we call them sleeping policemen."

"I think I like your term better," he says and pulls into a parking bay. "I always learn something from you."

I can feel myself blushing. "Thanks."

Mike gets out of the car, goes around to my side, and opens my door. I ask myself when was the last time that a man opened a car door for me, and I quickly calculate the answer—never. Mike takes my hand and does not release it until we are at the front door of the store.

A line has already formed, but when the bookstore owner sees Mike, we get in straight away, which surprises me a bit. We're led to two seats in the front row of the area where the reading is going to take place. Mike hands me a copy of the book, which I pretend to read. I didn't bring my glasses with me. No need to telegraph your age to all and sundry, now is there?

It takes more than half an hour to get everyone seated and while we are waiting, a parade of fresh-faced young women in tight jeans and blousy tops keep approaching Mike and saying, "Thank you" and "I appreciate it" and "You'd be proud of me, I'm still working on my novel." One girl with beautiful long blonde hair sways on her hips while talking to him, her eyes fixed on his, her hand lightly touching his arm.

Mike smiles and banters with her and all of his fans and then turns immediately back to me.

As soon as he does, a slight woman with unruly hair who can't have been more than twenty-three walks up to the podium carrying a book. She flicks the microphone to make sure it's turned on, and, as if by osmosis, everyone stops talking. You can see the woman is terribly shy but also terribly excited. She is shaking a bit, yet her face is open and her expression beatific.

"Before I start the reading," she says, her voice tremulous, "I would just like to thank my professor Mike Dutton at USF for all the help and guidance and encouragement he has given me over the past few years. He's sitting in the front row right here. I would not be here without him, and I know a slew of other graduates from USF's MFA program who feel the same."

All eyes are trained on Mike. He reluctantly does a faint wave. He is obviously embarrassed, but also pleased, and everyone is clapping and hooting and hollering for him. It opens *my* eyes a bit, I can tell you.

When the cacophony dies down, I whisper, "I thought you said you teach English."

And he whispers, "I do. Creative writing is part of it."

Most professors I've known are pompous like my father, only too willing to brag about their accomplishments. Mike is truly humble. It's so refreshing.

He takes my hand in his. I let it rest there, thinking how good it feels.

After the reading, we stand around and chat for a while with a bunch of people, all paying homage to Mike. He introduces me to everyone, whose names I forget immediately, but I keep smiling and make small talk about writing. I even mention my burgeoning reentry into the world of journalism. It feels good to be with someone who respects me and wants me next to him.

Several young women cluster around him, eyeing me suspiciously, but not for one moment do I see Mike responding to any of them. Finally, he puts his hand on my waist, nods good-bye to everyone in our path, and guides me out of the bookstore.

"I'm so sorry about all that," he says as we walk across the parking lot. "I hate these things, but I feel that I need to support my students' successes. I hope it wasn't too tedious for you."

"No problem at all. I enjoyed it."

He looks at me. "I'm glad. Dinner?"

"I thought you'd never ask."

"Good. Do you like Indian food? There's this great Indian place I know in San Rafael."

"Yes, I love it."

Within ten minutes we are in San Rafael's Canal area, driving into the ugliest and smallest strip mall ever built. It lies along the canal where people can rent slips and live on their boats.

Soon we're seated in a comfortable booth overlooking the less-than-picturesque docks. We order and I sit back, realizing I am happy and having a good time.

The food arrives, and we dig in. "Tell me more about your writing students."

He is wry and witty about his classes, regaling me with stories about the select group of young writers he has seen off to publication, the holy grail for writers. It's a delight to listen.

After dinner, we enjoy some chai. As the smell of cardamom invades us, we sip our tea and talk about a lot of things, particularly about how books were Mike's escape when he was a kid growing up in the South and how he had always wanted to have a book published.

"Have you?"

"I'm happy to say I have, actually."

My expression must show my shock, because Mike laughs. "What?" he says.

"Why didn't you tell me?"

"You didn't ask."

I roll my eyes. "Not only are you a great teacher, but you're also a published author. No wonder your students worship you and are themselves successful."

"Oh," he says. "I just hand out the matches. I don't light the fire."

On the drive home, the sky is blistered with stars, and as we emerge from the Waldo Tunnel, the city glitters in the distance and the lights of the Golden Gate Bridge twinkle. At my house, Mike stops the car, reaches in the back for something, and then gets out to open the car door for me. He hands me a book. "This is one of my novels," he says.

"I happen to have it in the car, because I was going to send it to my niece in Atlanta."

"One of your novels? You mean there is more than one?" I've been going out with a bona fide multi-published author, and I'd not even known it. I've been caught up in myself and paid too little attention to this nice, talented man.

"There are three," he says, smiling. "Let me walk you to your door."

When we are there, he leans into me. Alarm shoots through me, but he kisses only my cheeks. I can smell his cologne. "Sleep tight," he says.

"Thanks. You too."

I climb the stairs to our front door and turn my key in the lock. Tossing the keys on the foyer table, I pay Gracie and see her out of the house, and head immediately for the sunroom where I turn on a lamp, and throw myself onto the sofa. I take up Mike's book and start reading. And keep reading. It's a fictionalized account of the Donner Party, and the writing is so mellifluous, so fluid, and so poignant I wonder how I will ever be that good. It's a real tear-jerker, too. The story is inherently sad, but he writes in such clean and fresh language that it makes you hope that just this once, tragedy won't hit and people won't die.

I look at the clock. It's three o'clock in the morning, and suddenly I'm exhausted. Climbing into bed, I feel lucky for the first time in months. Lucky to start building my own life. Lucky to have met a talented man like Mike.

Chapter 40

We waste time looking for the perfect lover, instead of creating the perfect love.
—Tom Robbins

THE BLASPHEMY BOX

When you're going through a divorce, all of a sudden you're perceived by the newly separated as an expert, even though you're just stumbling along like everybody else who finds him or herself in this less-than-enviable position.

You go along, negotiating the relapses and bumps on the road to recovery, sometimes even thinking things are getting better, which mostly, they are, but only by inches. And you hope and pray every day that you will not feel miserable and terrified forever. But as for giving counsel and advice to others who are getting divorced, well...

The kids are with Anita and I am out with my friend, Candy Mendelsohn, for dinner in the Marina district. She's the woman who ran into Steven and Girl Bambi at the opera and came to tell me. She discovered recently that her husband was cheating, and a month ago, she threw him out. We saunter along Chestnut Street, with all its bright store lights showcasing Majolica platters and Dior sunglasses and copper cooking pots, and arrive at an Italian restaurant Steven and I used to frequent until it started to get popular. I tell her it will probably be very crowded inside, and she says that's fine by her, she needs to be around crowds to distract her from the thoughts of murdering her cheating husband. I have a headache just at the thought of it, but she really wants to go and get some of their great ravioli.

After ordering we get busy talking.

"So where are you in this whole divorce nightmare?" she says.

"Well, we're coming up to the mandatory settlement meeting," I say. "If we can settle the issues then, we won't need to go to trial, but if not..."

"What are the sticking points?"

"Well, money, of course, and he wants me to move out of the house so he can move in with his girlfriend and have the kids with him."

"Yeah, right," Candy says, tossing her gorgeous blonde hair to one side, "that ain't ever going to happen."

"I keep telling myself that, but..."

"Listen, Maddy," Candy says. "No judge is going to make a woman who has lived in her home for twenty years and raised three children there get out so the husband can move in with his hussy."

"I sure hope not," I say. "How are you faring?"

"I just hired an attorney and filed for divorce. It's all so horrible."

I take her hand. "Yes, it's been the worst experience in my life."

"Tell me how it is to be single after twenty years of being married. Are you dating at all?"

I don't know what to tell her. I'm still figuring it out myself.

"It's an eye opener, I can tell you that. Dating just seems so complicated, what with the kids' schedules and all." I don't feel comfortable talking about Mike or my online experiences. Candy's such a gossip, and I don't need the other women I know (and who know Steven) to start judging me.

"It was hard at first, relearning how to be alone, but I'm getting used to it. Mostly, I enjoy not having to feel limited by Steven's whims and wishes. And his mother's."

"Not having to deal with my mother-in-law will be a blessing, certainly," Candy says.

"Well, obviously she does still get the kids, and she still complains, but now I don't have to listen."

Candy downs the rest of her Martini in one gulp. "I'll be right back." She heads for the restroom. I settle back in my booth, and just at that moment, the door of the restaurant opens and in come Steven and Girl Bambi. She has a proprietorial hand on his arm, and they are walking in step, her stomach distended, his head bowed toward her so he can hear what she is saying, just like he used to walk with me. What she is saying must have amused him, because he has that half smile on his face, the one I know so well. I feel this huge weight of sadness descend on me.

I don't know how, but he doesn't see me. He's looking in front of him, toward the hostess station, and not to the left toward our booth.

I cover my face with my napkin as if I'm blowing my nose, and I keep it there until they have passed by and have been seated.

I am shocked at how upset I am. It hurts seeing him so close, so together with the woman he has left me for, assuredly. But I'm more upset at the fact that I've been thinking I'm getting over all this. I'm not in as much pain as I was, and have been feeling sensible and strong and able to handle whatever comes my way. And yet a chance near-encounter at a restaurant can throw me off-kilter in five seconds.

When Candy comes back, she says, "What's wrong?"

"Steven just walked in."

"With his floozy?" she asks.

"Yes."

"Where did they go?"

"To the other side of the booths, by the window. We have to leave."

"No, we don't. We're going to stay here and enjoy our dinner. Why should he spoil our ravioli?"

I look at her. "Damn right," I say. "Why should he?"

And we eat our ravioli with relish, drink far too much red wine, and stagger home, leaning on each other. Steven has not seen us. But when I get into the house and fling myself on my bed, a deep, abiding sadness takes me over again. The incident has unnerved me and makes me doubt I will ever be able to feel really normal again. I'm back in that state of confusion of not knowing where everything is and why, what to move toward, what to dismiss.

Chapter 41

A word to the wise ain't necessary. It's the stupid ones who need the advice.
—Bill Cosby

THE BLASPHEMY BOX

If we learn from our mistakes, why aren't I a genius?

Perhaps the wiser question is, do we learn from our mistakes? *In my case, there are so many, I really don't know. We've all had relationships with or been married to men we know are not good bets. And yet we continue to go down that path when we truly do know better. We even make mistakes knowing they're mistakes.*

Why can't we see what's good for us? Why, when we see it, do we go in the opposite direction?

It must be all the attention Mike has been paying me and the inner and outer confidence that it has given me, but all of a sudden, I am getting small flashes of attention from men again. Very unusual. Very nice.

One such man is a gorgeous Italian at the Starbucks I go to after the gym. He looks to be in his mid-forties and has been smiling quite effusively at me lately. Last week, as usual, when I arrived at Starbucks, he smiled and said, "Buongiorno."

I smiled and said, "Buongiorno," and then hurried to the counter to order my latte.

As I was walking out, he stood and invited me to join him. I smiled but motioned that I had to be going. He graciously conceded, and I left.

I didn't visit the Starbucks for a few days, hoping the friendly man might go elsewhere. (Even though he is someone who could put his shoes under my bed any day.) But it didn't work. This morning, he's sitting at his usual table as I walk in. This time, he greets me before I get to the counter.

"Buongiorno, Signora."

I greet him politely.

"Where have you been? I have missed you."

I blush.

"What are you having?" he says.

"Skim latte, please," I say to the cashier.

"Permit me," he says, handing three dollars over the counter. "Please join me," he adds, gesturing to his usual place.

Not wanting to be rude, I agree and walk over to the table and sit down across from him. "Sono Alessandro," he says, placing my latte on the table.

"Sono Maddy."

"Ah, so you speak Italian?" he says, surprised.

"Un poco."

He smiles broadly at me. He has lustrous dark hair that hangs over his bronzed forehead, and the most amazing languid eyes of peacock green. We sit there for a few minutes by the window, people passing by. His English is good, but accented in a wonderfully attractive way. I've always been a sucker for Italian men. They could be reciting the California Penal Code, but in that accent it sounds like *Romeo and Juliet*. We chat about the gym (which he expresses surprise that I even need), and work (he's a maître d' at some Mediterranean bistro in town). He spots my wedding ring.

"What does your husband do?"

I freeze, not knowing exactly what to say. "He's in finance, but we're not together."

"I cannot believe any man would willingly let you go," he says.

"Things happen."

"Yes, that is so. What do you do?" he says.

"Besides raising three kids, you mean?"

"Yes, besides being a mother."

"I'm a journalist." And then his eyebrows go up, impressed.

"It is a noble profession."

We sit there in silence for a moment. I ask him about his work, and he tells me some very funny story about an older couple who had a fight in the middle of the restaurant. He had to step in and got slapped by the lady for interfering.

"Passion doesn't weaken with age." He looks directly at me. My latte almost done, I stand and thank him again.

"Before you go, will you have dinner with me? I know all the romantic places." I want to say, I bet you do, but I don't. I am flattered, of course, and tempted, but keep my cool.

"Thank you, but I think not."

Alessandro shrugs his shoulders. "Perhaps another time then?"

"Perhaps," I say politely, surprising myself with leaving the door open.

"Until then, Cara Maddy."

Back safely in my car, I can't help enjoying what just happened. Food for thought.

≫≪

When the kids get home from school, they're all in a tizzy because one of the parents is sponsoring some big balloon excursion in Napa, and they all have been invited to go. Charlie finally has his cast off, and the event happens very early tomorrow. Since it's Steven's weekend with them, he has said he will take them. He'll pick them up in an hour, so they can drive up to Napa and get settled in some motel up there and be ready to get up early tomorrow morning.

Typical of Steven that he would not even tell me about this jaunt and that I would have to hear it from the kids at the very last minute. But I try to suppress my annoyance, and one by one, herd them into the shower while I pack a backpack for each of them with clean clothes, shoes, socks, toothbrushes, hairbrushes, books, power bars, bottles of water, and anything else I can fit in.

Just as I'm smoothing down the adorable cowlick on the crown of Colin's head, Amanda's phone rings.

"Dad's here," she trills and runs toward the door.

"Get your backpacks and hurry down to Daddy."

I go with them, and when I open the door, it is not Steven, but Girl Bambi behind the wheel.

I manage a tight smile. "Where's Steven?

"He's packing and asked me to pick up the children. I hope that's OK."

It's not, but no point in making a scene.

"Not a problem. They're all ready. Please have Steven call me."

"I will."

"Have a good time, kids," I call into the car.

The kids wave as they drive off. I'm not as upset as I would have been a while back.

I sit down to finish up a story for the *Chronicle* on a famous game show host's wife's new clothing line that is being sold exclusively at Neiman Marcus. Thank God for the distraction.

On another latte run, I see Alessandro again and say hello, and we chat for a while. It seems he has the night off and still wants to take me to dinner. Feeling a bit bereft because of the balloon trip, I agree. He is delighted, and we agree to meet at eight at E'Angelo in the Marina district. Popular, but understated.

I'm in a pair of jeans I've not been able to get into since Bush II was first elected. On top I wear the see-through black Emporio Armani top with ruffles and tassels and other frippery that I wore on that disastrous blind date with the oral surgeon. I have brushed my hair until it looks like burnished obsidian. Anyway, I feel good. And when Alessandro whistles when I join him at the table, I feel even better.

He gets up to let me sit down and squeezes himself in close to me until his thigh is touching mine. The sensation of body against body is strangely unfamiliar to me, but exciting.

"You look ravishing tonight."

"You are very kind. Thank you."

The waiter appears, handing us the menus. Alessandro orders a bottle of red wine.

I pick up my menu, and of course I can't see a thing because I refuse to wear my glasses on a date. Without my glasses, it's all a big blur, but you know what Marilyn Monroe said, and she was right.

"What do you recommend?" I say slyly. "I'm sure you know what I'll like."

When the waiter returns with the wine, Alessandro orders the pasta and salmon special with a simple salad to start. "I know the chef here, and it is his best dish."

The main course arrives, and I must say, it is quite good. He is pleased, and we happily eat and talk.

A pretty young brunette saunters by our table then, however, and waves at him.

"Cara!" he says.

"Call me," she says and walks away, her too-short skirt leaving precious little to the imagination.

"Who's that?" I say.

"Just a friend," he says, taking my hand. He shifts himself closer to me and puts his arm around me. I blush and squirm, but he doesn't seem to notice. I feel like an unadulterated, unmitigated fool. When a few more "caras" walk by and smile invitingly at him, I feel like the worst kind of fool—an old fool.

"This place is crowded," he says. "Perhaps we could find some place more private. The evening is young."

I can see where this is going.

"I have friends staying at my house. Do you live close?" he says.

I pull away. "Fairly close, but I live with my young children."

He is disappointed and releases me. I mumble something about going to the restroom, and he lets me out.

When I get back, Alessandro is gone. At least he paid the bill.

Mike is just back from an academic conference in Boston, and for the first time, he invites me to his place for dinner. I feel foolish about Alessandro and am looking forward to seeing him. Against my better judgment, the kids are with my mother, but under strict orders not to leave her house under any circumstances.

I drive over to Twin Peaks, two hills that, with the exception of Mount Davidson, are the highest points in the city. Mike's small, romantic cottage is charming and even has a garage and a driveway on which guests can park. Hooray! I feel like I've won the lottery. I've actually gone somewhere in San Francisco where I can park without:

1. Setting my stopwatch to ping at me every fifty-nine minutes so I can dash out and feed the meter.

2. Filling that meter with $4.25 every time I dash out.

3. Paying between $5 and $12 every twenty minutes in a lot.

As soon as he hears my car, he appears in the doorway. In a neatly pressed blue shirt and chinos, he smiles and kisses me on the cheek.

"I brought a white. I hope that's OK?" I say.

"Perfect. It will go well with the clams."

He leads me over flagstone steps and into the house, which is light and airy, with two skylights, bleached hardwood floors, and a peaked beamed roof. A small deck clings to the back of the house with unobstructed views of the city and the Bay.

"This is wonderful," I say, as I follow him to the kitchen.

"Well, it's tiny, but it suits me," he says, smiling.

I see a big salad on the counter and a soup tureen full of what smells and looks like clam chowder. Baguettes from a popular bakery lie ready to be buttered.

Mike opens the wine I brought and pours us each a generous glass. "Shall we go out on the deck?"

It's not warm, but who cares with a view like that? The lights of the city twinkle in the distance, and I sit there silently for a while, just looking.

"This is lovely," I say. "Just lovely."

"Thanks. It's modest, but it suits me."

"I should say so."

After a while, he points me inside the house for dinner. As we eat the delicious chowder and crunchy baguette, we chat a bit about the conference, my writing, and his novel. I can't say enough about how much I enjoyed it.

"I read your latest piece, by the way, the one about Paul Lee's wife's new clothing line," Mike says. "It was hilarious." And he picks up a copy of the *Chronicle* and reads: "'The question is not whether Annabel Lee's razzle-dazzle clothing line will play in San Francisco (it probably won't), but in Peoria, the seat of husband Paul Lee's popularity.

"'There, Lee's clothes, as overwrought as they are, will probably do gangbusters. Those middle-American women love the kind of faux

Hollywood glamour that Nolan Miller and Bob Mackie did first, and better.'"

"I can't believe you kept that," I say, so flattered that he did. "But thanks. I got some good comments on the paper's blog."

"I hope you're weaving your own blog into your book."

"What book?"

"The novel you're writing."

"I hadn't thought about it. Not a bad idea. Unfortunately, I haven't gotten very far."

"Give it time. It's not as if you're on a deadline."

As I get up to help him clear the dinner plates, Mike asks, "What's happening with the divorce?" He goes to the fridge, from which he draws out a fresh fruit plate and some yogurt. He has remembered my diet and made it easy for me to stick to it.

"We have our mandatory settlement meeting soon."

"Do you think you'll get all the issues resolved that way, so you don't have to go to trial?"

"I don't know," I say. "Who's going to have the house and how much money I get are sticking points. He's not fighting me on the kids. He can't handle them on his own anyway, and God knows Girl Bambi can't run after ten-year-old boys and a baby."

"You seem different about the whole divorce thing," he says.

"I feel different. More relaxed, yet focused."

"Good. In the mood for a walk? It's a lovely night."

"Sounds great." I hope the neighbors won't be snooping.

As we walk under the starlit sky, he tells me about the conference and the tawdry affairs of professors gone wild away from home.

"Oh God, it was awful," Mike says.

"What happened?"

"All those academics altogether for seventy-two hours? They're all nuts, truly. It was like Jonestown without the Kool-Aid."

I laugh out loud. "And you say I'm funny."

Mike chuckles.

"Any torrid sex?" I ask.

"For everyone but me, it seems."

I am silently pleased.

We continue to chat, he telling me about all those college professors and how insufferable they were. At one point I am laughing so much I get stomach cramps and beg him to shut up. He turns toward me then and brushes my lips with his. They are cool and firm, and he smells good. He takes my face in his hands then and kisses me deeply and longingly. I am frozen, unable to respond, suddenly terrified.

He steps back, obviously wounded. "Maddy, I'm sorry. I just got carried away."

"No need." My words snap in the air and fall heavily.

We walk to his car.

"Thanks for…everything. I'll call you."

"I'd like that."

At least I got that last part right.

When I check my blog for responses, I find this one, in answer to my question of why we knowingly make mistakes.

I did exactly what you seem to be doing when I was going through a divorce: ignored the decent guy who kept on calling for the hunky contractor who was working on my house while also working on me. It was a mess, literally and figuratively. The decent guy finally scrammed (can you blame him?), and I'm still living on a building site with only twenty-eight boxes of drywall nails and 527 square feet of ceramic Flandes tiles to show for my supposed remodel.

Posted by susanG

Chapter 42

---

*He is a wise man who does not grieve for the things which he has not,
but rejoices for those which he has.*
—Epictetus

THE BLASPHEMY BOX

*The first major family holiday without your spouse can be particu-
larly daunting. That empty chair, is, well...horribly empty. For years
you've followed a certain set of rituals that bolster your belief that you
are not alone in this cold, old world. And then—boom—all of a sudden,
everything you thought you knew and everything you were accustomed
to is stripped away, and you're like that poor friend of mine in Denver
who, on her first post-divorce Thanksgiving, ate a frozen turkey dinner
from Safeway and watched fifty-eight thousand episodes of "The Twilight Zone." I call it divorce depression, and I tell you, it must be fought.*

I've been dreading Thanksgiving. The first one without my husband; the first one for my kids without their father. I've been wondering
how I'm going to handle all the innate stresses of such a situation, not
the least of which is who the hell is going to carve that goddamn turkey?
The whole idea of celebrating family when a significant part of that family is now gone is really hard to get your head around.

And then you have to appear cheerful in front of your kids and
make the occasion as happy and fun for them as you can, when all you
really want to do is get into bed with a tub of mint chocolate chip ice
cream and weep till the cows come home.

Pondering all this in recent weeks, I decided that rather than the
kids and I sitting there at the dining room table, staring at each other

in silence, I would invite some friends over to fill up the place with noise and laughter and conversation. Mother said she would be happy (darling) to forego her and Dad's very-much-looked-forward-to annual Thanksgiving trip to Hawaii (darling) so that (darling) I wouldn't be all alone with just the kids (darling). But the thought of her pacing the kitchen asking me if Steven and I are going to reconcile and informing me that I've put too much sugar in the pies and too much butter in the yams causes me to deflect that huge sacrifice on her part, and instead say, "Aloha."

I thought of asking Mike, but it seemed too intimate of an invitation. I asked Candy to come over with her two cherubic-cheeked boys, who are around the same age as mine, and her daughter, Emily—the one who said, "Shit, I forgot my purse."

I also invited Myla from my support group. I figured she and Candy would get on well, because they shared the same interests: fashion and revenge against their exes. I was going to throw Rachel, the leader of my support group, into the mix too, but then I thought all those nose rings and belly-button piercings might give Amanda ideas. Both friends were happy to be asked, and Candy arrives first with the boys in tow and some Dom Pérignon, which she plants in the fridge and then roams around the kitchen, saying, "Now, have you got any real alcohol in this house? I really need a drink."

It's two in the afternoon, but I pour her a Scotch, which she downs in two seconds. A bit more relaxed, she sits down at the counter. "You cannot believe what a shit Ken is being. He's just been terrible about Thanksgiving."

"What did he do?" I ask.

"Well, first, he said wanted the kids, because he and his ho were planning on going out to a nice holiday-themed restaurant. How plebian. Then, when it became clear his ho didn't want the kids, he called and said I should take them, as if they're rolls of toilet paper that should go wherever they're most needed."

"Uh huh, what a jerk." I continue on making pumpkin and apple pies and sweet potatoes with marshmallows.

"I mean, really," she says. "Talk about being whipped."

"So Emily isn't coming?" I ask.

"No, she said she'd had enough of the pair of us and went to a friend's."

Candy seems unperturbed. If Amanda spent Thanksgiving at someone else's house, I'd be crushed.

Soon after, Myla arrives. She's in a Chanel jacket with nicely pressed jeans and lots of gold jewelry. Two minutes after she and Candy meet, they're on the couch, gabbing away about husbands and bastards and how they love Donna Karan's latest black jacket. I hear Candy tell her about the day a while back, when she desperately wanted her hair cut but couldn't get in. She put a paper bag over her head, cut out three holes for her eyes and nose, went to her salon, and said, "Now can I get a haircut? I can't go to the opera like this."

I turn on my forties music channel, and Dame Vera Lynn is singing "The White Cliffs of Dover." It reminds me of England, and I feel homesick and want to cry, but I don't.

The turkey is done, and so is everything else. I beckon Amanda to help me carry the side dishes to the table. I manage the turkey platter. Instead of going through the usual ritual of having the man of the house carve the turkey (because there isn't one this year), I carved it up myself in the kitchen.

"Everybody please come to the table," I say.

Candy stands up, sways a little, and meanders over with Myla close behind. The four boys run to grab seats together.

"How is everything?" I say, kind of into the air after everyone has been served and is eating.

Everyone murmurs the appropriate praise for the food. It's a pleasure to see my table filled up for a change. When everyone's finished eating, I get up and start to clear the table. Amanda helps too, miracle of all miracles. I announce that dessert will be out shortly. Everyone hastily beats a path to the living room, and soon we are all, including me, eating pie with fresh cream I whipped myself.

Myla and Candy get up and help clear away the dessert plates. The kids are excused. The four boys charge upstairs, shrieking the entire time, and Amanda disappears into the study. I carry coffee into the living room, and the three of us take a cup.

"Phew!" I say. "Some peace and quiet."

"This was all so delicious, Maddy," Myla says.

"So happy you enjoyed it."

"Yes, it was," says Candy, "and so nice of you to invite us."

"Well, I was just so happy you could come. We're all going through a difficult time, after all," I say.

"Yes, and I'm going to make sure Justin goes through the same difficult time," Myla says. She is still consumed with rage, and I can't blame her.

We trade lawyer stories, cheating-husband stories, being-a-single-mother stories, and being-a-single-woman-again stories, and we laugh and laugh and cry and cry so that when they finally leave, I feel like I just appeared on *Oprah*. (If Oprah still had that show on ABC, that is.)

It's around nine when both Myla and Candy get up to leave. "Boys!" Candy shrieks. Four boys charge down the stairs and screech to a halt in front of us, just like the Road Runner.

I find that although I do not want either friend to leave, I don't feel as bereft at the thought as I imagined I might. And I realize I haven't really thought about Steven much the entire time, either. We all exchange kisses and hugs, and then I am back in my kitchen, clearing away the last few things.

Amanda comes in then. "Hi, Mom."

"Hi, sweetie, did you have an OK time today?"

"Sure," she said. "What about you? Was it lonely for you?"

"Lonely?" I say. "How can I be lonely when I have you all?"

And I kiss her on the top of her head. Her eyes salute heaven, but she doesn't pull away like she usually does.

Chapter 43

All love is vanquished by a succeeding love.
—Ovid

THE BLASPHEMY BOX

In all this tawdry morass of divorce and feeling like you've been hit by a truck, there sometimes are wonderful little gems of surprises that bring you back to life. Let's call them epiphanies. Out of the blue, everything suddenly goes from blurred to in focus, and you're thinking not about being unhappy but about how to be happy again. And believing you can.

You clearly see what's good and what's not, and you realize everything else was a mere bagatelle.

The person who might offer you comfort, the one you've been resisting because you're scared to death not to, is standing right in front of you, and for the first time, you actually see him.

Yesterday, I woke up and suddenly thought, I haven't heard from Mike. Not even at Thanksgiving. He's never gone this long without calling. I debate whether to call him, but figure if he wanted to contact me, he would. Then I decide to e-mail him. He does not respond. I find myself missing his calming, steadying influence and obvious attraction to and concern for me.

After dinner, the kids settled in with their homework, I decide to give him a call. I get only voice mail, but leave a cheery message.

This morning, after I get the kids off to school and get back from the gym, I decide to surprise Mike with a picnic lunch. It's a scary thing to do, but it's time I took the initiative.

I rush over to Safeway to pick up a host of items. Once home, I prepare a picnic and insert all the items into a wicker basket I always take on picnics with the kids. If it's too windy or chilly, I think, we can always picnic in his office. Then I head for the shower.

I go on the USF website to research exactly where he works and his office hours, then drive up to the Lone Mountain campus, atop one of San Francisco's highest peaks.

I don't know how I manage to find a parking space, but I do, and I start to make my way over to office. I get a bit lost, of course, and all the left, right, left, right instructions some skinny young kid is kind enough to give me get me even more lost.

I finally find the place. My stomach is churning, but I try to calm myself. I'm not quite sure how Mike will react. I am so nervous I start to sweat, and I can hear my breath in my ear. I concentrate on not dropping the picnic basket, which is filled with delicately cut cheese and cucumber sandwiches, wine, and strawberries and cream. More summer fare than winter, but who cares?

I knock on the door.

"Come in," I hear him say.

"Hello, stranger."

"Maddy!" He jumps up from his chair and enfolds me in his arms. We kiss.

Immediately I relax.

"It's great to see you."

His office is no bigger than a restroom stall and jam-packed with books. "Three novels published, and they can't give you more room than a pantry?" I say, smiling.

"I'm not here all that much anyway, so it's fine. Sit." He clears a pile of papers on the chair opposite his desk.

He looks handsome and collegiate in his gray slacks and navy jacket. He has caught a little sun somewhere, and his skin is golden and clear.

"So, to what do I owe this pleasant surprise?"

"I thought you might need lunch," I say. "And I haven't heard from you for a while and didn't want you to starve."

He laughs. "Yes, I'm sorry for being out of touch. My sister and I went with our collective kids to Hawaii for Thanksgiving, and I'm just so behind on everything. I've missed you."

I'm relieved his silence has nothing to do with me. I smile. He's such a dear man.

"So what's for lunch?"

I proffer the picnic basket.

"Cheese and cucumber sandwiches and strawberries and cream," he announces, lifting the lid. "How English. How perfect."

Now I smile, a smile that engulfs me.

"Do you have time for a picnic? I know you're probably busy, and it isn't exactly picnic weather."

"Nonsense," he says. "Let's get out of this hole and into the fresh air. It's nice outside in the sun."

We go outside and sit on a bench and eat our lunch. It's all so perfect.

"Are you writing your novel?" he says, as we're finishing up the strawberries.

"I am."

"Good. Can't wait to read the finished book."

"You mean I have to write it and finish it?"

"Very funny," he says. "When will you be done with the first draft?"

"Probably by 2030. I really don't know. It's going so slowly some days, not at all, others."

"First novels are the worst. I know how tough it can be. But you can do it, Maddy."

"I wish I had your confidence."

He smiles warmly. "If anyone can, you can."

I feel a rush of excitement. "I hope so. It's so difficult."

"Nothing worth anything is easy, Maddy."

It's in that moment that it comes to me, this all-powerful, all-encompassing realization that I, me, myself, am sitting opposite this man and am *happy*. Not thinking of divorce, not thinking of loneliness, not full of fear, not consumed by hate and disillusionment, but just quietly content and optimistic.

Chapter 44

I'm an excellent housekeeper. Every time I get a divorce, I keep the house.
—Zsa Zsa Gabor

THE BLASPHEMY BOX

The end of a marriage is not easy—for anyone. All the squabbling over every last penny, all the hurt engendered, all the pettiness and vitriol that spills over and poisons the well, is natural, we know that, but you do not come away from it untouched. You see yourself and your spouse in ways you never thought possible. And even if you get what you want, every single last thing you want, it's a victory more Pyrrhic than triumphant.

We are almost at the end of the negotiations, which means we are almost at the end of this marriage, and though that has been true for nine months now, there's nothing like black-and-white legalese to seal the deal and make you feel like the big total failure you just know you are. The finality of the paperwork in my hands is disturbingly painful. I thought I'd be relieved once it was all over, but I'm not. I comfort myself with the deep and profound thought that without endings, there can be no beginnings. That without trying, there can be no success. I've always thought that in life you have to try. Because if you don't try, all that will have happened is that you didn't try.

It's cloudy today, the day of the mandatory settlement meeting. Figures. The office of Steven's lawyer is dark from the impending storm, visible through the huge windows overlooking the Bay. If we can't settle our differences today, we will go to trial with a judge getting to decide all points of contention.

"Is there a new offer from your side?" Alec asks Harrison.

Harrison looks at Steven. "This is our final one," he says. Steven is looking daggers at me.

I roll my eyes. I can't believe I loved this guy. This moody, withholding, disapproving guy. This guy who never understood me and never tried to. I cannot believe it is happening, but it is, and I feel powerful enough to compete with Steven on his own turf: money.

Harrison hands a piece of paper over for our perusal.

"As you can see, Mrs. Nelson gets to stay in the house until the twins are eighteen, which is in eight years. At that point, she will move out and return the house to Mr. Nelson. Meanwhile, she gets a nice big lump sum now—the settlement for the value of her part of the house— and a good monthly chunk for the kids and alimony. Amending somewhat the current arrangement, Mrs. Nelson has the kids during the week and every other holiday. Mr. Nelson has them the rest of the time. He stipulates he wants to have the children stay overnights with him and his partner. Mr. Nelson will pay for the children's education through college and their health care."

Sounds good to me. All that is left is for both of us to sign the papers, and the divorce will be done.

Alec leads me out of the room. "What do you think?" he says, showing me the offer.

I scan it quickly. "The alimony's a bit low, isn't it?" I say. "I can't live on that."

"Exactly," he says. "In we go."

We sit down, and Alec looks at Steven. "The offer is acceptable to us in all parts except the alimony," he says.

I can feel Steven snarling at me.

"Well, we think this a fair offer," Harrison says.

"We don't find it adequate." I look at Alec. His face is expressionless. "So what do we do?" he says. "If we can't resolve this, we will have to go to trial."

"Excuse us." Harrison leads Steven into the hall and closes the door. I hear shouting, but can't make out what is being said. Doesn't bode well. Suddenly the door opens, and the two men walk in. Steven plops down in his chair like a petulant child. Harrison hands Alec the settlement paper again. I watch Alec as he surveys the amendment, then passes it to me. I nod.

"I think we can work with this," he says, finally.

He directs me to sign the paper, then hands it to Steven. Steven scratches his signature, abruptly stands, and walks out.

The Marital Settlement Agreement is done. It will be filed with the court and made part of the final judgment. After the judge signs the judgment, it will become a court order. Soon, the divorce will be final. My marriage is irrevocably over.

Chapter 45

We must be the change we wish to see.
—Gandhi

THE BLASPHEMY BOX

Sometimes in life, just when you think things are going as badly as they can, something good happens and takes you by utter and delightful surprise. I've been bound by fear and beset by stress, wounded and believing I will be alone forever and will make the same mistakes I've always made. I've been terrified I will always be a dumped, fifty-year-old housewife whose career was gone long ago and who will never find love and contentment with the "right" guy. But the past does not have to repeat in the future. I learn that I can grow and find that silver lining, despite how dark it gets.

Mike comes for dinner. I sent my novel to him last week, and he was supposed to read it. He e-mailed me that he guessed we are a couple now, since I've opened up this secret part of me. I didn't know how to respond, so I didn't.

Either way, Saturday, when the kids are with Steven, Mike arrives with champagne and gives me a big hug. A little charge sparks through me, confusing me a bit. It feels good, though.

I'm desperate to gauge his reaction to the book, but he doesn't give anything away. I make us martinis, and we sit by the fire overlooking the Bay. The water is gray and angry, and being inside feels warm and comforting.

"So," I say, unable to keep quiet any longer, "what did you think? You haven't said anything. I'm terrified you hate it."

"I could never hate anything to do with you, Maddy," he says. "That's my problem."

I flush, of course, but say nothing. What, I think, will he—a published novelist—think of my writing? Somehow, so much seems to depend on this one moment in time, and if it doesn't go well, I don't know what I will do.

He takes both of my hands in his then and leads me to the window with that breathtaking view of the Bay, and he says, "Maddy, I really like your book. I could hear your voice all the way through it. It was fresh and fun and telling, just like you."

An insane kind of joy charges through me then, a feeling of light and brightness. "Thank you," I manage to say, overwhelmed with relief and satisfaction.

"However," he adds, "there are few things I'd like to suggest, if you'll let me."

"Of course. Let's go into the kitchen, so I can take some notes."

We sit at the counter. "Ready, maestro."

"OK. I think you could flesh out the early part of the novel. There isn't enough context in which to place this woman, her husband, and their divorce. The reader needs to know more about their past situation, so they can understand the present one." He continues on about the main character, her motivation, and her relationships with other key characters.

I am frantically taking notes. He continues to give advice and point out inconsistencies.

"Jeez," I say, finally, "how about I just throw the whole thing onto the fire and write a book on how to reuse old graves, bomb-proof your horse, or have lesbian hair?"

Mike chuckles. "It's all part of the process. You've worked with editors at the paper your whole career. It's the same thing."

I pout. "I know, but it seems so much worse when you're doing it."

He laughs. "Am I that much of an ogre?"

"Not really. It's just so daunting. I thought I had finished it, and it was done."

"It sounds like there's a lot to do, but there really isn't. Just a few tweaks in the beginning, that's all."

"Apparently so, " I cry, though secretly I am grateful to get feedback from someone who really knows what he's talking about, and really cares that that knowledge benefits me. "Now, let me just get the dinner on the table, and we can chat more."

I have made coq au vin, which turns out to be the best coq au vin Mike has ever had—or at least, that's what he tells me. I think of how rarely Steven complimented my efforts in any arena and how swift Mike's compliments always are.

"So what's going on with you?" I ask him as I clear the dishes and get out a bread pudding I made that morning. I cut him a piece and drizzle caramel sauce all over it.

"Mmm," he cries. "This is the most delicious thing I've ever eaten in my life."

"Now stop with all that flattery," I say, grinning. "You're laying it on a bit thick, aren't you?"

Mike pretends to look wounded. "Of course not. You really are a superb chef, and I don't even think you know that."

How right this man always is about everything.

Chapter 46

You are never too old to set another goal or to dream a new dream.
—*C. S. Lewis*

THE BLASPHEMY BOX

Sometimes dreams do come true. Even when you're afraid to have them. Afraid to hope because you may be disappointed, afraid to act because you may be deflected. Oscar Wilde said a dreamer is one who can only find his way by moonlight, and that's how I feel lately, as if I've been stepping gingerly along, in twilight or darkness, trying things out, attempting to regroup, willing myself to make a new life, a whole life. And finally, I must tell you, I'm seeing the sun.

I have made all the changes Mike suggested (three nights rewriting while the kids slept), and he has reread the novel and pronounced it to be good.

Then, the phone rings. "Is this Madeleine Nelson?" The woman's voice is warm.

"Yes, it is."

"This is Sonya Benson."

"I'm sorry, but do I know you?" I say.

The woman gives a throaty chuckle. "No, you don't, but I hope you want to."

This must be a telemarketing call. "I'm afraid I don't like salespeople ringing me. Please take my number off your call list."

The woman chuckles again. "Madeleine, I am a literary agent. I have been reading your blog, and I think it would make a wonderful book."

I can feel my heart thudding. I don't know what to say.

"Madeleine, are you still there?"

"Yes, I'm still here." My mind is racing, and excitement is firing through me like a cannon. I run to my laptop and put her name into Google's search bar. Sure enough, there it is. Sonya Benson and Associates. It's in New York. I click on a listing of authors it represents. Up pops a record of names, some of which I have heard enough of to know they are respected authors.

"Well, what do you think of the idea? I'd love to work with you on it."

"I've actually made the blog into a novel already."

"Really?" she says. "Great minds think alike."

"I'm not sure it's ready. I've still got some polishing to do, and..."

"Not to worry. That's to be expected. Could you e-mail me what you've got? I'll take a look, and we can talk about it." She gives me her contact information.

"OK. It may take me a few days, but I'll get it to you as soon as possible."

"Sounds like a plan. I'll look forward to reading it."

"Thanks for your call."

"We'll be in touch."

When I put down the phone, I shriek out loud. Thank God I'm alone, or the kids would think I'd lost my mind.

I call Mike to give him the news, but his voice mail comes on. I leave a message for him to call and hang up. Then I can't wait to tell the kids and Suzy and even my mother. But I must remain calm. I remind myself that nothing is set in stone and that Sonya might hate the novel when she reads it and/or ask for ten thousand revisions before she takes it on. I head for my laptop. I spend the rest of the morning fixing the few very last things I know need work and run several spell checks. I'm ready to send it, but decide to let it sit at least until tomorrow morning.

At 3:30, the kids come barreling into the house.

"Go wash your hands," I say. "Snacks are on the kitchen counter. I've got some wonderful news." They come back and are busy eating and talking about their days.

"So," Amanda says, "what's the big news? Are we finally getting an HD TV?"

I laugh. "Maybe someday. But my news is that some literary agent wants to read my book and maybe try to get it published!"

"Wow! You'll be famous, like J. K. Rowling, right?"

"I don't think so, but it's a start."

"Does your book have pictures and stuff?" Colin asks.

"Don't be dumb," Charlie says, nudging his brother. "It's a chapter book. Right, Mom?"

"Yes, sweetie."

"Well, it's cool anyway."

I give them all a huge hug, smiling through my tears of joy.

After dinner, when the children are in bed, the phone rings.

"Maddy, it's Mike. I just got your message. Is everything OK?"

"Well, I got a call from a New York literary agent."

"You did?" he says. "Which one?"

"Sonya Benson. She says she's been reading my blog and suggested I turn it into a novel. When I told her I already had, she asked me to send it."

"That's fantastic," he says.

"I'm going to send her the manuscript. She said we'd talk after she read it."

"This is the best news you could have given me. Congratulations, Maddy. We have to celebrate."

҂◦ৼ

It's a few days after my big news, and Mike says he wants to take me to Napa over the weekend. I say, "More wine tasting?"

And he says, "If you'd like. I was thinking about enjoying the countryside, even though it's a bit chilly, perhaps having dinner or something. We have to celebrate your blossoming career."

"Sounds wonderful."

It's a stunning day, the bright sun perfect for a drive in the valley.

The Yountville restaurant Mike knows is packed, but we manage to get a table. We both order burgers and onion rings. "I shouldn't be eating this, you know," I tell him.

"Oh, don't worry about it," he says. "You look great."

This is how it always is with him. I can't believe my good fortune. I can't believe I'm actually seeing it as good fortune. Believing it is good fortune. I have become wise. Or wiser than I was. I can recognize good from bad now, because I've had one, and now I have the other.

Over coffee, the conversation turns to my book.

"Have you heard from the agent?"

"She got the book and has started reading it. She e-mailed me an author's agreement, so I guess that's a good sign."

"I'd be happy to look it over, if you'd like. It's probably pretty standard."

"That would be great. Thanks."

On the way back to the car, we are holding hands and chatting.

"By the way," I say. "You never told me the name of your agent. Do you think he knows Sonya?"

Mike flushes. Very unlike him. "Er...well..."

Odd. Mike doesn't usually equivocate.

"Still, I would like to know as...a colleague. Maybe he could help with some advice."

Mike stops and looks at me. "My agent's name is Sonya Benson."

I should have known.

"It was you who contacted her and told her to read my blog and call me."

"Well..."

"Mike?" I say.

"I just suggested it to her. She wouldn't have called if she didn't think the blog is fabulous. She's a pro."

"I wish you would have told me."

Mike smiles, taking my hand again. "It's the way it works in publishing, Maddy. Despite all the websites and advice on how to get published, it's still about personal recommendations. It's how agents sort through the hundreds of submissions they get. Besides, I knew she'd love your work."

I stand there quietly then, thinking. Thinking how kind and special this man is.

And then I walk over to him, take his face in my hands, and kiss him deeply. A calmness descends on me for the first time in months. I feel safe. I'm not terrified of everything anymore. I have a partner. I have a best friend.

When we arrive back at his place, he invites me in. "Nightcap?"

"Sure."

The house is silent. He pours us some port, puts on some soft jazz, and we sit on the sofa in his living room.

"Maddy, you are very special to me."

I turn to look at him. "You are special to me, too. I've known it all along but was too afraid to accept my feelings."

He puts his arms around me. We kiss and kiss, deeply and more deeply, until I feel overwhelmed and need to break away. But he holds me to him, and I like the feeling of his warm body. Without a word, we stand, and he leads me toward the bedroom.

"Are you sure?" I whisper in his ear as we sit on the edge of the bed.

"More than anything in a long time."

We kiss and lean back onto the bed. As we undress each other, lost in the moment of passion and intimacy, I feel alive, truly alive for the first time since the whole horrible mess began. And safe. Safe in Mike's arms.

Chapter 47

Listen; there's a hell of a good universe next door: let's go.
—*e. e. cummings*

THE BLASPHEMY BOX

The first Christmas after a divorce, like the first Thanksgiving, is never easy. All the memories that are attached to this particular day can be painful to entertain, and don't even get me started on the music you all sang along to together that now provokes such profound sadness whenever it's on the radio, which is twenty-four hours a day. (If I hear "White Christmas" one more time, I might just have to jump off the bridge.) All those ads on TV of happy families celebrating the holidays are so jarring and upsetting that you really do find yourself giving way to all your negative emotions. However, thinking positively is just as easy as thinking negatively, I'm beginning to find. All that 'buck up and look on the bright side' stuff that you hear after a divorce really seems to work if you practice it. And even if you don't. You forge new rituals. You make new habits. You have to. And often they are more satisfying than the ones you had.

Though I got the kids for Thanksgiving and Steven should have had them for Christmas, he thought Girl Bambi should take things easy, what with her due date coming up. Fine by me! I have a lot to celebrate and would like nothing more than to have my lovelies at home with me. They are to go to their father for New Year's Eve. I am going to LA to see Suzy.

I decide Mike and I are sufficiently "together" to invite him for Christmas lunch, along with his daughter, Jenny, who is a friend of

Amanda's. (But, it must be said, one of those friends who actually does her homework, instead of—like Amanda—complaining that she has to do it.) Jenny will be with her mother, however.

Though all the kids have met Mike before (when he dropped Jenny off or picked Amanda up for playdates), I only told them yesterday that he and I are dating. The boys fell to the floor, laughing hysterically.

"What's so funny?" I said.

"Mom, you're too old to date," Charlie said.

"Yeah, Mom, *way* too old," Colin added.

Amanda just saluted heaven with her eyes and said she was going to pluck her eyebrows.

That is why I am nervous today about how they will react to his being here and sitting in Steven's chair.

Mike arrives at my house at noon, earlier than I had expected. I am still in my bathrobe, an old terrycloth thing that has seen better days.

"Hi, I didn't think you would be here until later," I say as he bounds up the stairs carrying Champagne, a bunch of white roses, and three gift-wrapped packages.

"I thought I would come help you with all the preparations."

When had Steven ever helped me with the preparations for anything, I ask myself, standing there, looking at what must be the world's only perfect man.

I smile and take the bottle and roses and place the packages under the tree. "How nice. But you shouldn't have brought presents for the kids. They get so much, you know."

"Can't have Christmas without presents," he says.

"Quite right," I say, smiling. "Shall we get cracking?"

"Absolutely," Mike says and follows me into the kitchen. He takes a quick look at the turkey in the oven and then rolls up his sleeves. "Now, what shall I do?"

"Well, you could boil the potatoes and then mash them," I say, "and I was going to make the pumpkin and the apple pies."

"Oh, I love to bake," Mike says. "Why don't I make the pies?"

"You know how to *bake*?" I say, incredulous.

"Of course. Doesn't everyone?"

I grin. "OK, know-it-all. There's the flour, butter, eggs, and sugar. The pumpkin filling is in the fridge, and the apple slices are in cold water in that bowl."

"I'll need a rolling pin," he says.

"In the second drawer," I say.

For the next hour, we boil and sauté and cream and blend, moving easily around the kitchen in some kind of sweet harmony, chatting as we work. Suddenly, the boys are there.

"Oh, hi, guys," I say. "You remember Mr. Dutton, don't you? Jenny's dad?"

Colin says, "Hi, Mr. Dutton." Charlie says, "Hi, Mr. Dutton. Mom, when's lunch? We're starving."

"Gosh, you just had that stuffed French toast a couple of hours ago."

"Mom," says Colin, "can we have a snack?"

"Lunch is almost ready. Just have a banana."

Amanda appears then. "Mom, when will lunch be over? Sarah's going to ride her bike in Golden Gate Park and wants me to go with her."

I almost tell her she can't go, that Christmas is time for families. But I don't. "We should be done around two-thirty," I say.

"Great," she says. "Hi, Mr. Dutton."

"Hi, Amanda."

When she's gone Mike and I look at each other and smile. "Not as awkward as I thought it might be," I say.

"Life is full of wonderful surprises," he says.

And he's right.

Soon, he's heaving the turkey out of the oven, and after it has sat a while, he starts to carve it. Without an electric carver! I call the children, and soon we are at the dining table. Mike makes to sit on one side, but, with one eye on the kids, I gesture to him to sit in what is Steven's place and has been for twenty years.

"Could you pass me the marshmallow sweet potatoes, Mr. Dutton?" Charlie says. As easy as that.

Over lunch, Mike tells funny stories about when Jenny was a toddler. Amanda affects her this-is-so-boring pose, but the boys listen carefully.

"Well," Mike says, "when she was two, she kept trying to blow out the lights on the Christmas tree."

The boys grin.

"And then when she was five, she heard in preschool that you should stand your Christmas tree in sugar water—it keeps it fresh—and before we knew it, there was a long line of ants coming from our front door over to the Christmas tree."

The boys laugh. So does Amanda. Yippee!

"This pumpkin pie's great, Mom," Colin says, spooning as much as he can into his mouth at one time.

"Yes," I say, "it is. Mr. Dutton made it."

Colin's mouth falls open. Even Amanda looks up from her iPhone.

After pie, Charlie asks if we can open presents. I look at Mike questioningly. Will he be terrifically bored and run back to his peaceful pad in the sky?

He nods encouragingly.

"OK, fine, but you each have to write down who sent you what for the thank-you letters. You're grown up enough to do it now."

I hand out three pieces of paper and pens, and we gather around the tree, which I spent three hours decorating with the kids, making sure to hang the latest framed picture of all of us, a family tradition that used to include me and Steven but now features just the kids and me. It is cozy and warm inside, and outside, the million lights of the city shimmer incandescently.

As the kids open their presents excitedly, the house fills with noise and torn wrapping paper and cries of "Look at this!" and "See what I got!"

I save the presents to the kids from me and Steven (something we managed to arrange with very little fighting) until last. Amanda opens hers first: a curling iron, some turquoise jeans, since colored jeans are hot right now, and the thing she wanted more than anything in the world, a Coach bag.

"Oh, it's beautiful, Mom!" she cries, even coming over to hug me.

"Open Mr. Dutton's present now," I say, handing it to her. Amanda looks at Mike shyly and tears open the package. Inside is the latest iPhone case in white, covered in vibrantly colored love hearts.

"Oh my God, I love this case," she cries. "Everyone wants this one."

I point her toward Mike. "Thanks so much, Mr. Dutton," she says.

"You're very welcome," Mike says. We look at each other then, and I have to look away, the feeling is too strong.

"OK, now it's time for presents for you boys." I hand them each a long, slim package.

"What is it, Mom?" says Charlie.

"Why don't you open it and find out?"

Both boys tear the paper off as fast as they can.

"Oh my God," cries Colin. "An electric Razor scooter!"

Charlie shrieks. "A Razor scooter! I've wanted one for ages!"

Mike and I smile at each other.

"Mom, can we go in the street and ride them?" Colin's face is flushed.

"Only if I'm there with you, sweetie. There are cars coming and going out there. We'll go soon, but why don't you open your presents from Mr. Dutton first?"

I hand them each a similar-sized package, which they rip open.

"Cool!" Charlie cries. "Wheels for my scooter. In lime green!" And he jumps up and down with joy.

Colin has the same reaction. His wheels are cobalt blue. "Thank you," he says to Mike.

"Yes, thank you," Charlie says.

I look at Mike and in a whisper say, "How did you know to get those?"

"You mentioned that you and Steven were giving them Razor electric scooters."

"That was very considerate and generous of you," I say, so warmed by this decent, giving man.

"OK, time for scooter riding!" Mike cries.

"Are you sure?" I say. "I can go out with them."

"No, you stay here and relax for a bit; you've been going all day. I'll supervise."

An hour later, he is still supervising and as I watch him and the boys from the window, my heart is so happy, so grateful, so relieved.

Chapter 48

WEEK 51 OF SEPARATION

Cheers to a New Year and another chance for us to get it right.
—Oprah Winfrey

THE BLASPHEMY BOX

Getting divorced sets you up for a long, enervating series of firsts. The first hour without your spouse, the first dinner without your spouse, that first night when the empty bed in that silent room trumpets the awful, irrevocable truth. The first church service, party, shopping trip, school event, holiday without your spouse—all of these are difficult. (You don't know how much, for instance, you lean on a partner to get out of social engagements until he's gone, and you can no longer plead his having swine flu as a reason to stay home.) Probably one of the most difficult firsts, however, is the first trip. Alone. You without him or the kids.

But all those firsts have to be met and breached. Once they are, you no longer have to say to yourself, last time I was on a plane it was with His Majesty and the kids on the way home from a fabulous trip to Mexico.

On New Year's Eve, Steven and I would always get a babysitter, paid at double the hourly rate, and go out to dinner at one of those restaurants with those outrageously priced prix fixe menus where you get three spoonfuls of soup, a chicken leg, and some butterscotch nonsense that tasted like it came out of a box from Safeway, all for the grand price of $150 per person. Then we would go to a show, often at the Fairmont Hotel's gilded Venetian Room, where, they never tire of reminding guests, Tony Bennett first sang his signature tune, "I Left My Heart in San Francisco." We didn't see Tony, but we did see James Brown.

Since the kids are meant to be with Steven and Girl Bambi and Anita, Suzy kindly invited me to spend New Year's with her and her kids, her ex, Rex, and his partner, Craig. And I could not think of any reason not to go.

Suzy said spending time in LA would make me feel better, because people get married and divorced in LA faster than a lion spots a limp, and I won't feel so sidelined and like I'm wearing a big D around my neck. Apparently, a study put the state of Massachusetts with the lowest rate of divorce in 2009 and California as having one of the highest. (Does that mean that divorce is a function of an unhappy marriage, or it's just what happens if you live in the wrong state? Does it mean, for instance, that if Steven and I had lived in Boston instead of San Francisco, we wouldn't be divorcing?)

I take myself off around 8 a.m. to SFO and drive around and around the long-term parking lot for twenty minutes, until a young kid with a mullet pulls out of a space, and I pull in. To get to the terminal, I take the shuttle, which throws me back and forth and rattles my insides for a full ten minutes until depositing me at the international terminal so I can get my Virgin flight.

I already have my boarding pass, so I go through security and then try to find somewhere to have a drink and a snack. Most of the restaurants look as God-awful as they always do, serving up eight-thousand-calorie pieces of pepperoni pizza or oil-laden fried rice, and every single one of them has people screaming into their cell phones while they eat. Besides, I don't like eating alone. Especially at those plastic tables with plastic knives and forks that break the moment you stick them in something.

I wander over to Peet's, where the line is long. I don't feel so lonely doing this, since I do it every day, and no one pities you if you stand in line alone. (Only if you eat alone.) I dutifully wait my turn and get a coffee and a low-fat apricot scone for an outrageous price.

I sit down near the departure gate and eat my scone. Everywhere I look, I see couples—some with kids, some without—but couples all the same.

Once on the plane, I settle in for the one-hour flight with my book. We're all told to turn off our phones, and soon we are in the air. Everyone seems to be traveling in pairs—everyone except me. I am used to making all the family travel plans, packing for everyone and settling everyone on the plane to wherever we are going. Now it's just me. I keep looking around, expecting to see my kids bickering or engrossed in their electronica. I only see other people's kids. I keep looking across the aisle to see Steven, who would sit only on the aisle, and all I see is a man in a gray suit reading the *Wall Street Journal* and picking his nose.

The flight is uneventful, and as we approach LAX, a million turquoise pools come into view, and a labyrinth of freeways snake right and left into oblivion. I have been to LA several times and never really liked it much. It's not really a city in the way San Francisco is. And all those palm trees make it seem as if you are on a movie set.

When I arrive in the terminal, I know I'm definitely in LA because most of the women are blonde and tanned with smooth skin and small noses and wearing Lily Pulitzer-esque pedal pushers, mile-high platforms, and tight, cropped T-shirts, emphasizing boob jobs and unnaturally ripped abs. In the restroom, a row of women stand at the sinks, primping their hair, touching up their makeup, and gauging their attractiveness factor in the mirror. I've never seen so much taut skin and puffed-up lips since *The Real Housewives of Orange County* went on the air. Out on the curb, blinded by the bright sun, I call Suzy. She's circling outside in her car and comes by in a few minutes.

"Did you have to wait long?" I say, getting into her van.

"Not long, by LAX standards."

We smile at each other, and I can feel myself relaxing. "I'm so happy to see you."

"Me, too," she says.

We make our way out of the airport and onto Sepulveda. It's warm and smoggy, and I find myself coughing.

"Sorry," Suzy says. "This is how it is here."

"No worries. I have my allergy pills. And it's so nice to have some warm weather."

"Yes, at this time of the year, it's lovely during the day but gets pretty chilly at night."

As we inch along in the traffic, we chat about everything, like real friends do, able to take up immediately where we left off.

"I like your new look," she says.

"Highlights," I say.

"Rex's boyfriend has highlights, too."

We both burst into laughter.

"What's happening with all that?" I ask.

"Well, the latest is they are debating having their own baby. They want to find a surrogate to carry the child."

My mouth falls open.

"And how do you feel about that?"

Suzy grimaces a bit. "Not as bad as I would have imagined. But when I told my mother, we had a bit of a row. I told her to tamp down all that bigotry inside of her. I didn't hear from her for at least two weeks, which was not a bad thing."

I laugh. "Sounds like your mum. She was always a bit doctrinaire."

"Well, then there was a bit of a blowup over the Christmas holidays. Because both I and Rex want to be with our boys for the holidays and because Mother and Father want to be with their grandsons, and because Rex also wants to be with Craig, we thought it would be a good idea if we all spent Christmas this year in London. But then my Papist mother got herself into a terrible lather about it."

"What did you say?" I ask.

"I just told her that it's either a visit from all of us or none of us at all for Christmas. So we didn't go, and here we are."

What seems like hours later, we arrive at Suzy's house, a large, Spanish-style stucco affair.

"What a beautiful place."

"Rex and I agreed that I'd keep the house. He moved into a condo not too far from here."

"That's great," I say. "I had to fight Steven over everything."

"That's because he's a selfish turd. I'm sorry."

She pulls my little suitcase out of the back seat and wheels it in through the front door.

"Are the boys here?"

"No, they're with Rex and Craig. But we'll see them tonight."

"Great," I say, setting my purse down on her foyer table so I can survey the house.

I look around. "This is lovely," I say.

And it is. An unspoiled classic with lots of period details, it has a tiled entry in front of a sweeping staircase with an intricate, wrought-iron banister. The living room and dining room have gorgeous carved ceilings and pretty picture windows looking out to a lush, English-style garden. There is a sunroom, a kitchen with vivid cobalt blue tiles, and the room I will stay in has its own balcony. Everywhere I can hear birds chirping and smell the fragrance emanating from the garden. It all so feels warm and cozy.

"You haven't seen this house?" Suzy says.

"No, you moved in just after my last trip here."

"That's right," she says, pouring two glasses of iced tea. "I love it here. Shall we go sit outside?"

We step out onto a small flagstone patio shaded by magnolia trees. It is quiet and inviting, and we sit sipping our tea and chatting.

"How are Amanda and the boys?"

"Great," I say.

"And Steven?"

Surprisingly, I find I do not want to talk about Steven. A few short months ago, he was all I thought about. Now, not so much.

"The same."

"How do things stand with Mike?" Suzy is smiling coyly.

"Well, we see each other."

"See each other?" Suzy says. "Have you..."

"Yes."

"Good for you," she says, pouring me another iced tea. "He sounds like a good guy."

I love her for not questioning me further.

"Now, what would you like to do? We could go wander around Westwood Village and have lunch in the sun. It's actually close enough to walk there. A rarity in LA, as you know."

"That sounds perfect. I'll go wash up a bit first."

In fifteen minutes we are walking down Lindbrook into the controlled chaos that is LA. The streets and cafes and stores are jam packed, and drivers are getting into verbal matches over illusionary parking spots. Suzy takes my arm, and I press her hand with mine, so warmed at being enveloped in her love and affection.

We wait for half an hour to get a table at a restaurant with some cutesy name Suzy says has great salads. When we finally get seated, we promptly order chicken salads with mandarin oranges and candied walnuts and catch up on all the family and England news.

"Julia Anstruther-Eaton-Stuart rang me up from London the other day, and she asked after you. I told her you were doing great and getting a divorce. She said, 'It's about time.'"

"That cow."

"Exactly," Suzy says. "So I told her she wasn't a great expert on successful marriages herself, after her own two divorces, one from a fake Romanian count."

I scream with laughter. "You didn't."

"I did. It was worth it to hear her gasp."

"Then what else did she say?"

"Nothing," Suzy says. "She hung up."

"You've always been my best friend," I say.

"Always will be."

A woman approaches our table. "Suzy!" she cries.

"Jill!" Suzy says. "Come here and meet my best friend, Maddy Nelson."

Jill is as thin as a strand of vermicelli. She's in tight jeans and a low-cut ruffled top that looks like frisée lettuce. "Pleased to meet you," she says to me.

"Same here."

She sits down next to Suzy. A waiter immediately appears to take her order. She passes.

"Jill is going through a divorce," Suzy tells me.

"Yes," Jill confirms. "My ex just couldn't keep his hands off the babysitter. Well, he'll think again the next time."

"I assume the hearing went well," Suzy says.

"It pays to have a good lawyer. I got nearly everything I demanded."

"You did?"

"The house, one car, the vacation house in the desert, two IRAs, alimony, and the kids!"

"Well done!" I say, before I can stop myself.

Jill smiles. "Yes, it wasn't easy, but it worked out in the end." She looks at her watch. "Must rush. The kids are almost done with yoga. Enjoy your visit, Maddy."

"Everyone I know is getting a divorce," Suzy says.

"I only have one friend who's getting one."

"Like those women over there," Suzy says, pointing to a table by the window that's peopled with five women in too much makeup. "They work at UCLA. I see them a lot, and they're all getting divorces. Three women in our lab are getting divorced, and two mothers whose kids go to my kids' school have split from their husbands."

I know Suzy is sharing this with me to make me feel better. But it doesn't.

"Why does marriage seem so difficult for so many people?"

"I don't know," Suzy says. "Divorce is acceptable now, unlike with the older generation. No matter how miserable they were, they still stayed together. We just don't. Are we smarter for it? Can't say."

"I guess you're right," I say. "But it's so sad." I remember the story I told Mike about Suzy's father.

"It is, but it is what it is. It's up to us to stay calm and carry on, isn't it?"

We both laugh. So nice to be with a fellow Brit.

The bill paid, we saunter out and walk up and down the streets, looking into the stores. Suzy picks out outfits for her boys, and I get LA T-shirts for my three. I have brought down Giants shirts for Suzy's boys.

"I wish you were staying more than one night," she says.

"Me too. But I have things to do at home and want to do them while the kids are away."

"I see," Suzy says. I realize then she is as lonely as I am.

"What time are we going to see Rex and the kids?"

"I said we'd be there at seven. Craig's making dinner. Apparently, he's a gourmet chef."

When we get back to Suzy's house, we both go for naps. When I wake up, I lie languidly in bed, knowing I don't have to get up and tend to anything or anyone straight away. I don't have to go to the grocery store. I don't have to make dinner. I try to call the kids but can't reach them. Suzy comes in and sits on my bed, and we chat about things—life, our lives. She finishes my sentences. I read her thoughts. Nothing is more valuable than friendship.

On the way to Rex's, I have Suzy stop at Bristol Farms so I can buy a bottle of Perrier-Jouët for him and Craig. I call the kids again. I am missing them so much. Amanda answers her iPhone.

"Hi, Mom."

"Hi, sweetie, how are you?"

"OK," she says. "How's the weather?"

"Beautiful and sunny. Are you having fun?"

"Sure," Amanda says.

"I miss you all very much."

"We miss you too, Mom, but I gotta go now. Dad's taking us out for dinner."

"Can I talk to the boys?"

But Amanda has hung up.

Soon we are at Rex's place in Beverly Glen.

"His condo is hideous," Suzy says. "It was built in the seventies and looks like it, but they are fixing it up, and it should be quite nice."

We park outside and walk up an overgrown path to the front door. I can't imagine how Suzy must feel, having to ring the bell to the door of the house where her ex-husband lives with his lover. The door opens, and the aroma of a roasting chicken wafts toward us. And there in front of us is Rex, tall and lean in khakis and a T-shirt.

"Maddy!" he cries. "How lovely to see you. I begged Suze to get you down here for New Year."

"Lovely to see you, Rex," I say, kissing him and handing him the Champagne. I have always loved Rex. Everyone loves Rex. So different from Steven.

Before I can say anything more, two lean teenagers in shorts cry, "Aunty Maddy!"

I turn to Crispin and Christopher. "And who are you? And why did you kidnap my godchildren?"

The boys laugh, and Suzy smiles indulgently.

"Come here, you two monsters," I say, hugging them. "Oh my God, you're so gorgeous and so grown-up! Presents!"

They take their shirts happily, give everyone a sheepish grin, and head back to the couch with their laptops.

Rex leads us into the family room, where a man I assume to be Craig is straightening up. As soon as he hears us, he turns around.

"Hi, I'm Craig," he says, extending his hand to me after kissing Suzy. "You must be Maddy." He has bright red hair, a smile wider than the Grand Canyon, and laughing eyes.

"Happy to meet you," I say.

Craig gestures us to sit down. "I'll go get iced tea, unless you want something stronger?"

"Oh no, that's fine," I say.

Rex sits down in an armchair. "Sit, Maddy, dearest. So, how are you?"

"Oh fine," I say. "I'm almost divorced..."

"Yes, Suze told me. I hear it has been rough."

"Well, it hasn't been easy," I say.

"Never is." Sadness passes across his face and then across Suzy's.

We sit quietly then until Craig bursts through the door with a tray of iced tea.

"Here we are, then," he says, serving Suzy first. "Dinner is almost ready. Just waiting for the vegetables and potatoes."

"I hear you're an excellent chef," I say.

"He's an excellent everything," Rex says quickly. I look at Suzy, but she is smiling.

In half an hour, we are sitting at a table beautifully set with shimmering crystal, Limoges china, and heavy linen napkins. Craig brings in a huge chicken on a porcelain platter, while Rex and Suzy carry in green beans, roasted potatoes, and butternut squash and pour wine for the adults.

"This is delicious!" I tell Craig once we start to eat. And it is.

Craig raises his glass. "So happy to hear it. Now, here's to friends and family!"

I raise my glass. "And here's to the chef."

Craig smiles happily. I miss my kids so much.

After dinner, we adjourn to the family room, and Craig brings in coffee and gooey, delicious Princess cake. When we all have our coffee, he sits down on the sofa next to Suzy and puts his arm around her. I am shocked when she snuggles into him and rests her head on his shoulder.

"I love this woman," Craig says.

"Almost as much as you love that man," Suzy says, mischief in her eyes.

We all laugh. "Exactly. Hey, do you like the window coverings? I just made them."

We turn our attention to the room's windows and some very attractive Roman shades in a golden damask.

"You know how to make Roman shades?" I say.

"I should. I'm a designer."

"Well, they're perfect," I say.

Craig smiles.

"How long are you in town?" Rex asks.

"Just until tomorrow."

"Too bad. We could the tourist thing. And there's a wonderful new organic Thai-French fusion place."

"Maybe next time."

The rest of the evening is so relaxing, I hate to leave. At midnight we open my Champagne and do a toast. Suzy and I hug, and I am comforted.

The next day, Suzy parks at the airport, and we share lunch in the terminal before I have to go the gate.

"Thanks so much for the wonderful time," I say, hugging her tightly.

"It was too short, but great to have you. I'm sure everything will work out. Keep me posted."

"Promise. Talk to you soon."

When I get on the plane back to San Francisco, I feel amazingly cheered up, courageous, and more optimistic about the future.

The house is so empty and cold when I return, however, it's hard to retain my cheerfulness. If I were not divorced, I think, Steven and I and the kids would be tumbling off the plane about now, brown as hazelnuts, fresh from the beach in Cabo. He would, as usual, be grumbling about how much it cost and about having to haul my suitcase up the steps to our front door, asking me if there was a dead body in it and if I cared at all about his bad back when I packed enough changes of clothes for a visit to Balmoral. I would be ignoring him, as usual, not knowing the day would soon come when I would be hauling the suitcase myself, alone.

I make some Earl Grey tea and collapse onto the sofa. I think of calling Mike, but I don't want to sound maudlin when I talk to him. He has taken Jenny to Vermont to see his parents and won't be back for a few days. The kids are meant to be back tonight, but I haven't heard from Steven and don't feel like calling him.

I get up and start unpacking, a chore I loathe. I love packing. It means you're going somewhere. But unpacking…

I turn on the Sinatra channel and move from suitcase to closet to laundry room until everything is sorted out, and then collapse back onto the sofa. Tossing my phone onto the kitchen counter, I make more tea and toast a bagel. I've started to eat them again, now and then. And nothing terrible happens when I do. It's amazing. I settle on the sofa again, drink my tea, and watch CNN. And discover that it's not so bad there on my own, all alone.

Chapter 49

Every new beginning comes from some other beginning's end.
—Seneca

THE BLASPHEMY BOX

If divorce is the end of one life, it's the beginning of another. And while that can be a terrifying thought, there is good news in it. Your new life might be better than your old one, the one you fought to keep but now accept along with the chance at a new, other kind of happiness. A year ago, I would never have believed that I would be ending one life and starting another. That my husband would have run off with some bimbo, embroiled me in a less-than-friendly divorce, and left me to mostly raise our three kids by myself, and him expecting a new one. But where I am right now isn't that bad, is it? My kids are healthy and happy, I have readers of my blog, a novel that will be published, and a new romance that is infinitely more satisfying than the old one. And I don't curse anywhere near as much as I used to. What the heck is wrong with that?

The kids are home! I am so happy I would wag my tail if I had one. They arrive rushing in as they always do, in a great hurry to get somewhere—where, I have never figured out. There are only so many rooms in the house, and they've been in all of them.

"Daddy's baby was born, Daddy's baby was born," Charlie cries.

"Yes, it came last night, Mom," Colin says.

I have been dreading this moment, but now that it is here, I find I am facing it with something approaching equanimity. I know I have to seem pleased and happy for the children, but I actually do feel pleased and happy for Steven and his Bambi. Children are gifts from God.

"Well, that's good news, isn't it? How much does he weigh?"

Charlie and Colin look confused.

"Eight pounds, ten ounces," Amanda says.

"Who does he look like?" I ask.

"Dad says him, and Gabriela says her," she says. "But we haven't seen him yet."

"Who stayed with you when they went to the hospital?"

"Nana," Charlie says.

Why didn't she bring them home to me?

"How nice. What did you do?" I say.

"Nana took us to some stupid kids' movie," Amanda says, rolling her eyes.

"We're going to see the baby tomorrow!" Colin cries.

I smile. "What did they name him?"

"Fernando," Charlie says.

"Hmm...I guess it's OK," I say.

"Yeah, we don't like the name either, Mom," says Colin.

"Well, just as long as he's healthy and has got all of his fingers and all of his toes, who cares about his name? Right?"

"Right," says Charlie.

Soon we are eating dinner, and I'm bathing the boys and putting them to bed. After all the nightly negotiations of how many books I will read them and how long they will have to read on their own, I make my way to Amanda's room. She's flopped on the bed on her stomach, punching away at her iPhone.

"Are you happy to have a new brother, Amanda?" I ask, leaning on her doorjamb.

She grimaces. "More to the point, are *you* happy, Mom?" she asks.

I am silent for a moment. Then I say, "It doesn't upset me, if that's what you mean. I think I have moved beyond that."

She watches me carefully. "Yes," she says. "I think you have."

I kiss her, turn out her light, and go to tuck the boys in.

Just then the doorbell rings. It's Steven, come to drop off some of the things the kids had left at his mother's house.

"Congratulations," I say as he stands awkwardly in the doorway.

"Yeah," he says. "Well…"

"You don't sound too happy about the baby."

He sighs. "No, I'm fine. I just haven't slept."

"A new experience for you, I guess," I say, mischievously.

Steven isn't amused.

"So how is the baby?"

"He's healthy and looks just like me."

I smile. Typical Steven egotism. And then I thank God it's not me who has to deal with that again. Ever.

He lingers in the doorway, as if wanting to say something more.

"Everything go OK with the kids for New Year's?" I ask.

Steven ignores the question. "Gabriela and I have to look for another house."

"Babies take up a lot of room."

"And we're getting married. It's hectic."

They're getting married. What do I feel? Nothing.

"Congratulations," I say.

Steven ignores my comment. "And by the way," he says, "I heard about this supposed novel of yours. I hope it's not about me."

"Don't flatter yourself, Steven," I say. "It's fiction, after all."

I want to tell him what a stupid, insufferable twit he is, but I stop cold. What's the point? He is who he is, and I'm through with him. I remember Mike whispering to me once, "Forgiveness heals the forgiver," and I say nothing.

"Well, it'd better be," he says. "Or I'll fucking sue."

And I say, "Twenty-five cents in the Blasphemy Box."